Sisters Between

A Novel of the Beguines

by Molly Connally

For my family:
Jim, Mike, Lori, Kathy, and Sallie
Your help and encouragement were invaluable.

My thanks to Pat Meder for her assistance with the cover design.

CHAPTER ONE

Flanders: Summer, 1330

A ragtag troop twenty leagues from the town tramped through the heath, churning it into mud that sucked at their boots. The new recruit lagged behind, wearing a makeshift uniform that hung on his lanky frame: it was no more than a dark pair of work pants, an old gray shirt, and a tunic held by a worn belt. A cap with the insignia of the militia that had impressed him shielded his face from the warm drizzle. Its brim hid a recently healed scar the length of his thumb that pulled the corner of his right eye down and left his cheek puckered and red. The sergeant turned and drilled him with a stare, and he stepped up his pace.

Toward late afternoon the sky cleared and the spires of a town came into view. The recruit stared at the town wall and the buildings rising behind it, far away across the fields. Until now, he had never seen a group of dwellings larger than his own hamlet. He imagined the town crowded with people going about their business, heedless of any strangers in their midst.

If I'm going to get away, there's where I want to go, he thought. All he had wanted, since he had been conscripted by this band of soldiers scouring the countryside, was to get away. He knew nothing, cared nothing for the cause its leaders espoused, nor for the king they supposedly served. The recruit looked down at his dirty clothes and muddy boots. He had been wearing these same clothes ever since he had been impressed, at least fourteen mornings ago. The townsfolk might spot him for a deserter if they saw him like this. But would they care? He had no idea, but he thought he'd better wash up, just in case.

Later, after the troop made camp, he chewed the tough bread that served as their only meal, drank the thin ale, and plotted his escape. He should leave at least an hour before dawn, so he could arrive at the town early and perhaps slip through the gate unnoticed. As he trudged away from the campsite to relieve himself he scanned the fields, looking for a stream or a drainage canal. Narrow canals drained most of the low-lying fields and he soon spotted one, cutting its way along the edge of the heath, separating heath and field.

The troop bedded down on the damp ground that night and the young recruit tossed and turned, trying to get comfortable. At last he fell into a restless sleep, waking early to find himself wrapped in a blanket of fog, a soft gray blanket like the one his mother used to tuck around him when he had the winter fever. He could barely see the other men, though he heard the low rumble of their snores.

This is the day, he thought. He had saved a hunk of the hard, dark bread and had tucked it in his knapsack after the midday meal. He had few other possessions: the knife he had been issued, tied to his belt; the tunic and a worn coat of his own; an extra pair of hose, and string to tie them on just below his knees. Quietly he slipped out of the camp. The sentry, a commandeered country lad like himself, was fast asleep.

The recruit tramped a long way before shedding his clothes and slipping into the canal. The cool water soothed him, and he reached for his clothes and washed them as best he could. They would dry quickly in this warm weather. Struggling into the wet clothes, now appreciably cleaner, he tugged on his dry hose, and then his boots. At least they are in good repair, he thought, and well padded with rags torn into thin strips. The damp hose went into his knapsack, but the knife, a good one, and newly sharpened, he kept tied to his belt. He dropped the cap and tunic into the canal and sank them with a large stone.

The fog held as he trudged toward the town, but it seemed as far away as when he first saw it. Hunched over, he stopped frequently to listen for steps behind him, but heard only birdsong. Dawn found him striding with more confidence, chewing the tough bread as he walked. When he finally arrived at the open gate the sun had burned off the fog and was high overhead. Immediately a sentry challenged him. The recruit drew himself up and declared that he had come to find work as a carpenter.

"Good luck," was the gruff response as he was passed through.

He walked the streets of the town most of the day searching for work, bewildered by its size and the many shops and crowded streets. By late afternoon he was exhausted, and spent his few coins at an alehouse for a mug of ale, a great hunk of fresh-baked bread, and a small bowl of gruel. The heat of the day had left him sweating and disheveled. He knew he should get off the streets before too long, so as not to arouse suspicion by wandering the town after dark. He wished for the cap left behind, as it had shielded the puckered red scar, and he found himself cupping his hand over it. Many wore scars from the pox, but they were grayish things and commonplace.

As the evening shadows lengthened, he found himself walking along the street that bordered the town wall. The street suddenly dipped slightly, almost becoming a separate walkway, and the wall joined a slightly lower and perhaps newer section, if its smoother stone and lighter color were any indication. Behind the lighter wall tall trees shielded the buildings, one with a small spire. Perhaps it was a hospice, a place of rest for travelers. His thoughts were fuzzy from fear and fatigue.

By now it was nightfall, and the moon was rising. He stepped into the walkway, and luck was with him: it was deserted. He decided to scale the lower wall and try to find shelter behind it. He wedged his boot into a crevice where the lower wall met the thicker town wall. Thrusting himself onto the wall, he dropped down on the other side, clutching at the branches of a tree. His heart was pounding, and he leaned against the wall to catch his breath.

Looking around, he found himself in a vegetable garden flanked by trees heavy with fruit, like dark globes in the moonlight. Grabbing a soft shape, he bit off a large chunk of the sweet pear, its juice tracing a path down the dirt on his chin. He stuffed several more pears into a pouch in his knapsack and followed a path out of the garden. Passing several outbuildings, he drew near a stone building; its large, evenly spaced windows were three floors high. The intruder had never seen a building of such size. Was this the hospice? The windows closest to the ground were tightly shuttered, but the upper windows were open to the evening breeze. Curious, he came closer, and placing his boot on a lower sill, was able to hoist himself up to an open window and peer inside.

Moonlight flooded in through the window, illuminating the room. Close by a woman lay on a carved wooden bed, a coverlet on a heap in a nearby armchair. Her face was turned toward him and it was a comely one; her skin was fair and unmarked and long, blonde hair fell in loose curls over her shoulder. The recruit gave no thought to the oddity of a woman sleeping alone in a large room. How long since he had seen a woman? Touched a woman?

He quickly heaved himself up onto the sill. Stepping into the room, he crept to her bedside. She was young, barely a woman. Dare he touch her?

3

Desire flushed his face, and he reached out a rough, dirty hand to stroke her hair. She stirred, lifting her shoulder towards him, and her gown slipped down, exposing part of her breast. Kneeling by her he hesitated, then tugged urgently at his clothes, and prepared to heave himself on top of her. But she felt him brush against her, awoke and cried out before he could clap his hand over her mouth. Suddenly strong hands grabbed his arm, and dragged him off the struggling figure.

"Get off her, you devil!" A short, thickset woman in a long shift struck him a blow that nearly dropped him to the floor. He tried to throw her aside and get to his feet, all desire leaving him in his need to escape, but she kept pummeling him with her fists, keeping him down on one knee.

Her face was freckled and pale and only a hand-width from his and her eyes were fixed on his face, marred by that scar. In desperation, the intruder pulled his knife from his belt and tried to hack at her bare arm, but he was off balance and the sharp blade made only glancing cuts. She screamed, footsteps sounded in the hall, and the door was flung open.

With all his strength he shoved the woman off him, and waving his knife, stumbled to the window. In a moment he was on the sill; then he dropped to the ground below. He found his way back through the garden, scrambled over the wall, and stumbled into the alley. This was not the shelter he had sought. He ran off into the night, again seeking safety.

The room filled with beguines in plain muslin shifts, pushing against each other, some crying, some supporting Mergriet, who was dizzy, others comforting Clare, huddled on her bed, crying, her arms cradling her blonde head. Some sisters held candles that wavered and dipped, reflecting the disquiet of those carrying them and casting frightening shadows on the walls. There seemed to be blood everywhere.

One of the sisters ran to the grand mistress' little house to rouse her, and Beatrice rushed downstairs in her nightdress. The two hurried back to the reassuring solidity of the main building. When they reached Clare's room, Beatrice was greeted by the smell of hot tallow from the candles, the press of bodies, noise and confusion.

"Quiet! You will wake the children!" she exclaimed in a voice that throbbed. She trembled, feeling a swirling darkness reach out from the shadows, trying to envelop her. The sisters gave way as she went to Clare and knelt beside her bed, quickly grasping that while frightened and almost hysterical, the young woman appeared to be unharmed. Beatrice got to her feet, and taking a deep breath, tried to speak calmly.

"Sister Celie, stay here by Sister Clare." Then she turned and saw Mergriet by the window. She was swaying, one arm dripping blood, her shift splotched in red, her unbound auburn hair illumined by a candle one of the sisters was holding. In an instant Beatrice was at Mergriet's side, wrapping an arm around her. She called to Sister Marie, bent her head close to her friend's ear and spoke urgently, lowering her voice.

"Sister Marie, please go to the kitchen and warm some milk for Sister Clare and Sister Mergriet, and get some of the honey salve we keep by the hearth for cuts and burns. Then fetch some clean bandages from the infirmary, and several pinches of the powder we use to induce sleep. Please, take everything to my receiving room." Beatrice straightened. She was tall, her thick braid held back by her nightcap, but even in her nightdress the grand mistress' air of authority pulled all eyes to her. She raised her voice slightly.

"Sisters, go back to your rooms and please try to sleep, or at least rest. I will give you a report of Sister Clare's and Sister Mergriet's condition in the morning." Beatrice's voice allowed no room for objection, and beckoning she moved them toward the doorway and out of the room. The sisters filed past her, whispering among themselves. Beatrice went back inside.

"Sister Mergriet, let me look at your arm." Beatrice spoke softly, sounding like the solicitous aunt she had been years ago, and bent over Mergriet. "I need to see how serious this is." Mergriet clenched her teeth against the pain and stretched out her arm. The cuts seemed to be shallow, but they were bleeding freely. Beatrice tore off a strip of cloth from her own shift and bound Mergriet's forearm tightly with the cloth, still warm from her own body. Then she gently eased her niece onto a small chair in Clare's well-furnished room. "Now, rest a moment, Grietje."

Beatrice moved to Clare's bedside and again knelt beside her. "Sister, I am going to leave you for a short time so I can tend to Sister Mergriet's arm. But I will be back very soon, and Sister Celie will stay right here by you." And indeed, Celie appeared at the grand mistress' elbow. Clare nodded, her sobs already subsiding. Celie pushed aside the bedcovering that had been tossed on the large armchair next to the bed, and eased her body into it, feeling for its padded arms with her curved hands, their knuckles swollen and bent with age. So small that she was nearly lost in the chair, Celie gently took Clare's hand, and held it on her knee.

Beatrice helped Mergriet to her feet and the two walked slowly down the dark hallway and then downstairs to the grand mistress' receiving room. She carried the candle in one hand and wrapped her free arm around Mergriet, being careful not to touch her bandage. Mergriet stepped tentatively, cradling the bandaged arm in her other hand. As the two approached the main entrance of the building, the candlelight caught the gold threads in the tapestry hanging on the wall near the door.

Mergriet hung back as they moved on to the receiving room, but Beatrice, taking her hesitation for weakness, only clasped her more firmly. Neither spoke as they entered the room, dimly lit by one flickering candle. Sister Marie, her dark, curly hair freed of its nightcap, was there to greet them, having placed the things the grand mistress had requested on the large wood table that served as her desk. With her usual efficiency, Marie took Beatrice's candle and placed it in a candlestick, helped her settle Mergriet into the chair behind the table, and placed a light shawl over her shoulders. Beatrice added a pinch of the sleeping powder to each of the cups of milk Marie had waiting, and Marie left with the cup of milk for Clare.

Beatrice urged Mergriet to drink some of the still-warm goats' milk and with cautious fingers loosened the makeshift bandage, now stained a deep red. The bleeding had almost stopped. Beatrice let out her breath: she felt as if she had been holding it in since she first saw the wound. She blotted the cuts with the strips of muslin Marie had handed her and waited calmly for her return, trusting her Sister's unflagging energy, such an asset in a crisis.

In a few minutes Marie appeared with fresh cloths over her arm, carrying a bowl of warm water with a small piece of soap floating on top. Beatrice washed the cuts and then Mergriet's entire arm. Mergriet winced and sucked in her breath as Beatrice gently rubbed away a few bits of dirt, but allowed no tears to fall. Then Beatrice dampened a fresh cloth and gently wiped her face. She was imitating the nursing sisters she had observed, who bathed patients with warm cloths to calm and soothe them. With a feather-light touch, she smoothed the healing ointment over the wound and bound it with strips of clean muslin. Beatrice nodded in response to Marie's questioning glance and Marie left, closing the door behind her.

Mergriet felt uneasy sitting in the receiving room, and in the Grand Mistress' chair. She had acted without thinking when she saw the intruder bending over Clare. Then she had felt sharp, searing pain. Now her arm was throbbing, but as the potion worked its way through her body the pain subsided, and she slumped in the chair, dizzy, exhausted and anxious.

"Grietje, I can take you to the infirmary; the sickroom is empty, thanks be to God. Or you can come to my house and spend the night with me. Which would you prefer?"

Mergriet tried to concentrate on Beatrice's words, but kept her eyes fixed on her injured arm. She had been the first to come to Clare's aid, yet her room was far down the dormitory hallway. Her aunt had not failed to notice that, she was sure. She looked up and felt the floor shift under her feet. Then she reached for the cup of warm milk.

"I am not afraid to be alone. I think the infirmary would be best, Aunt Bea." Mergriet spoke hesitantly, responding to her nickname by using the familiar form of address from her not-so-distant childhood.

Beatrice took up her candle again and the two left the room, Mergriet supporting her injured arm. Reluctantly, Beatrice guided her down the hall to a side door that opened on a path to the chapel. She chastized herself for leaving to Mergriet the decision as to where she should go. Off to one side of the chapel, almost hidden by shrubs, the infirmary was a small building where ill sisters and those who could no longer care for themselves stayed.

Beatrice opened the door and stepped into the sickroom on the main floor. Dried herbs hung from the ceiling on twists of hemp, perfuming the air with bergamot, pennyroyal, lavender, angelica. A table by the door held a mortar and pestle ready to crush the herbs for healing potions, and a candle in a simple wooden holder. Six cots with coverlets over them lined the opposite wall. Beatrice lit the candle on the table, and led Mergriet to a bed in the corner furthest from the now-dark fireplace. She settled her under its coverlet, firmly tucking the shawl around her shoulders. Then she carefully rested the bandaged arm on a pillow from the nearby bed. Finally, she woke the nursing sister sleeping in the adjacent room, told her what had happened, and asked her to look in on Mergriet and change her bandage if necessary.

"And I will look in on you in the morning," she murmured as she left Mergriet's side. Her eyes were open, but she did not stir.

Beatrice walked slowly back to the main building, her head drooping with fatigue. Celie was keeping watch over Clare from the chair by the bed. Her head was propped on her hand, but her dark eyes were wide open. The cup of milk Marie had brought rested on a small table beside her. Clare lay on her side, knees drawn up, her hair a pale gold curtain over her face. She started when Beatrice bent over her. Beatrice eased her to a sitting position and urged her to finish the warm milk she had only tasted, and soon the sleeping potion began to take effect.

"If you would like, Sister Celie may spend the rest of the night here with you. We can bring the bedding from her room here."

"Oh, yes, please," Clare managed a faint smile. Celie's room was only a short distance away, up the stairs and across from the girls' dormitory. Soon Celie's bedding was moved and Clare fell into a restless sleep; it was Celie who lay awake. Beatrice rose, ready to leave.

Her nightcap had come undone and fallen off as she hurried to the main building, and now her hair was a curtain around her shoulders. It was spring and she was barefoot, and had given no thought to wearing

7

clogs in her haste to respond to the summons. Now she stumbled in the dark, striking her foot on a stone in the path. She slowed her pace, but only slightly.

It was not the bats flitting high above her that made her so uneasy; it was her fear that the intruder might still be inside the begijnhof walls. She bent her body forward and hunched her shoulders, trying to make her tall form smaller. At last she reached her house and stepped into the parlor, locking the door behind her. She climbed the stairs to her bedroom and slowly knelt on the padded shelf of the prie-dieu beside the bed. Resting her clasped hands on the upper shelf of its sturdy frame she recited the paternoster, but felt no comfort in the familiar words. She opened her prayer book and paged through many of the psalms, still finding no solace. Finally she closed the psalter and prayed for the safety of the community.

"Lord Jesus, hear my plea. How can I protect us, and keep us safe?" She spoke softly. "How can I make sure that such an attack will never happen again?" Beatrice had heard that the countryside was rife with banditry and even warfare, and she had witnessed street fights and heard screams in the night. She knew that stabbings were not unusual in Sint Joric, but she had never before witnessed the effects of such an attack.

"Please, Lord. Without thy help, I am nothing." She continued to pray, leaning on the prie-dieu, and at last wept a little. For the first time since she became grand mistress, she felt uncertain of her ability to lead the community. Uncertainty was an uncomfortable, almost intolerable feeling; she tried to shrug it away.

Exhausted, she climbed into bed, closed her eyes, and tried to relax, but soon felt the swirling darkness that had enveloped her when she first entered Clare's room. She could feel something unsettling. Was it Satan's messenger pulling at her? A crow cawed close by her window. Some said the devil's emissaries at times took on the shape of a crow. She got out of bed and went to the window, pulled the shutters closed and locked them, in spite of the warm night. The crow flew off, still cawing. She shivered as she got back into bed.

At last she slept, and when she awoke her shift had twisted around her, and was damp with sweat. The room was turning from impenetrable dark to gray. She began to see the outline of familiar objects: the chair by her bed, the prie-dieu, her clothes hanging on pegs on the wall. Best of all, she felt the comfort of day pushing back the horror of the night before.

Beatrice rose, bathed her face with water from the bowl Ingrid had left, and scrubbed her teeth with a damp scrap of cloth dipped in a bit of salt. She dressed in the plain gray-brown beguine habit that fell to her feet, then combed and twisted her tangled hair and tucked it under a clean, white cap. It was too warm to wrap a headcloth around her head. Instead, she simply framed her face with a gray linen wimple, finding comfort in the daily ritual of placing the wimple on the crown of her head and adjusting it so it fell evenly along both sides of her face. She slipped on her softest lightweight wool hose, attached the calf-length tops to her garters, put on her leather shoes, and left the room.

Downstairs, she slipped outside to the privy. Then she stirred up the fire in the main room until the embers glowed red, added some lumps of coal, and swung the kettle over it. She sat for a moment in one of the padded chairs drawn close to the shuttered window, the ones brought from her old home years ago, now recovered in heavy beige linen embroidered with flowers. The seats, comfortably worn, invited rest and refreshment. But Beatrice stood, rinsed a favorite mug, made herself a strong infusion of chamomile, and added a pinch of yarrow. She opened the shuttered window to watch the sun rise, then slipped on her clogs and left for the infirmary.

The nursing sister whispered that Mergriet had slept fitfully but now was fast asleep, so Beatrice went on to the main building to reassure herself that Clare was resting comfortably. Clare too was asleep, as was Celie, sleeping in the cot close by her. Celie should have been up by now, urging the schoolchildren in the large dormitory room upstairs to dress and comb their hair. They were boarding students who lived in the begijnhof during the school term; their homes were on farms or estates in the countryside, or in the small hamlets near Sint Joric. Beatrice could hear giggling, their bare feet slapping on the smooth floor, and the sound of splashing water in the large basin placed just inside their room. Quickly she roused a sister to take Celie's place, and very soon the splashing ceased.

Beatrice slipped out the side door of the building and walked to the plain stone chapel, its large glass windows reflecting the morning sun. Soon everyone would be gathering for morning prayers, but now the chapel was quiet as she walked to the marble altar, its carved wood crucifix suspended on a long chain. Kneeling on the stone floor, she prayed for healing for her two beguine sisters. Then, rising, she stood silently wondering how she could bring calm to her sisters and help them feel safe again.

When the service was over, Beatrice asked Sister Celie to take the children outside to play so she could speak to the sisters about the events of the night before. She stepped in front of the assembled beguines, feeling their eyes fixed on her as though she alone could cure this ill that had befallen the community.

"Sister Clare and Sister Mergriet are both sleeping." She began with what she hoped was a reassuring smile, hiding her shaking hands in the folds of her habit. "With God's grace and our prayers, I believe that Sister Mergriet's arm will heal and she will be restored to health. And I hope that Sister Clare eventually will recover from the shock of last night; thanks be to God, there was no damage to her person. At least for tonight, Sister Celie will again sleep in her room.

"I have thought much about this unknown intruder who dared to attack one of our sisters. We must pray that God will grant him forgiveness for what he has done." There was murmuring among the sisters, and some frowns, but she pressed on. "We do not know what brought the man here; perhaps he was simply a thief or a vagabond who dared to climb our wall and violate the security of this community.

"We could try to keep secret what happened last night, but one way or another word of the break-in will get to the townsfolk. Remember the words of the psalmist? I think it is Psalm 19: 'One day tells its tale to another, and one night imparts knowledge to another.' Thus, our response to questions should be that the intruder was repulsed, and no harm was done. After all, break-ins in Sint Joric are becoming more and more common in these difficult times. But no one, not even family members, must know that Sister Clare was attacked." Sister Beatrice spoke firmly and the sisters nodded, but they looked at each other questioningly. Why shouldn't they let people know that one of their sisters had been threatened? As if she had read their minds, Beatrice responded to their objections.

"What would the parents think if they learned that a man assaulted a beguine who was sleeping just steps away from their child? The attack on Sister Clare must be kept secret from the children living with us: in fact, from all of our students. Otherwise, their parents might decide that their children are not safe here, and withdraw them from our school. We cannot let that happen, sisters. We teach because it is our mission, but also because we need the fees parents pay us, in order to sustain ourselves. Both our livelihood and our mission are at stake. Please, please do not speak of the intruder's wicked act to anyone, not even your own families." Beatrice exhaled slowly; she felt as if her plea had been made in just one breath. She paused and then hurried on, her voice growing stronger.

"Outside these begijnhof walls the world is becoming more and more dangerous; thieves and other desperate men abound, and we must keep our begijnhof safe. After what happened last night, we can no longer assume that a wall is sufficient protection for us. It is not enough just to have a gatekeeper who screens our visitors during the daylight hours. Heretofore, we have simply locked the gates at night. But now I think we must hire a guard to patrol our walls from dusk until dawn. He will be instructed to challenge anyone who lingers near the gates or loiters along the part of our wall that is inside Sint Joric. Our outside wall is of course part of the town wall, which as you know, is patrolled by the town's watchmen.

"This begijnhof is a sanctuary; not just for the women of this community, but also for the children who live here with us. And it must remain so." By the time she had finished speaking, Beatrice's voice was hoarse. She took a linen cloth from her sleeve and wiped her face, her hand shaking.

The sisters looked at one another in silence, some with foreheads wrinkled in bewilderment, a few so agitated that they covered their faces with their hands and began to weep. Still others clenched their jaws in frustration, or shook their heads, uncomprehending. Clearly, their confidence in the begijnhof as a place of safety had been shaken.

"Now, let us pray." Beatrice knelt and clasped her hands together to keep them still, and listened to the familiar sounds of rustling dresses and scraping shoes as her sisters got down on their knees on the stone floor.

After petitions for the safety of the community, healing for Clare and Mergriet, and a prayer for the intruder, Beatrice rose and in silence led the women out of the chapel. Those who were teachers gathered their pupils and walked to the schoolhouse. A few went to the kitchen to prepare the midday meal, or fill baskets with loaves of bread to be given to the poor, already gathering at the main gate. Still others went to work in the garden. Beatrice went to her receiving room in the main building. Her head in her hands, she prayed that her sisters would not lose confidence in her.

By afternoon, Clare seemed her usual self, though Beatrice thought nightmares and fears would surely linger. When she suggested that Sister Celie continue to sleep in her room for as long as she felt the need, Clare was quick to accept.

Beatrice walked slowly to the infirmary, her head down, trying to gather her thoughts. Mergriet, awake and restless, her face taut with pain, was nevertheless anxious to be up and about.

"Please, Mergriet, be still so the bleeding does not start again," Beatrice cautioned, and then unwrapped her bandage and examined the cuts. "The cuts seem to be healing, but a hot poultice might help." Beatrice swung a kettle of water over the small coal fire in the fireplace, and then left to consult one of the sisters who had more knowledge of herbal remedies than she. On her return, she ground the recommended herbs in the stone mortar, wrapped them tightly in a cloth, and soaked them in hot water. Then she wrapped the poultice firmly around Mergriet's arm. Soon it cooled.

"I would like to return to my own room." Mergriet's voice, usually boisterous, was so low that Beatrice had to bend down to hear her.

"Grietje, you should stay here at least one more day, so that your bandage can be changed, and another poultice applied." But Mergriet shook her head, her hair slipping out of her headcovering. Beatrice sighed, helped her up, and put an arm around her sturdy body. Slowly they made their way to Mergriet's room in the main building, where she insisted on sitting in the chair by her bed. Beatrice pulled up another chair and the two women sat in silence for several minutes, their heads bowed. At last, Beatrice raised her head.

"Please accept my thanks and the thanks of the community for saving Sister Clare from an assault that could have ended in defilement, and perhaps abduction, had you not acted so swiftly. You were very brave and acted without thought for your own safety. I do not think she fully realizes yet the danger she was in, but when she does, I am sure Sister Clare will thank you also." Beatrice leaned down, trying to look into Mergriet's eyes, but Mergriet kept her head averted.

"Can you tell me more about what happened, or would you rather wait until you are feeling better?" Beatrice spoke gently but persistently.

Finally Mergriet looked into Beatrice's eyes and realized that any evasion, anything less than the whole truth, was out of the question. "It is true, what you are thinking. I-I was already in Sister Clare's room when the intruder entered. I was in a dark corner by the door, ah…thinking, and I saw this shape move into the room. I was stunned. I couldn't move. It looked like a shade from the dark side, silhouetted against the window, moonlight pouring around it. I could not see any features at all, just a looming form. Then, when it bent over Sister Clare, the moonlight shone on him and I realized it was a man, and I was horrified!" Mergriet's face tightened, her eyes widened, and she clenched her fists, holding them taut in her lap. For a few moments, neither woman spoke.

"Now, if you can, tell me what brought you to her room." Beatrice waited, hands folded in her lap, while Mergriet collected her thoughts. She willed herself to be silent, remembering that Mergriet was a young woman who had joined the community at seventeen. Her only experience of all-encompassing love was that of a young girl for her mother, and with her mother's death that love was lost to her. At last Mergriet met her gaze.

"Sister Clare is so beautiful, and she sparkles with life. Yet she keeps herself apart. I have only watched her; I never tried to be close to her. She is dainty and feminine and I…I feel sometimes like a clumsy field hand on my father's farm. Only in the kitchen, or when I'm playing games with the children, can I feel…comfortable." Mergriet paused again, looked down, and combed her hands through her wiry auburn curls, releasing them from the cap that already was slipping off. She tried to find the right words.

"I knew I should not have been in Sister Clare's room, I knew it was against the rules. But all I did was look at her. I did not touch her. I have not broken my vows.

I knew when I came here that this life would be difficult for me. I had never thought of becoming a religious. But I—father was pressing me to marry." She finished in a rush, raised her head, and looked straight into Beatrice's eyes.

"Aunt Beatrice, I have found a place here, baking bread for the poor. Baking gives me such pleasure; it is the thing I do best. And I have felt more unfettered behind these walls than I have felt since I was a small child, before I was bound by women's clothes and father's rules. I will never be a scholar like you"—at this Beatrice drew in her breath—"but I can offer up my humble gifts to God.

"I have learned much about prayer, and to be still and listen for God, but it is hard, hard. My faith is growing—slowly, but it is growing. I am trying to be a friend to my beguine sisters. Please, Sister Beatrice, do not make me leave the community for this transgression. Please give me another chance." And Mergriet began to cry, tears trickling down her cheeks, and her tears upset Beatrice more than her words had. She had not seen Mergriet cry since her mother's death, more than six years earlier.

Beatrice leaned forward and took her hand. "I do not judge or condemn you, Sister Mergriet." She spoke firmly, but her voice was soft. "This is a matter between you, and me, and God. There was so much confusion last night that I do not think anyone else realized you were already in Sister Clare's room when the intruder came. We will keep this to ourselves. You and I must spend as much time as we can in prayer about this matter. With God's grace, an answer will come."

Mergriet lifted her head, sniffled once, and straightened her shoulders. "Thank you, Sister Beatrice." Beatrice rose and helped her to her feet. Mergriet took off her shoes and climbed into her bed, relieved that least Aunt Bea had not summarily dismissed her from the beguine community.

Beatrice straightened as she made her way down the hall, nodding a greeting to Sister Elisabetta, who was preparing to leave for her town-house. Blinking in the bright sunlight, Beatrice walked to her own house and found herself, as always, comforted by its familiar surroundings. She climbed the stairs to her bedroom, took down her prayer beads and knelt on the prie-dieu by the window. She prayed for strength against the demon she thought had invaded Mergriet, and against those demons that had visited her in the swirling darkness. She prayed that God would hear her pleas and answer them; most fervently, she prayed that no one else had realized Mergriet was in Clare's room when that awful man climbed through the window.

CHAPTER TWO

Ten years earlier, 1320

One side of the townhouse rose straight out of the canal, and two of the windows on its upper level looked down on the murky water. The house was larger than most on the street in order to accommodate the shop on the ground floor. Carved into the shop's big door was a sewing needle as long as a dagger, painted a dull gold. Its large eye was threaded with roughly hewn yarn made of wood and painted bright red. There was no need for a sign: every matron in town knew that this was the best place to shop for thread, yarn, every kind of sewing need except the fabric itself. One went to the cloth merchants for that.

The rising sun lit the gold needle just as Old Bess, largest of Sint Joric's church bells, rang out to greet the dawn. The storks on the rooftop across the canal from the townhouse answered Old Bess by clacking their beaks and rising up from their nest of sticks and debris. Slowly a window on the upper floor of the house creaked open and Beatrice, wrapped in a plum-colored shawl of fine wool, leaned out. There was movement in the nest and she could see two scraggly chicks stretching their beaks up toward their parents, demanding food.

Willem, when he was small, loved what he called the 'giant whites.' The sound of their big bills clacking would bring him running to the window, and scrambling up on the stool Beatrice kept there just for him. The storks' legs looked like sticks and their habit of dipping their necks while flapping their black-tipped wings made him laugh and try to imitate them.

Willem had been a solemn child, but he gave himself over to joy when the storks arrived each spring.

He was born when Beatrice was nineteen, and the birth was difficult, with much bleeding. When it was all over, the midwife said she doubted there would be more children, and time proved her right. Gerard, Beatrice's husband, hid his distress and did not abuse her or treat her with contempt because she was now barren. And Willem, praise be to God, grew up strong and healthy. But now Gerard was dead, of a sickness that seemed to strike at the same time every spring. He had been swept away in three days, and buried a week ago. How she missed him! His warmth next to her at night. His arms around her as they came together. His smile greeting her when she came downstairs to help him in the shop. His comforting words in times of crisis: "Beatrice, my blessing, all will be well."

Theirs was the usual arranged marriage, but while most women of her class married in their early twenties, she was betrothed at sixteen because her father, in failing health, wanted her future settled before he died. Gerard was older, and well established in his business. He was as tall as she but somewhat portly, his hair already thinning when they met. Steady and patient, he had a ready wit and a sense of humor that Beatrice sometimes found disconcerting, having come from a family that took themselves, and life, very seriously. He countered her intensity with an ease that calmed her, the ease and confidence that charmed the patrons of his shop—and his father-in-law. Gradually they had come to love each other.

Gerard brought Beatrice to this house above his shop, and it had been their home for twenty years. She had made it a place more befitting their status, gradually adding to the rooms spare furnishings and replacing the oiled parchment windows with glass ones. The main room was warmed by the sun through polished windows that faced both the canal and the street, and was bright even on the frequent rainy days.

Benches and a trestle table of fine wood were placed against the wall facing the street, the table crowned with finely-wrought iron candlesticks twisted into vines whose leaves ended as spikes piercing their beeswax candles. Two armchairs with embroidered seat cushions sat before the fire, and a large dresser nearby held bowls and utensils. Straw on the floor absorbed some of the damp and the dirt, and herbs were strewn over the straw; pennyroyal and rue to repel insects, lavender and thyme for their pleasing aroma.

Beatrice stepped back from the window and glanced at the small trunk in the far corner. Her mouth curved upwards when she thought of her school and she brushed her hand across her lips, feeling her first smile since Gerard's funeral.

16

Teaching children was Beatrice's passion. Her collection of storybooks, most in Flemish, a few in Latin, was kept in that trunk. The children's favorites were old folk tales, some on parchment rolls saved from her own childhood. The wooden boards with scraps of parchment attached, that the children used to practice their writing, were stored there too.

Beatrice had "read" to her younger brother as soon as she could talk, pointing to the drawings and re-telling the stories her mother had read to her. So teaching Willem his letters had been pure pleasure, and when he was reading by himself, Beatrice set about trying to teach others. Her first pupils were her brother's children. Then her neighbor asked if she would teach his son. Soon she had a school of a half-dozen children, and the big, sunny room became a schoolroom each weekday morning. Gerard had supported her teaching, giving her money for new books written on parchment, illustrated with ink drawings, and bound with hemp. The respect the neighbors had for her teaching skills made him proud, and he enjoyed the occasional sounds of laughter that drifted down to his shop from the big room upstairs.

Beatrice's smile broadened, remembering her youngest niece's mischievous laughter. Mergriet, with her copper curls and plump body, her lips always about to break into a smile, wanted only to run and play. It was a challenge for Beatrice to capture her attention long enough to teach her to read and write, to learn her numbers, and then simple arithmetic.

Sighing, Beatrice closed the window and pulled the plum shawl closer around her. It had belonged to her mother, who had died during childbirth when Beatrice was ten. Her father, a scholar in a family of merchants, had insisted that she, as well as her brother, be well educated; thus she could read and write in both Flemish and Latin. But Father was always buried in his books, unable to show the feeling she felt sure he had for her. Except in his marriage gift, a beautifully bound and illuminated psalter containing all of the psalms and other devotional readings. She had clutched it tightly during Gerard's funeral.

Gerard had had little use for the church and less for Father Johan, their parish priest, but would willingly take young Willem for a walk along the canal so that Beatrice could go to mass by herself. Father Johan's sermons repelled her with their constant emphasis on sin and retribution. Yet sometimes, on those special holy days when the consecrated bread was actually placed on her tongue, she could feel something deep inside her swell and her faith was renewed.

Now Beatrice felt abandoned, by Jesus as well as by Gerard. She hunched her shoulders to shrug off such thoughts, lest she be overwhelmed by her guilt. Her prayers of contrition left her empty, lonely, and fighting off tears. Why couldn't she feel Jesus' compassion now, when she most needed it?

Her jaw clenched at the thought of Father Johan's conduct at Gerard's funeral mass. He said the mass, but his homily was perfunctory, conveying to all in attendance that Gerard was not a faithful member of his parish. Yet he bowed and smiled unctuously when she gave him a generous offering for his services. Then his mouth immediately resumed its thin line, and she turned away to hide her disdain.

At the sight of the table piled with sheets of parchment, Beatrice sighed and her head drooped. It was time to take Gerard's will to the town clerk, so that the deeds to the shop and the house could be transferred. She owned their business now: Gerard had bequeathed it to her, a not uncommon occurrence. But the building itself he had willed to Willem, as was proper. Naturally, Willem assumed she would take over the shop and he had urged her to continue living here. But she had no talent, nor interest, in shop-keeping.

Gerard's eye for color and his skill in showing his wares to advantage had made theirs a prosperous business. Bourgeois ladies of the town embroidered their fine woolen dresses with his beautiful threads and yarns, sometimes using bright hues to accent the muted colors their class required. Their workmanship was all that was needed to complete the ensembles that advertised their positions as wives of the most powerful merchants in Sint Joric. Even ladies of the minor aristocracy who favored brighter colors in brocade or silk frequented the shop on the "gold needle street."

Once, when Gerard fell ill, Beatrice had to run the shop by herself for a whole week. Her face perspiring and her hands clammy, Beatrice had stammered as she gathered together different colored yarns, trims, and thread and attempted to provide advice as to how they could be combined. It was obvious that her skills were woefully inadequate. She remembered in particular one afternoon when she had allowed her impatience to show in her voice, as she was forced to bargain with a demanding patron over the price of every item. And the guilt she had felt later. Now the shop was hers, but she did not want it.

Beatrice rolled up the parchment containing Gerard's will and went to their bedroom. She laid the parchment on the big bedstead's burgundy coverlet, its canopy draped with curtains, tied back now that spring had arrived. Then she slowly unwound the plum shawl and pressed it to her cheek before folding it and placing it in her clothes trunk. Slipping on a plain black dress over her linen shift, she smoothed it carefully, pulled on her hose and buckled on her shoes. Straightening, she went to the small sheet of polished tin hanging on the wall. On this bright morning it reflected the straw-colored hair falling around her shoulders and her clear gray eyes, deep-set under arched brows. Altogether, she gave the impression of calm, of one not easily upset. When at Gerard's deathbed her face had suddenly crumpled and reddened, her younger brother Hans scarcely recognized her.

Stepping back a little, she combed and braided her hair, secured it with long hairpins, and covered it with a close-fitting cap of fine linen. Next she arranged her wimple over the cap, letting the fabric fall on either side of her face. Finally, she pulled a plain black shawl from the trunk in the corner, picked up the parchment, and headed for the hall. At the sound of footsteps on the stairs she started, a hand on her chest. For a moment she thought the steps were Gerard's, but it was Willem slowly clumping up the stairs.

"Mother, how are you?" He greeted her with a restrained hug, but Beatrice gripped him tightly, dreading the conversation she knew would follow. Willem stepped back awkwardly. He was tall, with her gray eyes and his father's curly, dark hair, and he wore his usual working clothes: well-worn brown wool pants, sturdy boots, and a somewhat wrinkled linen shirt. He managed of one of his Uncle Hans' warehouses, and lived in the few rooms in its loft. As far as Beatrice knew, he spent most of his spare time there. A quiet young man, he had stifled his grief for his father's death by hardly speaking at all.

He followed Beatrice into the front room. "It's such a fine morning; I thought the shop might be open. Isn't it about time to…to get on with things? I think that is what Father would wish."

"Yes, your father would want us to go on as before, and I think we should open the shop again before long." Beatrice turned away, twisting the ends of the shawl in her fingers. "But…but not yet, Willem. The shop has been closed but a short while, and we are in mourning; surely it can stay shuttered a bit longer." Willem nodded silently.

"I am not ready to manage the shop just yet, to take it over by myself. But it is my responsibility now, and I should—be assured, Willem—I will see that it continues to prosper."

Their conversation had all the warmth of a stately dance between two strangers, and they soon parted with an awkward embrace, both uneasy in the knowledge that their relationship had changed. Willem was now the titular head of the family; but Beatrice had made clear that, as far as she was concerned, the head of the family was no longer present, and they would have to sort out their differences without him.

Beatrice waited until the door downstairs thudded shut, then dropped her shawl on the bed and started down the stairs. Even the decision as to whether she needed a shawl or her coat seemed a challenge these days.

"Mevrouw, can I get you a mint infusion and some bread from last night's supper?" Her servant Ingrid met her at the bottom of the stairs. She was thin and fair, her eyes a faded blue. She had served the family since Beatrice's mother died and now waited, noting her mistress' determined chin.

"No, thank you, nothing now, Ingrid; I will have something to eat later." Ingrid, though not much older than she, often chided Beatrice for neglecting to eat regularly. "And, I promise to buy food for a proper midday meal on my way home."

Beatrice pulled on her coat and stepped into the crisp morning. The air was fresh after the night's rain, the cobbled street cleaned of waste and debris. Children were spinning tops and playing tag, their wooden clogs clattering on the stones. Her step lightened as the children greeted her, and she smiled as one of them ran behind her to escape being caught. She let him hide behind her coat for a moment.

"Mistress, ah, Mevrow Van Belle, good morning." Stumbling over her words, Gretta, a neighbor, appeared in her doorway, and stopped Beatrice to express her condolences. Funerals were frequent; still, the sudden death of someone as strong and vital as Gerard came as a shock. To cover her distress, Gretta quickly began chatting about her cousin. "...Sister Marie is a beguine, and the family will gather as soon as she arrives. She is coming to pray for an aunt who is ill. Would you like to meet her?"

Beatrice demurred, and after thanking Gretta for the invitation, continued on her way. But the word "beguine" stayed in her mind. Beguines were often asked to pray for the ill or the departed, they fed the poor, and some were teachers, she knew that much. She knew little else about them, though their walled begijnhof was only a few streets away. Picking up her pace, Beatrice turned toward the center of town.

After presenting Gerard's will at the town hall and requesting that an official copy be made for the family, Beatrice strolled along the market stalls in the sunshine, listening to the sellers singing out their wares. Once a week farmers brought their goods to town, and today there were spring vegetables in abundance, and even fresh meat. She pressed her forehead, trying to remember what she needed and finally selected leeks, young carrots and peas, and a piece of spring lamb. And of course bread from the bakery nearby. Then she started home, first stopping at her parish church.

Sint Agustin was a simple church, its "Roman" style limiting its size. But a deep porch had been added, providing shelter from rain and wind.

Beatrice stepped onto the porch and pulled open the door. The church was empty at this time of day and dark, lit only by patches of light slashing through the narrow glass windows to the floor.

A massive marble altar and the wood crucifix hanging over it caught the eye upon entering the sanctuary. The crucified Christ was painted in excruciating detail, the colors softened by time. Behind the altar hung a worn tapestry of Saint Augustine in prayer, his once-bright halo and colorful robes now muted by disrepair and damp. A few tallow candles sputtered in a metal tray near the altar. Beatrice set down her market bags and lit a candle for Gerard, using the taper provided. She placed the candle in the tray and added a coin to the wooden box nearby. The heavy smell of melting sheep's fat filled her nostrils as she knelt on the stone floor to offer prayers for her husband. Fingering the prayer beads around her waist, she prayed for her family and for herself, then for the means to escape the shop, and continue teaching. The word "beguine" again flitted across her consciousness. For the first time since Gerard's illness she felt Jesus' presence in that place, and a faint hope that her prayers might be answered.

As she left the church, Father Johan came walking towards her. His small stature and slight build, and his dark hair and narrow face were unremarkable, until he had something of import to convey. She greeted him and on impulse asked him about the beguines. Suddenly his eyes bored into her and he thrust his body forward with a barely repressed energy that instinctively made her step back a little.

"Beguines? They're called 'religious women,' but I call them <u>loose</u> women. They are not nuns, they belong to no order. They are not sanctioned by the church, yet they dress alike and live behind walls as if they were a recognized religious community! They supposedly take vows of poverty, chastity, and obedience. Obedience to whom? They make their own rules. Beguines are women without men to control them, an offense against man and God." After repeating himself several times in slightly different form, Father Johan finished his diatribe, his face by now a deep red, his mouth an angry slash. Beatrice nodded briefly, her lips pressed together. At last she went on her way.

How foolish to ask Father Johan about the beguines. She knew well his views about the place of women. He sometimes railed from the pulpit against the rules allowing women to work in weaving, spinning, and candle-making trades, and to help husbands who were merchants sell their wares. Beatrice had heard from one of her cousins that he agreed with St. Thomas Aquinas' belief that women existed for only two reasons: to assist procreation, and to provide food and drink for men. Naturally, Father Johan would condemn the beguines and their way of life. After all, he

21

had implied that the beguines lived outside the authority of the church. That hardly seemed possible, but if it were true, it might explain why he disliked them so. And why had they chosen to live apart if they were not nuns?

Beatrice arrived at gold needle street with her purchases, the bags woven of twisted strips of cloth heavier with every step. When she reached home she entered by the side door, which opened onto the hall leading to the kitchen, and soon she and Ingrid had a fragrant pottage bubbling in the iron pot hanging in the fireplace.

That night as she undressed for bed, Beatrice tried to think of a way to keep the shop open and yet still continue teaching. She stood in her shift, slowly shaking her head. She could not escape it: she would have to run the shop. They employed a clerk, who had been with the family for years, but their customers would expect her to be there also, to provide advice on the best yarn or thread to go with a particular fabric, and of course to bargain if they felt her prices were too high. And she would have to do the ordering and see that goods were delivered on time and in good order. No, there would be no time to teach school. In frustration she splashed water on her face using more force than necessary, leaning over the basin Ingrid had brought her. She scrubbed her teeth with a scrap of cloth dipped in the mint infusion left there, then in a bit of salt. Relaxing, she unwound her plaited hair, ran her wide-toothed comb through it, and tied it back with a thick piece of yarn. The night had turned cold, and she shivered as she knelt on the wood floor beside the bed. She prayed for Gerard's soul, for Willem, and then for herself.

"Lord Jesus, thou knowest all my thoughts, all my failings. Help me to pray, Lord. And help me to go on teaching." She murmured the paternoster and the twenty-third psalm, her favorite. At last she felt calmer, and a feeling of warmth imbued her in spite of the cold floor. The fireplace in the main room next door hissed. She got to her feet, crawled under the goose-down coverlet and fell into a fitful sleep. Her dreams were of Gerard, solid, smiling at her lovingly as he invited her into the big bed. She was smiling, too.

Next morning she awoke, stirred up the fire, and swung a small kettle of water over it to make herself a cup of her strongest infusion, mint with hyssop, and for a treat added a bit of sugar. Soon she heard Ingrid's step on the stairs; she brought bread and some dried pear slices, determined that Beatrice would not again skip breakfast.

That afternoon Beatrice forced herself to go down to the shop, guiltily noting the dusty counter and dirty floor, feeling the abandonment of the place. She was reluctant to open the shuttered window, now striping the

22

worn wood floor with a thin light, lest passersby think the shop was open. She made her way behind the long counter, stroking the skeins of yarn in every color and shade as she walked by them. There were vibrant reds, lustrous purples, bright blues, pale and deep golds, and her favorite, rich plum. She settled on the wooden stool that fit her so comfortably. And no wonder, she thought, after the countless hours she had spent there, bent over account books and greeting customers when Gerard was out searching for new merchandise. In truth, though they never spoke of it, both knew that she was better at keeping accounts for the business, while he excelled at dealing with customers and getting the best price for goods for the shop.

The room was almost dark, shadowed by the townhouses across the street, when Beatrice finally roused herself, lit a candle and slowly climbed the stairs. "Beguines." The word slipped into her mind again as she prepared for bed.

Several mornings later, Beatrice rose and dressed with great care. Her head-covering confined her thick braid, her best wimple was carefully placed, and her finest black wool dress newly pressed. Finally she put on her coat and left the house. She had not far to walk but a light rain was falling, so she tugged the hood of the coat up to cover her head. The town was noisier than usual; she had forgotten that today was Sint Joric's feast day, and she could hear the crowds around the buskers and puppeteers in the market square. Beatrice had to push past a few people and rise on tiptoe, tall as she was, to see the blossoming chestnut trees and the spire of the begijnhof chapel above its wall.

An elderly cousin had told her that long ago the begijnhof had been on the outskirts of Sint Joric, beyond the town wall. But as the town grew it had incorporated the begijnhof wall into its own expanding wall, and now the begijnhof was part of the town itself. She looked down the alley for the place where the begijnhof wall began but almost missed it, so seamlessly did the two walls meet. A casual visitor passing by might not know the begijnhof was there, but one more observant would notice a slight crumbling of the mortar in a place where the wall curved, and would wonder why such large trees had been left standing behind what appeared to be a protective wall. By now many of the trees in town had been cut for fuel, yet these remained. Perhaps the beguines had planted them all those years ago for the cooling shade their leaves soon would provide. And of course for the chestnuts, roasted and eaten out of hand, or ground and mixed into bread flour to help sustain the community during the long winter.

Beatrice stopped at the iron gate, pulled the bell rope, and was passed through by an old man who touched his cap and smiled at her. A cluster of gray stone buildings stood beyond the chestnut trees. The wealth and power of the aristocratic benefactresses who had built the Sint Joric begijnhof were evident in the glass windows in its buildings and in the large plot of land its walls encircled. Off to one side, almost hidden, was a chapel with its own bell tower.

That building with the wide porch might be the school, and the large one perhaps a dormitory for boarding students. Behind a small building that could be the kitchen was a fenced vegetable plot, and next to it, fruit trees blossomed. A bread oven with its large chimney and bulging, rounded sides sat nearby. A number of modest townhouses, some with small gardens behind them, formed a semicircle close by the walls. She imagined the begijnhof as a small village unto itself. All seemed calm and quiet here after the noise and activity of the streets.

Beatrice stood in silence. Could I give up my home to live here, give up my freedom to come and go as I please? Forgo time with Willem, and gatherings with my brother and his family, and my cousins? And what would happen to the shop?

Yet the idea of being part of a community of women intrigued her. In conversations with family members she had learned a bit more about the beguines. "Those women seem to live much like nuns; they keep to themselves and are seldom seen in town, except on market day," one cousin had remarked at a family gathering. "That's all well and good," responded another, pursing her lips. "But they're not nuns—they're not even recognized by the church as 'religious', Father Johan says."

"Nonetheless, their school has an excellent reputation," a younger cousin remarked quietly. Beatrice talked with her later about the beguine school.

Suddenly a group of young children ran out of the schoolhouse. Followed by one of the beguine sisters, they began to play tag under the trees, their skirts billowing out from under their wool coats. Beatrice watched them, smiling, as she followed a path of smooth, flat stones that led to the door of the largest building, where she was admitted by a tiny old woman with a face like worn parchment, and a smile that seemed to illumine her whole being.

"I am Sister Celie. Welcome."

"I have come to see the grand mistress, and find out more about this... this interesting place."

"Of course, please, this way." Celie led Beatrice to one of the chairs near the entrance hall. On the wall opposite hung a beautiful tapestry of

Jesus feeding the crowd on the shore at Galilee. "Now, if you will wait a bit, I will tell Grand Mistress Anna that you are here." After what seemed a very long time an elderly woman, her head held high and wearing the plain beguine habit as if it were the dress of an aristocrat, approached and Beatrice rose, curtseying in greeting, her head bent.

"No, no. No such formalities here. I am Sister Anna. Sister Marie told me that you might visit us. Come, Mevrouw van Belle, and we will talk." The grand mistress led Beatrice down the hall and into a sunny receiving room, furnished with a large table at one side and several chairs pulled up to the fireplace. As she seated herself Beatrice felt a trembling inside, almost a premonition. She looked into a patrician face surprisingly unlined, yet with deep-set eyes that appeared to have seen everything. "Now tell me what you know about us, and what you would like to know."

"...and so I do not know whether I am suited to this life or not." Beatrice leaned back in her chair and took a deep breath, having poured out her thoughts about the beguines and the possibility of joining the community. "I love teaching, and I would want do that here, in this beautiful place. But I have no idea whether I can, or even if I should, live in a religious community."

"No one knows what this life is like until she tries it." Anna's voice was gentle. "If we should invite you, you would live here with us for a few months and then we would decide together if this is the place and the life for you." Anna asked questions about Beatrice's family, and Beatrice spoke of her husband's death and her reluctance to continue his business; about Willem and her reluctance to leave him, even though they had little in common, and were growing apart.

"Part of my interest in coming here is a desire to choose for myself how I should live, now that I am alone. Yet should I be invited to join you, it would also mean giving up much of my independence." Beatrice dropped her gaze from Sister Anna's face. Had she spoken too freely about her misgivings, her difficulty in making choices now that Gerard was gone?

Anna sat back and smiled faintly, as if she had heard such confessions before, and continued to explain the pattern of beguine life. "We beguines promise to live a life of chastity, frugality, and charity. Thus no men may visit here without my permission. We teach children in order to support ourselves and to be of service to the community. We do not live in poverty as the Poor Clares do, but we do believe in the careful use of what we have, so that we may serve others. We produce most of our own food; and most importantly, we bake bread for the poor who come to our gate, as well as for ourselves. And in these uncertain times more and more people are coming to us, knowing that we share our bread.

25

"We conduct our services in the little chapel twice daily, and study our Flemish Bible together most evenings. Only on the occasions when a Cistercian priest comes to say mass, do we use the Latin Bible." Anna paused to see how Beatrice would react to this radical departure from the church's practices. She seemed unmoved, so Anna moved on to more practical matters.

"Each of us, when we join the community, rents a room in this building—which also houses our boarding students—and we provide our own furnishings; those who can afford it may rent a house after a time, as one becomes available. Anna sighed audibly, and paused again.

"As you may know, not everyone approves of us." Beatrice recalled Father Johan's tirade when she had asked about the beguines. "But we have been in this place for over half a century now. It was founded with a gift from two widowed cousins of noble blood. Our school has a fine reputation, and most of the townsfolk approve of the work we do in feeding the poor. And there are many, many beguines living in communities such as this, taking similar vows, and governing themselves, I believe, much as we do." At this Beatrice's eyes widened. She felt uplifted, suffused by a warm feeling that settled in her chest.

"We would welcome your teaching experience and your fine education, should you join us." Anna rose, signaling the end of the interview, and went to the door. "Would you like to visit our school?" Celie rose from a chair outside, nodding, eager to show Beatrice the schoolhouse.

The calls of children greeted them when they stepped outside. Play time was over; the children were skipping or running down the short path to the building opposite. The sisters followed at a stately, unhurried pace. It was as though there was no need for haste: their days were measured by prayer, work, and gathering for meals, each in its own time.

As Beatrice had guessed, the wide porch led into the beguine school. The room for the younger children was large, sunny, and swept clean; coats hung on hooks by the door, with clogs beneath them. The children seated themselves on benches pulled up to long tables and resumed their work without chatter. There were a few dolls, and even tin soldiers, piled in a chest nearby. All rose when she and Sister Celie entered.

"No, no, please go on with your work; I don't mean to interrupt. I am just here to see your bright schoolroom," Beatrice smiled. Class continued with, surprisingly, a young boy reading aloud a folk tale Beatrice immediately recognized, and she smiled as she walked over to the shelf of books nearby. Soon she and Celie moved on to a room where older students studied with their mentors. Again the children rose, and one of the sisters, a small woman with dark eyes and a broad smile, joined them at the door.

"I am Sister Marie. Welcome. Here we teach our older girls household management, needlework, and if they show talent, the lute. If their parents agree and are willing to allow an additional time of study, we teach Latin to those who wish to learn more." Marie showed Beatrice a treatise on the use of herbs to treat illnesses. "I am teaching my students how to use common herbs to treat certain illnesses." Marie's enthusiasm and her pride in the students shone as she led Beatrice around the room. "One of our patrons gave us this, a copy of the latest Latin dictionary; just what we needed." And, "Ah, see how fine Sara's stitches are; she has a real eye for color." Beatrice smiled, admiring Sara's work; how smooth and even it was, compared to her own efforts.

Then Celie took her back to the main building, where several beguines were waiting in a large room. An elderly woman rose, extended her hand and spoke in very cultured Flemish.

"I am Sister Elisabetta; my surname is De Lu." She lifted her head, as if waiting for acknowledgement of her status as a member of one of the town's elite families. Beatrice merely smiled and introduced herself. "Oh yes, yours is the shop in gold needle street." Elisabetta's nostrils flared faintly as she replied. The introductions continued, and polite inquiries were made of Beatrice over cups of mint infusion. She would learn later that she had met many of the elders of the community on that first visit.

"Jesus, help me to make the best decision about my future. I feel so alone in this place, so empty." Beatrice knelt beside her bed that night, a lighted candle her only company. Finally, she blew out the candles, climbed into bed and lay back, unable to sleep. Her duty to Willem, to the rest of her family, and to the business, all weighed heavily on her chest, pressing her down into the soft bed. Yet her thoughts kept returning to the beguine school. She could see herself there, seated among the children, teaching them to read, to do sums, to sew—well, maybe not embroidery, but simple stitching. And Latin, how she would love to teach Latin to those eager young girls.

Mistress Anna and the elders met later to discuss the possibility of admitting Beatrice for a trial period. Her family was well known in the town; still, inquiries must be made about her husband's family, her son, her piety.

"But she would bring no—distinction to the community." Sister Elisabetta's view that the begijnhof should be a refuge for widows of the elite was well known.

27

Grand Mistress Anna pursed her lips. "Sister Elisabetta, we would find ourselves a very small group indeed, if we admitted only women from the 'elite' of Sint Joric."

"Mevrouw DeBelle's teaching skills and her fine education would be a great asset." Sister Marie spoke up, pointing out that from the beginning the beguine sisterhood had been charged to provide for themselves, and teaching was the means the beguines of Sint Joric had chosen. Each of the elders had her say, and then the community decided: after her time of mourning was over, Beatrice would be invited to stay in the small room used for guests, to see if she might be a suitable addition to the community.

The year of mourning dragged on, and Beatrice chafed at her long days in the shop, sitting on her stool behind the counter. She chatted with the customers and cajoled them until she felt her face was a mask with a smile fixed upon it. The nights were long too, and her bed cold. But the seasons turned, and at last spring arrived again, and she put away her black dresses. Then word came that she had been invited to a trial period in the begijnhof.

Beatrice looked forward to going, yet felt a strange reluctance at leaving the shop. She hugged herself, gripping her shoulders to shake off her unease. *Perhaps it is because the house and the shop are linked,* she thought, *and not just by wood and stone; together they have held my life for twenty years. But this is only a trial period; I have not decided to become a beguine, and they have not yet chosen me.*

Soon after she received the news, Beatrice asked Willem to come to the house. She knew he would be dismayed at her decision to stay with the beguines for a time. And he was.

"Mother, what are you thinking of?" Willem paced the floor of the front room, warm in the morning sun. "What about the shop? You cannot expect me to run two businesses at the same time. Are we just to close up this business while you are gone?"

Since his father's burial, Willem had gone back to work without thinking much about the shop: his mother had charge of it, since it was now hers. He ran both hands through his thick hair. "Why do you want to go to these—these beguines to stay, when you have a comfortable home right here?"

There was a long pause. Beatrice thought that nothing she could say would help Willem understand what the beguines were about. She went to Willem, put a hand on his arm, and spoke softly.

"I think your cousin Pieter might agree to run the business during my trial period at the begijnhof." Beatrice had carefully considered that possibility, had even spoken with young Pieter about it.

"So you're just going to go, is that it?"

"Yes, Willem, I am." Beatrice felt a knot in her stomach, but she took her hand from his arm and straightened to her full height.

"Well then, Mother. I must go now." Willem could hardly bear the hot stuffy room a minute longer. There was not much he could say: they both knew that his mother could do what she liked with the shop. Soon he was clumping back down the stairs.

Beatrice wandered about the flat after he left. She leaned over the stairwell and shook out the down comforter with more energy than usual, smoothed it back on the bed and punched up the pillows, rather than plumping them. Willem had a right to be upset, even angry, and she felt it was not just about the shop. It was also about her leaving him, and putting herself first.

Pieter agreed to take over the shop temporarily and he worked alongside Beatrice for several weeks, greeting customers with an easy smile. Meanwhile, Ingrid helped her prepare the things she would take to the begijnhof, her presence a constant reminder to Beatrice of what she was leaving behind.

"Of course I understand, Mevrouw. You are lonely now that the Mijnheer is gone." Ingrid stood folding one of Beatrice's shifts, which she had washed and carefully ironed, her head bent slightly to avoid looking into Beatrice's face. No need for the mistress to see that tears had suddenly blurred her vision. Carefully, she placed the shift in the mistress' trunk.

One night about a month after she had arrived at the begijnhof, Beatrice awoke in the guest room, her cheeks wet. Had she been crying? The moon was almost full, and she could see her "schoolroom" trunk in the corner, stacked with books, and her clothes hanging on pegs on the wall. What had she done, coming to stay at this strange place? The loss of Gerard was a hollow ache deep inside her.

At last she fell asleep, and dreamed that she was walking down a long, dark road, tall trees bending over it on either side. She kept stumbling over obstacles in her path, and her feet hurt from walking on the rough ground in her soft leather shoes. Finally she could see a faint light ahead, and when she reached the light at the end of the road she was enveloped in warmth. There were smiling faces around her and a voice said, "Welcome. We are so glad you made it here."

Beatrice again awoke, to a room still dark but with dawn a dull gray curtain at the window. Birds had begun their morning songs. She felt strangely calm. The dream was still vivid, and she wondered at the welcoming voice and the warmth she had felt. Her dreams often seemed portents, and she tried to remember what the faces around her had looked like. They were comforting faces, angelic even. At last she roused herself, but by the time she had dressed the dream had faded, and all of her aching uncertainty again pressed down on her.

Next morning she joined Marie on a bench in the shade, watching the youngest children at play after the morning lessons were over. Marie was always ready to laugh, was adored by the children, and they were instantly ready to learn whatever she had to teach them. Beatrice had friends among her large extended family but until she met Marie, no one she had known, except her father, had shared her love of learning.

The light spring shade dappled their bench and played over their faces. Some of the older children were chasing a large hoop down the dirt path, trying to guide it with their sticks. Others tossed a ball back and forth, still others played a running game. The day students played unencumbered by the street traffic in town, and the boarding students were free from the duties that occupied much of their time at their homes in the countryside.

"Mevrouw de Belle, how do you find this life?"

Beatrice jerked her head; she had been daydreaming while she watched the children. She rubbed her forehead, thinking how best to respond.

"It is almost unbelievable to be in a community where women sing the prayers and conduct the daily service all in Flemish, with no clergy present. It is a life I never could have imagined. And teaching again is—well, it is a privilege to be here. But I just do not know if I could stay, should you invite me." Beatrice's voice had gradually become fainter, until she almost was speaking in a whisper. Marie did not press her.

The next day Beatrice asked to speak to the grand mistress. The receiving room was gloomy and rain poured in sheets down the window panes. A small fire in the grate, and a candle on the table between the two padded chairs provided the only interior light. Beatrice seated herself at Sister Anna's invitation and leaned forward.

"Mistress Anna, I have been selfish, putting my own desires before my duty to my family, leaving my son behind. I—I think I have made a mistake in coming here."

"Mevrouw van Belle, almost every woman who comes here leaves loved ones behind—parents, children, grandchildren." Anna looked deeply into Beatrice's face. "True, we do visit our families on rare occasions.

"But here we have an opportunity to live a simple life of prayer and service, offering whatever gifts we have to God's glory. I have seen your face filled with joy when you are with the children. God gave you the gift of teaching.

"I suggest that you devote more time to prayer and meditation before you decide if you are willing to make the sacrifices this life requires. Ask God what He has in mind for you. Then be still and listen... Listen." Anna rose, smiling. "And then come to me, and we will talk again."

Beatrice struggled to discern God's will for her over the next several weeks. There were days when the joy of teaching a child to read wiped out the guilt she felt about the selfishness of choosing this life. But then came the sleepless nights when guilt overcame her. Often she tossed in the narrow bed until dawn, and then knelt beside it to pray.

"Is it sinful to choose the life I want, Lord? Willem is a man now, and he must make his own way. Why can I not do the same? Must I drag this guilt with me like the cross penitents drag behind them in the Good Friday procession? Allow it to follow me into beguine life?" There was no answer, no sign from God. Her faith was sorely tried.

"Why does God not answer my prayers, Grand Mistress?" Beatrice was almost pleading. "I have prayed, I have fasted, but as you said when we last met, the burden of this decision is left to me."

"I can sympathize with your distress, Mevrouw. But you are right: the decision to choose this life is yours alone. I feel certain that the sisters will invite you to join us, and then you must give us your answer. But remember, there is no stigma to leaving if you decide later on that this is not the life for you. No one, within the community or outside it, will count it against you."

Several months after she came to stay at the begijnhof, Beatrice was invited to join the community; she rejoiced at the news and accepted with alacrity, but that nagging voice inside kept nudging her: "You have chosen to do what _you_ want to do, and to be where _you_ want to be." Yes, she knew that she could leave the community at any time. But she also knew her pride would never allow her to do so.

Again, she waited in the front room of the house on gold needle street on a warm day. But the room, the entire flat, looked different; it had faded somehow, in spite of Ingrid's care. The things that mattered—Gerard's favorite hat on the peg in the hallway, her "schoolroom trunk," the stool by the window across from the storks' nest—were gone. Beatrice rubbed her forehead and straightened as Willem came in. They hugged briefly.

31

"I have to say it, Willem; it pains me to be here." Beatrice began. "Much as I loved our home and our life here, it is a hollow shell without your father. And yes, I know you miss him too." Beatrice's voice faltered. "I do not want to live here alone." Yet, there was that knot inside her, reminding her that if it were not for the pull of beguine life, she undoubtedly would have stayed in this place. "I want very much to continue to teach, Willem, and I can do that only in the beguine community—"

"But mother, you could start your little school again, right here at home, if you wanted to." Willem interrupted, not realizing how patronizing he sounded. He paced the room with his hands behind him, sweating in the room's sun and heat.

Beatrice bristled at his words. "My 'little school' could not support me, Willem, and I do not want to be dependent on you, nor go back to the shop. I am not suited for shopkeeping: I have neither the skills nor the patience for it. I would end up driving customers away, and we certainly do not want that. And I want to spend more time in prayer, to try to become closer to God. I know it is hard for you to understand, but please try." Beatrice stopped, her face flushed.

Willem was silent.

"There are some things I should do soon." Beatrice hurried on, to fill that awful void. "I must move my belongings to the begijnhof and I must pay for my lodging there, in a building with large rooms, where most of the sisters live. I will have to pay for my own living expenses as well, provide my own clothes and so on." She paused and took a deep breath. "You see, beguines are expected to provide a dowry for themselves, if they are able. Or their families provide it for them. Nothing like that required by a nunnery, but still…

"And there is the matter of Ingrid." Her throat suddenly filled and she paused and swallowed. "We must continue to take care of her. Eventually, I would like to rent one of the smaller houses within the begijnhof grounds, and bring Ingrid to live with me there. That is, if I can afford it and she wants to come. I have no choice but to sell the business in order to have the money I need."

Willem's face had reddened and he tugged at his shirt collar. "Sell the business? The business that Father built so successfully? And what if you change your mind about being a beguine and want to leave? What would you live on then?" He paced the front room. One of the headaches that sometimes plagued him was coming on; Beatrice could see it in his frown and his tightened jaw.

"I have some rights as a beguine, Willem." Her voice softened. "The furnishings I bring with me are my property and if I should decide to leave, most of the money I bring into the community would be returned to me." She continued with more assurance. "If I stay, the community will care for me if I should become ill, and I will be cared for when I can no longer work."

"Well, Mother, you have made up your mind, that is clear. There is nothing more to be said." Willem slapped his hat against his thigh, then turned and left. But there were many more conversations, and finally Willem agreed to buy the business from her in two installments, several years apart. With the first payment, which he took from the money his father had left him, Beatrice had enough for her initial contribution to the community. She was eager to be off, impatient with the details of transferring the business and preparing her belongings.

But leaving Ingrid behind was a continuing source of guilt and pain. She had agreed to continue living behind the kitchen, taking care of the shop and the rooms upstairs as she always had. She had come from the country and had no family in Sint Joric. But Beatrice knew she had a few friends whom she met during her frequent trips to the shops.

"Ah, Ingrid, some day I'll have a place of my own in the begijnhof. Would you consider living with me there?"

"Mevrouw, I will come if you have a place for me, but only if I do not have to join the community. As you know, I have no wish for beguine life. I want to be with my friends, as I always have."

"Of course, Ingrid. And I have made inquiries; there are other sisters living in the townhouses who have made that same choice." Beatrice embraced Ingrid for the first time since she was a child, bereft at her mother's death.

When she told her brother Hans of her plans, he was dumbfounded. "Give up a successful business to be a beguine? At least there is some respect accorded to becoming a nun. You bring no credit to our family by going into that begijnhof. Think it over, Beatrice."

"Hans, I have made up my mind. If it is the wrong choice, I am free to leave. That would be near impossible if I were a nun." She summoned all her patience, knowing she would have to make this announcement to every family member, and undoubtedly not one would understand why she wanted to become a beguine.

Finally, Beatrice moved her belongings into the begijnhof, pleased that the room provided for her was a spacious corner one, with windows on two sides. She hung her coat and the gray-brown wool dresses Ingrid had made for her on pegs on the wall, her clogs and shoes beneath them. Her shifts and finer garments were folded into her trunk. The stories for children and the writing boards she stored in her small "schoolroom" trunk; her precious books were stacked on the chest of fine-grained, dark wood she had brought with her. It had been in the main room of their upstairs flat, and its deep drawers had held the account books for the shop. A chair from home was pulled up to a large table, and above its comforting solidity hung a remembrance of her mother.

It was made from a deep blue wool shawl, a gift from her father to her mother. Her mother had embroidered one corner of the shawl with field flowers, wrought in fine yarn, and so intricately made that the blossoms were almost brought to life. Beatrice had worn the wrap occasionally, and one afternoon left it on the end of her bed. That day the storks had arrived, and on hearing them Willem came running through the bedroom waving a toy soldier of bright red metal. The toy caught one edge of the wrap and tore it. Rather than mending it, Beatrice had chosen to edge the flow-ered portion, back it with sturdy cloth fastened to a thin piece of wood, and hang it on the wall.

Her beloved psalter rested on a small table beside her bed, a brass can-dlestick beside it. She hung the prayer beads she received when she entered the community on a peg above her bed. She had become a beguine, and she told herself again and again that she would never regret her decision. Yet she had to accept that nothing she could say would assuage Willem's hurt and anger. She had not seen him since the day they had met to sign the papers transferring the business to him. She knew it would be a long time before she saw him again.

CHAPTER THREE

Summer, 1326

eatrice bent forward as if she had been struck a blow. Anna, the venerable grand mistress beloved by her sisters and respected by the townsfolk, was dead. She had been failing, they all knew that; still it was a shock. Beatrice was rising from her prie-dieu when word was brought to her. She sank back down on her knees for a few moments' prayer for Sister Anna. Then it was time to go to the chapel, where the sisters would be gathering to mourn their leader.

Many in the town, including her large family, attended Anna's funeral at the begijnhof; there was barely room enough in the chapel for all the mourners. They had to crowd together, and though the windows were open the space soon became too warm, and all were perspiring in the stifling heat.

The sisters sang the requiem in polyphonic harmony, the music floating up to the peak of the sanctuary. Abbot Paulus came from the Cistercian abbey, a day's journey away, to celebrate the mass. Burial followed in the chapel's small graveyard, the family acceding to Anna's wish to lie within the walls of the place she had loved so well.

Selecting a new leader for the beguine community was a matter of great import. It was customary to choose the grand mistress from the elders, or "wise ones" though all were not wise and a few were not old. Some were included by virtue of their families' wealth and position. Others because they were judicious and prudent, able to make wise choices for the welfare of the community, and Beatrice was one of those. She knew that her willfulness, the determination to go her own way that had brought her here, also had enabled her to step out and become an elder in the community. Yet her headstrong nature was like a spirited horse, always ready to run. And though her need to prevail in any contest of wills sometimes caused her to stumble, she had yet to fall.

When the elders met, usually in the receiving room after dinner, the meetings at times seemed endless; each sister could voice her opinion, and most often they came to an agreement. But they looked to their grand mistress to guide them, and she had the last word. She was also the arbiter of any dissent, and the disciplinarian, should any of the sisters stray from her vows, a rare occurrence.

"This young lady is simply not suitable! She wants to become a beguine only to escape marriage to that squat, pox-marked, wealthy man her family has chosen." Sister Elisabetta knew all the gossip in town, and she was correct. The woman was not invited to join the community.

"We need to plant some flowers along the paths, perennials or bulbs perhaps. This place, especially when winter is almost over, looks drab and uninviting." Sister Sara spoke up.

"Sister Sara loves to garden. Wouldn't she welcome the job of planting those flowers by the front door?" One of the elders whispered to another.

On one occasion a desirable house in the community was vacated unexpectedly, when its elderly occupant died suddenly during the night. After the funeral and a decent interval, it was time to decide who should be given the opportunity to lease the house.

"This is one of the largest houses in the begijnhof," said a sister who lived in a similar one. "It should go to Sister Olga. I know she wants it, and she can well afford the lease."

"I think we should consider giving the house to Sister Margaretta." Beatrice spoke up. "Yes, I know she cannot afford it unless a contribution is made to the lease. Still, she has been a wonderful teacher here for so long. I think one of our patrons might be willing to contribute to the cost of her lease."

"But Sister Beatrice, if we offer the house to Sister Margaretta and a patron does not come forward, the community would suffer a loss of income, and we don't want that." This from Sister Elisabetta.

In spite of Beatrice's impassioned plea, she did not prevail. Grand Mistress Anna stepped in, and the house was leased to Sister Olga. It took all of Beatrice's will power to accept defeat with good grace. But she acquiesced with a tight smile.

Beatrice paced in front of her sitting room window, open to catch the faint breeze. Bright sunshine lightened her hair, now showing a bit of gray at her temples but still wound in a thick braid. She had furnished this small house with the belongings from her room in the main building, adding only a bed for Ingrid's room and, at Willem's urging, two comfortable armchairs from the house in town. She sat down in the one closest to the window.

Ingrid had settled into the small room next to the keeping room, free to come and go as she pleased. She greeted the sisters stiffly, and continued to visit with her friends in town. Yet her ties to the DeBelle family were strong, and she felt it her duty to keep Beatrice abreast of family news when she visited the house on gold needle street. Her only complaint was that she had few meals to prepare, since the mistress ate most of her meals with the community.

They had lived in the house only a few years, but Beatrice felt as though it had always been hers. The flat above the shop had become a distant memory. A knock at the door, and Beatrice pulled herself out of her chair. It was time for the elders to meet.

The deliberations were long and solemn and when they were over, Beatrice was asked to be the new grand mistress. Why had she been caught by surprise, when she herself had been present for most of the discussions? Only Sister Elisabetta had expressed her reservations about Beatrice aloud.

"I agree that Sister Beatrice would be a good leader of the community. But I am not sure that she has the stature this position requires. Will our school continue to attract students from the best families if she is our grand mistress?" Everyone knew that Elisabetta was distantly related to a family of the minor nobility.

"Sister Elisabetta is such a snob," whispered one of the elders, her voice a bit loud as she was hard of hearing. "After all, status is not what makes a good grand mistress." Elisabetta flushed and said no more, but her downturned mouth expressed her displeasure.

"Thank you for offering me this great honor." Beatrice's voice shook a little, but she was smiling. "I will try to discern if it is God's will that I should accept it, and I will give you my decision soon." The sisters nodded approvingly.

Beatrice went immediately to the chapel, seldom occupied during the day. Like the buildings around it, the chapel was of stone with large windows. Its altar was a simple slab of marble, polished by reverent beguines since it was first placed there.

She knelt on the stone floor at the altar rail and prayed for a sign that she should accept the elders' invitation. But no sign came. Deep in prayer, she hardly noticed the lengthening shadows. Then the chapel bell tolled; she got to her feet just as the door opened and the sisters and the children filed in, gathering for evening prayer.

The next afternoon Beatrice asked Sister Marie to share a pot of mint infusion in the quiet of her parlor. Ingrid crushed the dried mint leaves and placed them in a pot, poured boiling water over them, and steeped them for a long time, brewing them just as her mistress preferred. They two sat silently in those comfortable chairs placed before the window in the small sitting room. They blew on their mugs to cool the fragrant drink.

"Sister Marie, I don't know if I am the best choice to be grand mistress. Why did we not ask Sister Clothilde? She knows everyone of importance in Sint Joric, she has been here a very long time, and she has a commanding presence."

"We did consider Sister Clothilde; you were part of that gathering, though you said little. But remember, we were looking for someone younger. Sister Clothilde has indeed been here a long time. But you, Sister Beatrice are healthy, a strong woman, and very capable. It is that strength, and your readiness to respond when others need help or advice that make you our best choice. Sister Anna once told me that you had become wise at a young age."

"Ah, how kind of her. How we all miss her." Beatrice smiled, warmed by the compliment from a woman she had so admired.

"Indeed. And I believe you truly love God, Sister, you just do not talk about Him much."

At this, they both laughed, but Sister Marie, unknowingly, had touched upon what Beatrice felt was her greatest weakness: How could she lead these women when her own faith was lacking? That lack felt like a stone lying deep inside her. The weight had been there since she first heard of the beguines, first stayed at the begijnhof, and was with her during every prayer since, asking, begging for a stronger faith. She looked on with envy at the ecstasy of faith that caught up some sisters when they celebrated the feast of Pentecost, or mourned during Good Friday prayers. At dawn, she was on her knees at her prie-dieu, her psalter open, and after evening prayers she often retired to spend the last of the day on the prie-dieu as well. And still that weight was with her.

"Sister Marie, do you ever feel sometimes that your faith is faltering? That Jesus seems so far away that no prayer of yours can reach him?" Beatrice leaned toward Marie and spoke almost in a whisper. "There was that time when Willem was so ill. I was caught up in remorse for my absence from his life. I wept at his side, I prayed for him and for myself, yet in the end I believed it was his own strength that brought him back to life. Or was Jesus truly there, supporting him?" Beatrice bent her head, her shoulders hunched, trying to shrug off her guilt at such thoughts.

"Yes, Sister, there have been times when I felt my heartfelt prayers were of no use, and I was so discouraged that I could not speak. And when I finally felt a stirring of renewed faith, it was like a drink of cool, refreshing spring water." Again the two sat silently for a long time. Suddenly Beatrice shivered, even though the room was warm. *Dare I tell Sister Marie the whole truth?* she thought. *That imagining myself as grand mistress frightens me?* Finally the sun dropped behind the begijnhof wall, a reminder that their sisters would soon be gathering for evening prayers.

~~~

The late summer days were long, and this had been an especially long day for everyone. The sun was beginning to slide behind the tallest trees, and their shadows fell across the pathway to the chapel. The bell rang for evening prayers, and the boarding pupils and sisters gathered and walked down the path, the beguines' steps slower than usual, the oldest ones leaning on the arm of a younger sister. As they entered the chapel once again, they began to chant one of their favorite hymns of praise:

> "Of the Father's love begotten,
> ere the worlds began to be,
> He is Alpha and Omega,
> He the source, the ending He…"

Daybreak seemed an eternity ago. The sun had lightened the walls of the children's dormitory from almost black to deep gray. The room was quiet, the children sleeping in their low beds, a trunk at the end of each bed and next to each bed, a chair. The chair served as a place to sit when pulling on hose and shoes, or as a handy spot to put a treasure acquired during the day; perhaps a found object, such as a shell from long ago, when the whole area was part of the North Sea.

Each family had brought a trunk, usually made of leather, and filled with clothing when their child entered the beguine school; the family was expected, if they were able, to provide additional clothing as needed. A favorite toy might be included, to ease a child's parting from her parents.

As the room brightened, the children began to stir. Soon Sister Celie appeared. The children could not remember a day that had not begun with a procession to the chapel. But on this day Sister Celie led them in some simple prayers right there in the dormitory, they went down to the privy and then proceeded to the kitchen to eat.

Breakfast had sealed this day as special, for in addition to the usual small cup of goat's milk and thick slice of bread, there was pear honey spread on the bread, a rare treat. It was fragrant, sweet, and thick. The youngest girls smacked their lips, and all of them licked their fingers when they had finished. At last breakfast was over, and the children wiped their sticky faces and hands on clean, damp cloths provided by Sister Celie.

Back upstairs, they dressed in fresh shifts and their best dresses, the ones saved for special occasions. The little girls' hair was brushed free of tangles and left unbound. The older ones' hair was braided in two plaits that fell obediently down their backs.

"There will be a special service today," Sister Celie announced to the children, "and some very important people will be there. It is a celebration." She smiled, but all she would say in answer to the children's questions was "You will find out soon enough."

There was more than the usual talking and giggling as the girls guessed at what the day might bring. They tried to think of what saint's day it might be, but they did not have special treats for a saint's day— there were too many! Milling about in the hall, they waited to proceed to the chapel.

Peeking out of the window on tiptoe, one of the littlest girls gasped, "I think I see Jesus!" At this they all ran to the windows and there, with his back to them, stood a figure dressed in white, his feet in sandals and his hair flowing freely around a bald spot on the top of his head.

One of the older girls said with a disdainful expression, "That is Father Alban. He's a Cist...er...a priest who comes here sometimes. I saw him once." Father Alban's hair was thick and long and he wore the simple habit of undyed white wool of the Cistercians; he did indeed look like a holy man. He turned, smiled, and waved to them. Sister Celie called them back to order, covering her smile with one hand to hide her missing teeth.

At last Celie led them in single file to the chapel. The day students were already there, a few of them boys, all dressed in their best clothes and standing like statues. The statues came alive as they made way for the newcomers; there was shuffling of feet and a few whispers and then all was quiet.

The children came to the chapel every day for prayers, yet today it looked different. The altar shone in the strong mid-morning sunshine, the crucifix upon it glowing with a special light. The triptych mounted on the wall behind the altar was made of beautifully carved wood painted in bright colors, and it too shone with reflected sunlight. In the center

40

panel Jesus the Good Shepherd was holding his staff, carrying a lamb, and smiling faintly. To the children he looked friendly, as though you might climb up into his lap sometime to listen to a story. The sun lit his gold halo. Would it burn you if you touched it? On the panels to his left and right were saints on their knees, praying. All had haloes of gold leaf, and looked heavenward, as if they were in some other world, which they probably were, some of the children reasoned. In a bottom corner of the right panel a tiny figure of a woman knelt, her eyes cast down.

Finally the service began. It lasted a very long time, but there was so much color and music that it seemed more like an entertainment than a mass. There was a real procession: first came Father Alban's assistant, carrying the cross; then Father Alban, Abbot Paulus' appointed representative, who had waved to the children; and finally Father Matthias, the rotund Cistercian priest who sometimes came to say mass. Next came the sisters, two by two in freshly pressed gray-brown habits, their wimples snowy white, and their prayer beads swinging at their waists. They chanted plainsong in a canon. The two strands of melody twined together, swirling upward toward the chapel's ceiling, filling the sanctuary with an ethereal sound that gradually faded away as all took their places. Finally Sister Beatrice, impressive in height and demeanor, proceeded alone down the center of the aisle. She was immaculately dressed: her gray habit of the finest linen, her head covered with a fresh white wimple so fine it was almost diaphanous. She wore a large chain of prayer beads around her waist, alternating white beads that looked as if they were made of ivory and larger ones that looked like beads of coal. She carried her beautiful psalter, which the children had never seen before.

"Sister Beatrice is the new grand mistress," breathed one of the children. Only a few girls around her heard her, and she was instantly shushed. But a ripple of anticipation passed through the children and soon the entire congregation felt it.

Beatrice took her place next to Father Alban at one side of the altar. As she looked out over the gathering of sisters and children, she saw the small knot of townspeople, most of them families of the beguine school's day students. She noted, unsurprised, that Father Johan was not there. Then she saw her son Willem; she was thrilled that he had come to witness her investiture. He was dressed in his best dark gray suit but he looked grave, his lips pressed together.

Beatrice bowed her head for a moment. Would Willem always feel she had deserted him by becoming a beguine? Would there always be that gulf between them? They had visited together but a few times since she had entered the begijnhof. She felt guilty that she saw so little of her son, and her brother and his family, but pushed away her feelings of regret, as she had done many times before.

She straightened, and took a deep breath, remembering Sister Anna's words about the gift she had received in exchange for her sacrifice. I am not the uncertain, grieving widow who entered these walls years ago, she thought. This is my home now, and I am proud of the honor I have been given.

The service itself began with music, so important to the beguines. This time it was a polyphonic melody chanted by the sisters. They must have been practicing in secret to sound so heavenly, Beatrice thought, and allowed herself a slight smile. Prayers and Bible readings came next. Father Alban gave a brief homily, exhorting the sisters to be true to their calling.

"...and so I bid you, sisters, to obey your new grand mistress and the rules you set for yourselves when this community was founded: to live chastely, as befits a community of women living apart from men; to cultivate a humble and frugal lifestyle; and to practice charity, by feeding the poor who come to you hungry." Then came more prayers, and finally the mass, with Father Alban wearing a beautifully embroidered chasuble of soft white wool over his monk's robe.

By the time the service was over, the children felt as though Sister Beatrice had been blessed and prayed over by most of the adults present. The chapel bell was rung to mark the joyous occasion. The children left the chapel, some skipping and others almost running in relief after all that time alternately standing still and kneeling on the stone floor.

Everyone proceeded to the dining hall in the main building and gathered around the tables. Father Alban said the blessing and wine was served to the adults, weak ale to the children. The main dish that day was too fine to be called a pottage. There were big thick chunks of chicken in a rich broth with turnips, parsnips, mushrooms and onions, and each guest had their own bowl and spoon. Hard-cooked eggs were passed; the bread, spread with butter, had been baked with their finest wheat flour; and there were little cakes covered with sweetened fruit afterward. The children ate their fill and then ran outside to play games while the adults lingered at the table.

Talk turned to recent events, and the beguine sisters listened intently, as their only news came from their occasional visits to town. Crops were drying up for lack of rain, and the merchants would have to import more grain from southern Europe in order to mill enough flour for the winter months. Thus, the price of bread was rising. The sisters were seeing the evidence of hard times in the lengthening lines of the poor waiting at the gate each morning for their fresh-baked bread, the loaves now of necessity a bit smaller and made of coarser flour.

All were relieved at the lull in the fighting between England and France. However, there were rumors that England would restrict trade with the powerful cities of Flanders. But surely England would continue to sell Flanders the wool upon which her weaving industry depended. There were also rumors of tension mounting between the King of France and the Count of Flanders.

By late afternoon the room quieted, all sated with food and wine. The children were tired, and those who lived at the begijnhof were happy to go upstairs to their dormitory room to play quietly or take a nap. Sister Celie followed them. The day students found their families and sat leaning against a mother, an older sister, or an aunt. At last the visitors gathered up their children and their belongings and said their good-byes. All agreed it had been a fine celebration.

Willem lingered by the door of the main building until all the others had gone. He had come to please his mother, but felt out of place in this world of women. He spent his days at the warehouse, and seldom went out at night. Recently, at a cousin's marriage feast, he met a woman who returned his glances with a smile, and he had managed to overcome his shyness and stay by her side. Willem and Ilse had spent much of that afternoon talking together, and he had met her parents. Her father was a wealthy burgher who had visited Willem's warehouse on occasion. The two had a good conversation, with Ilse's mother looking on approvingly.

Finally Willem stepped forward. "Grand Mistress Beatrice," he bowed slightly, and both smiled. "I—I felt proud today. The respect everyone here has for you is obvious. I can see why you were chosen to lead these women. It is an honor and I congratulate you." Willem clasped her hands warmly, and told her that both shop and warehouse were doing well.

And he had met someone...was even thinking of marriage. Of course Beatrice wanted to know all about Ilse. Her smile, worn thin from overuse, was now genuine again, and she felt comforted by their exchange. Yet, as he turned to leave, she knew that the closeness that remained when he had first left home to go to work was gone now. Beatrice was absent from most family gatherings, and they communicated with an occasional note, usually concerning a family business matter. They were mother and son, but now no more than acquaintances. Again she felt that loss: it lay inside her, along with memories of Gerard.

Upstairs, in the long twilight, the girls chattered about the events of the day as they hung their good dresses on pegs on the wall beside their beds, and in shifts and bare feet, prepared for bed. Sister Celie nodded in her chair at one end of the room. Much of the children's talk was nonsense; they were too tired to be coherent. But it was a very special day, they all agreed. "Yes, it surely was," one girl declared, "for this is the first time we have ever been excused from evening prayers!"

The girls' laughter drifted out the window and was faintly heard in the chapel, now lit by flickering candles for the evening service. Without the children, the chapel was unusually quiet. The sisters were tired from the events of the day. Sister Beatrice led the prayers and when the sisters finally rose to their feet, their knees aching from what seemed like hours on the stone floor, she stepped out in front of them.

"I am not going to talk for very long, because we are all tired, but I do have some things to say. This is not a homily; women are not allowed to preach, and certainly not beguines, as we all know." The sisters hid their smiles.

"We often say we are trying to lead an apostolic life. What does that really mean?" Beatrice opened the New Testament the beguines used, the Flemish text translated from Latin. "In the Book of Acts we find this verse: 'They devoted themselves to the apostles' teaching and fellowship, to the breaking of bread, and the prayers.' I think that description of those first apostles also describes what we beguines try to do here. We teach children about Jesus, we live simply, we study the Bible, we pray together every day. And, we bake the best bread in Sint Joric, and share it with those in need.

"We are respected in the community. Our service to the poor and our teaching skills are well known and appreciated. But we are exceptional women: we do not fit the accepted roles for women. Some bishops speak out against us, though Bishop Christophe has assured me of his support for this community and the other begijnhofs in his diocese.

"The Council of Vienne, while condemning beguines as 'women without vows' did allow beguines living in community to continue to do so. But as some of you may know, any woman wandering the streets with a begging bowl and no roof over her head can call herself a beguine. I am told some so-called beguines are even selling their bodies to keep from starving." There were gasps from some of the older sisters; Elisabetta frowned at the unseemliness of hearing those words in church.

Beatrice continued. "In this community we let our good works speak for us. We have always lived quietly, and we shall continue to do so. Today there was enough excitement to last us for a long time." The sisters nodded in agreement. All had worked hard—in the kitchen, or preparing the dining room for the many guests; helping the children get ready; or escorting the visitors, a privilege reserved for beguines from the best families. Beatrice concluded, "With your help, I hope to lead this community for a long time. Please go with my thanks, and pray for me this night, as I will for all of you."

The candles on the altar were extinguished, the smell of hot tallow lingering as the sisters filed out of the chapel. By this time the sky was darkening, so those in the lead held lighted candles, and the rest trod like moving shadows, all softly singing the hymn they often chose to end evening prayers.

> "Come down, O Love divine,
> Seek thou this soul of mine,
> and visit it with thine own ardor glowing;
> O Comforter, draw near,
> within my heart appear,
> and kindle it, thy holy flame bestowing...."

Beatrice went straight to her prie-dieu when she arrived at her little townhouse. In spite of the accolades she had received, she felt uneasy. She had come here to teach and, she told herself, to seek a closer relationship to Jesus. There it was—she saw herself first as a teacher of children. She bent her head, fingering the cross on her prayer beads until sleepiness made her dizzy; she had to grasp the edge of the shelf holding her psalter to keep from falling.

Elisabetta was preparing for bed in her comfortable bedroom, her lips pursed. She was still shocked at the grand mistress' words; how could she know that there were women calling themselves beguines who were selling their bodies to men to keep from starving? And why, why would she speak of such a thing in front of the whole gathering? It was unseemly.

CHAPTER FOUR

Summer, 1330

It was several days after that awful night of the intruder, and the time had come for truth-telling. Mergriet sat in one of the large chairs in the grand mistress' receiving room, Beatrice in the other. Mergriet remembered the chairs from the flat on the gold needle street. They reminded her of the schoolroom in her aunt's parlor, where she had sat on the floor barefoot, wearing simple, short shifts and squirming with impatience until she had finished her sums and was released to play stick-ball in the street with the other children.

"Sister Beatrice please, I need to stay here, where I feel at home for the first time since Mother's death." This, at least, was the truth. Her mother's death was a dull ache that still pressed down on her, like an iron pressing clothes. She had birthed six children, but only Mergriet and one of her brothers lived past infancy. She had watched her mother's figure become frail and weak from childbirth, until at the end she lay on her bed like a scrap of faded linen worn thin from long use. Mergriet had leaned against Aunt Bea and felt her comforting warmth as they sat at her mother's bedside....

...Then there was that unforgettable late summer day, just before it was time to begin school. Mergriet's father had roused the family at dawn, and taken them on a long journey to their farmhouse in the country. She loved everything about that journey, even the bumping of the large cart over the rutted roads. The countryside was flat and almost treeless; the newly mown fields cut by drainage canals looked like a giant puzzle.

"Father, what are those great wheels?" Mergriet had tried to stand up and point, but was quickly jerked down.

"They are not wheels, they are windmills, child. They pump water out of the canals and into the river, so that the fields do not flood when it rains. Otherwise we could not grow feed for the animals, nor vegetables for ourselves."

At last they arrived at the farm, and Mergriet and her brother scrambled out of the cart. Scrub vegetation and small trees were allowed to grow along the canals to help hold the banks. But after a heavy rain the water rose up and eroded the banks in places, creating still pools for small animals to thrive in—frogs, newts, minnows. Mergriet and her brother, who had pulled off his tunic, waded barefoot in the water, trying to catch the small creatures. Seagulls cawed and tilted their heads as they circled overhead, waiting impatiently for their turn.

Mergriet climbed out of the water when her mother called, her shift soaked with muddy water. No matter, such amazing discoveries were surely worth a scolding. She knew her mother could not bear to whip her—and that she had packed extra clothes for herself and Hans.

After a midday meal of pottage and bread, they played with the lambs in the barnyard and then it was time to go home, loaded down with ripe pears and summer vegetables from the farm, and a tiny kitten from the barn that Mergriet had begged to keep. She held the mewing, tawny bundle of fur and watched the town walls grow nearer, solid and reassuring. But when they passed through the gate, she felt them, for the first time, confining as well.

Mergriet hated school. Though Aunt Beatrice was patient and kind, she could not bear to bend over a parchment board for long. Soon she would begin to squirm, then she would slide off the bench and stroll around the room. Beatrice would reprove her, but after a short time at the table, the wriggling began again.

A few years later, as soon as her father acquiesced, she stayed at home to help her mother, who taught her the domestic skills necessary for a wife and mother. Mergriet had been a willing pupil, at first just to please her mother, whom she adored. Then Mama began taking her to the market, where she could finger dusty leeks and smooth purplish turnips, and inhale the aroma of fragrant herbs.

Most of all, Mergriet loved baking. Just outside their kitchen door was a bread oven, rare in a merchant's home. It allowed her mother to indulge in her favorite pastime, baking breads of all kinds. Bread was on the table at every meal, and day-old bread often became a plate of sorts, to hold the delicious meat roasted over the hearth in the kitchen's fireplace.

As a child Mergriet thought bread was magical. It grew from soft, gray-white lumps of dough into crisp, brown, airy loaves, sometimes sweetened with honey. The soft center of the bread melted on her tongue. Her mother demonstrated bread making, and patiently let her experiment. She never forgot the glow of her mother's praise when she drew her first perfect loaves of bread from the oven. The odor of just-baked bread was her mother's perfume... Mergriet jerked herself out of her daydream and assumed a penitent expression.

"...and so, Sister Mergriet," Beatrice was saying, "you need to pray for guidance to discern if this begijnhof truly is where God wants you to be. And you should ask God's forgiveness for your impure thoughts." Beatrice rubbed her neck; it was aching again. "When you became a beguine you took a vow of chastity." She leaned forward, spoke slowly, and looked directly into Mergriet's eyes. "I need assurance that you can keep that vow."

"I have asked for forgiveness every day since it happened," Mergriet blurted out, slumping in her chair, "but my heart feels as dead as a stone, and God seems very far away." Well aware that she had evaded the request, she could not meet the grand mistress' gaze.

"I think you need to spend some time in reflection and prayer apart from the community, Sister Mergriet. A pilgrimage might help you open your heart to God and allow His love to wash that stone you speak of away. Perhaps I could look into the possibility of your joining one?" The last was spoken as a question, yet it sounded more like an order.

A long silence, as Mergriet fixed her mind on the word "pilgrimage" and what it might mean. A reprieve? Another chance?

"Oh yes, please, Sister Beatrice." She looked up, her face brightening at the prospect of a penance she could fulfill that at the same time would give her a chance to explore the world outside she had dreamed of since she was a child. But leaving the begijnhof for a long journey? What if she were not allowed to come back to the community? Her aunt had said nothing of atonement or forgiveness.

Smiling faintly, Beatrice rose, signaling that their conversation had ended, and Mergriet left the room, murmuring "Thank you, Grand Mistress."

Beatrice paced the room. She had in mind a pilgrimage the Cistercian community was organizing for their tertiaries, a group of devout women who lived in tiny huts close by the abbey's walls, under the monks' protection and guidance. Word of the pilgrimage had reached her just the day before.

She must write a note to Abbot Paulus, the head of the community, seeking permission for Mergriet to join the pilgrimage, and then find a way to send it to him as soon as possible. Fortunately, Father Matthias would soon come to say mass. She sat down at her desk and looked for a clean sheet of parchment, ready to turn her thoughts into words.

"Grand Mistress, I beg pardon for interrupting you, but it is Sister Clare." Beatrice, frowning, looked up from her task a few moments later to find Sister Celie standing in front of her desk, her head slightly bowed and her clasped hands bent as if clutching one another. "She has been having awful nightmares, and she doesn't want to talk to me about them."

Clare opened her eyes, struggling against the heavy, dark, strange-smelling form on top of her; she gasped for breath, and with one great push threw it off. Her heart pounded as she sat up and looked around. The room was dark, but the moon was full and she could see Sister Celie stretched out on the low cot nearby, snoring gently. The form Clare had thrown off was her coverlet, with its normal smell of her own body. Her shift was damp with sweat, her hair a limp tangle that fell over her face, her nightcap a crumpled heap on the floor.

When would these nightmares end? They seldom varied: always someone or something, a shade perhaps, trying to smother her, to wind itself around her or otherwise force her to bend to its will. I came here to escape my father's house, which is now <u>her</u> house. And here I am, accepting more rules and as helpless as ever. She lay back in her bed and slept fitfully.

When the sky lightened, Celie awoke in her cot next to Clare's bed. One glance told her that Clare had had another nightmare. Her face was flushed and moist, and her eyes had dark smudges under them, as if she had rubbed them with ash.

"What would make you feel better this morning, Sister Clare? A nice hot infusion, perhaps? I could bring you one."

"A bath, Sister Celie, to wash away this…this awful, soiled feeling."

Celie did not know how to reply. The beguines long ago had chosen not to visit the public baths, even though women were given one afternoon a week to use them. Rather, the sisters bathed once a week if they wished, using their big copper bath, dragged into the kitchen after supper and filled ankle-deep with water heated in the big kettle swung over the fire. But a bath in the middle of the week? And in the morning?

"Would it help if you told me about the nightmare? Were there evil spirits in it?" Celie shuddered. She feared mightily the power of evil spirits.

But Clare shook her head. She did not want to talk and, more distressing, tears began to wet her cheeks.

Several days later, Mergriet and some of the youngest, strongest beguines moved Clare's large, carved bed, her chair covered in dark green velvet, and the heavy chest from her old room to one at the far end of the hall. The women huffed and shoved and carried Clare's furnishings while she trailed behind, carrying her books.

The view from the window of her new room was of the neat rows of attached houses following the curve of the begijnhof wall. She wished she could have one of them. Her own place, perhaps with a servant from home to take care of her; away from so many women going to and fro from one room to another, as if the rooms belonged to them all. But this room was larger and brighter than the old one, and on this day sunshine lit every corner. It had been scrubbed clean, and fresh-smelling rushes laid down, even dried lavender, Clare's favorite scent. Perhaps when she had moved in the rest of her things and had arranged them as she wished, she would feel safe. Perhaps the shades from the nether world would not find her here, and the nightmares would cease.

Clare could not remember the details of that awful night, only that a man in the filthy clothes of a common workman had flung himself on top of her. She shuddered at the thought. And blood, she remembered blood everywhere, but knew it wasn't hers. Whose was it? Oh yes, Sister Mergriet's. But why was she injured, when it was I who was attacked? I really should speak to Sister Mergriet, Clare thought. But she could not bring herself to do so.

And none of the sisters ventured to speak to Clare about the attack. She had always kept to herself, and now was even more distant. She seemed more at home with the children than with her sisters. When the grand mistress asked her to speak about what had happened, Clare shook her head, bit her lip and said nothing. Beatrice noticed that her hands, once carefully groomed, were dry and her fingernails bitten and ragged.

"Surely the grand mistress would agree that rest at home might help you. This awful thing that has befallen you…it is worse than an illness." Sister Celie had moved back to her own room, but was uncomfortable leaving Clare to sleep alone. She thought time with her own family might help her.

"Oh no, Sister Celie, I cannot go home. How could I explain to my father why I suddenly wanted to visit him? He would know immediately that something was wrong. And if I told him about that night, he would never allow me to return." Deep down, Clare feared that the whole town would find out what happened to her and she would be disgraced.

51

After evening prayers, Clare felt the stiffness in her shoulders ease as she left the chapel and walked to the main building. She smiled and nodded to her sisters as she climbed the stairs to her new room, closing the door behind her. She could find little to say to them, and knew that her restrained manner did not invite friendship. The terrifying creatures from the dark side had ceased invading her dreams, yet she still did not feel at home in this place. When she looked in the polished tin mirror before leaving her room, she often felt she was putting on a mask, play-acting at being a beguine, much as the players did when they put on the mask of "Good-body," or "Satan," before appearing in the morality plays performed in the town square on holidays.

How Clare missed her father! He had been her teacher as well as her loving father. And from the time she was a small child, Clare had been an apt pupil, quickly learning to read and write in Flemish, then progressing to studying Latin, and reading the Bible. She loved stories, and the best stories were in the Bible, yet their priest discouraged his parishioners from reading it. He said the Holy Scripture would only confuse them, and he would tell them what it meant. Clare asked her father why Father Johan felt that way.

"Father Johan seems barely literate himself," she remembered Henri saying. "He just repeats the dogma of the church; that is why I stopped going to Sint Agustin. But I did not make that decision lightly, Clare. I sought more information about Father Johan. I found that he dutifully visits the sick, gives unction to the dying, hears confessions and metes out penance. His sermons are forceful, often, as you know, focusing on the devil working in those daring to deviate from the church's teachings. Though his judgments are often harsh, he is respected for his devotion to the church."

Henri knew the priest's message appealed to many in Sint Joric who were trying to understand why their lives were becoming more and more difficult, as crops failed and prices rose. They were looking for someone, something, to blame for their troubles. Perhaps God was angry at them, he had heard some say, and had sent Satan to plague them.

Clare sat quietly and waited for Henri to begin again. At last he looked up, and they went back to their Bible reading. Their chairs were drawn up to the fireplace in the library, close together so both could make use of firelight and candlelight. Clare viewed those evenings as a retreat into a world all their own. The Book of Genesis, with its tales of war, intrigue, love, hate, and betrayal especially fascinated her.

Her father skipped over the Song of Solomon when they came to it, but Clare read the lyrical love poetry in the seclusion of her room, by the light of one of the new oil lamps. She was amazed that such feelings could be put into words—and in the Bible! She felt an unexpected tingling in that place down below, the place that tingled when her fingers sometimes found it as she lay in bed at night. Feeling guilty and not knowing why, she decided not to mention to her father that she had read the Song of Solomon on her own.

Under Henri's tutelage, Clare began studying the New Testament. What Jesus preached was the goal of a simple life in service to others. She could not imagine such a life: she had servants to prepare her food, wash her clothes, and clean up after her. She re-read the Sermon on the Mount; there was no "Blessed are the comfortable" to be found in it. At bedtime she began to recite the few prayers she knew and was soothed by them.

Then, suddenly their Bible study together before the fire became much less frequent. Her father was out in the evening more and more often. After one such evening, Henri sat with Clare and tried to explain, stumbling over his words.

"I have met someone, and I—I have been a widower for so long, Clare. I have decided to take a new wife. Marta is beautiful, she is…I know you will like her." But Clare did not.

"My dear, this is a large house; why should you not have a sitting room of your own? We can make the room next to your bedroom into a comfortable place for you. Of course you are always welcome to join us in the parlor." But there was no fireplace in that room next to hers; it was as cold and uninviting as Marta's invitation. Clare pictured her father and Marta downstairs in the library, heads together near the fireplace where she used to sit.

For her part, Marta swiftly made it plain that she was mistress of the house. "You must not give cook instructions on what to prepare at midday, Clare. She is to come to me. And there is no need for you to go to market; I will take care of that." Clare felt pushed aside, unwelcome in her own home, and bored. She had not considered leaving her father's house until Marta came. She could have married; she had met a number of eligible men, but none of them attracted her, and her father did not press her. The only occupation Clare could think of to occupy her time was teaching. After all, she had her father as a model. But how did a woman become a teacher?

She had heard about those curious women called beguines from a friend of her father's, who spoke of them favorably as devout women who taught the burgers' children. And so she had visited the begijnhof to find out more about this place where so many women had begun a new life. Then it was time for the trial period, to which her father had reluctantly agreed.

The same tiny, ancient beguine who had greeted her upon her first visit answered the door when Clare and her father arrived at the main building, accompanied by a cart with her belongings. Again she was greeted with a welcoming smile.

"Come in, Mistress Van Aelst, we've been looking for you. I am so glad you're here." Sister Celie beckoned her. Clare suddenly found herself so overwhelmed at the thought of leaving her father that she was unable to respond. Celie turned to Clare's father. "We are pleased to have Mistress Van Aelst with us, Mijnheer. If you would ask your servant to bring the cart around to the back of this building, we'll unload her things there."

Clare's belongings had been placed in the small room that would be hers for the next few months, and then it was time to say goodbye. Neither father nor daughter could find much to say as they stood on the path outside the building.

"Father, I—I am not sure..." Henri reached for her hands and drew her closer, speaking softly.

"Clare, you can come home at any time. That was made clear to me when I wrote to the grand mistress to arrange for your arrival." Henri knew that his daughter was apprehensive about leaving home; that was natural. He also was aware of the antagonism between Clare and her stepmother. But he was enchanted by his beautiful young wife, and was unwilling to accept that Clare was leaving home because she felt unwelcome there.

"If you would like me to begin seeking a suitable husband for you, I would be glad—"

"No, Father, please, I must see if this is where I belong. If at the end of the trial period I do not choose to stay, well, then..." At that moment, Henri's servant began to pull the donkey's head around, and Henri turned to speak to him.

"I will walk home, Lukas. You can return the cart to the stable."

Henri hugged Clare, unable to articulate his feelings of love and loss. "Clare, you have only to send word to me if you want to leave, and I will come and fetch you." Clare had buried her face in his coat for a moment, and then turned away. At the doorstep, she looked back and saw her father walking up the path, his shoulders slumped like an old man's.

"Well, we all knew that you have not been...comfortable here. And now this...this..." Celie's voice trailed off. Clare barely heard her. She was hanging her mirror on the wall; there was a peg at just about the right height. She examined her reflection, and frowned.

"Celie, would you please help me wash my hair after supper tonight?"

CHAPTER FIVE

The old porter slowly pulled the gate open, peering suspiciously at the dusty, unkempt woman and the donkey she led. The animal was unable to lift its head and each step elicited a soft grunt of pain.

"Oh, my, it is Sister Mergriet, I beg pardon, please come in. I—I din't, that is, the grand mistress did not know when you mought return; only that it could be any day now, with the cold coming on." And indeed, the day was cloudy and the wind strong.

"It is all right, Niklaas. I am not surprised you did not recognize me. I look like a great lump of dirt." The porter hid a smile and pulled the gate wide open. Mergriet passed through and the donkey followed behind her, heading slowly for a patch of grass close by the path.

"You are please to go to the grand mistress' house, and I am to tell her right now that you have arrived." Niklaas hurriedly took the donkey's lead.

"Just a moment, Niklaas." And Mergriet untied the leather satchel attached to the heavy, padded saddle she had sat upon for so many days. She pulled the bag to the ground, and it landed with a loud thwack, startling the donkey, which stumbled forward and bumped a young woman who had stopped at the open gate. She fell to the ground with a cry, and Mergriet rushed to help her up.

"I am so sorry, this is my fault. Are you hurt?"

"I—I don't think so." Mergriet quickly reached out a hand to steady her as the young woman struggled to her feet, obviously dizzy. "I am all right. Thank you for your help." She began brushing off her skirt and her coat, and attempted to pull up her hose. At last she straightened up.

"My name is Annalise, and I am here to see the grand mistress. Should I just follow this path to that large building?"

"Yes, that's the one." Mergriet pointed. "But please, I would be glad to accompany you."

"No, thank you, I am fine now." Yet Annalise's voice trembled, and she walked slowly down the path with a pronounced limp. Mergriet saw that her hose had slipped down to her shoe tops, and noticed that her shoes were oddly made. One sole was much thicker than the other. Immediately, she stepped forward and took her arm.

"Please, let me help you. I am Sister Mergriet. Shall we sit for a moment on the bench there by the path? I would like to rest a bit myself. I've just come back from a long journey." Mergriet spoke resolutely, and Annalise allowed herself to be led to the stone bench.

The two women sat quietly for a moment, Mergriet rubbing her cheek where the satchel's strap had scraped it. She looked at Annalise and then dropped her eyes, so as not to appear to be staring. The woman was very young, fifteen or sixteen at most, the bones of her face still hidden by soft flesh. Her eyes were a pale gray, and her brows faint. Her light brown hair was braided and pinned to the crown of her head. She hugged her worn sheepskin coat to her body, shivering a little, and pulled her skirts down over her sagging hose. With her skirt covering her shoes, her deformity was hidden; she simply looked like a timid young woman. After a brief silence Annalise lifted her head, and spoke softly.

"Tell me, please, Sister Mergriet, is there any way that the beguine community would consider admitting someone who limps, as I do? I learned a little about your sisterhood from two women dressed like nuns that I met one day at the shop in the gold needle street. But I knew they could not be from Sint Anne's, since it is cloistered. They were very friendly, and urged me to come here and speak with the grand mistress. They told me they were teachers, and said the women here work to support themselves. I—I cannot teach, as they do. I can read and write and do sums, but that is all—"

"Ah, well, not all of us are teachers," Mergriet interrupted, smiling faintly. "I am a baker and a cook. Can you tell me what sort of work do you do at home?"

"Well, my mother is a seamstress; I do the cooking, laundry, and cleaning, so she can keep to her sewing." Annalise squared her shoulders and lifted her chin. "But I can even read a little Latin, Sister. My father is an illuminator of manuscripts and books, and he worked long hours so that we could attend the nearby school. Occasionally he brings castoff parchment scraps home with him. I studied the strange words on them and when he saw how interested I was, he helped me learn to read those words, and they were in Latin.

"Sometimes he brings home a frayed brush and a discarded inkpot, and shows my brother and me how he decorates the border of a text, or makes a picture out of a capital letter. His work is beautiful, with tiny flowers and animals; the pictures are magical, like illustrations for a fairy story. He gave me some scraps of parchment so I could try drawing; he said I have talent and a steady hand, but of course women are not allowed to be paid for such work." Annalise blushed at her boldness in talking so freely about herself.

"Ah, yes. One of our sisters sometimes copies a text for a patron and illustrates the borders, as you described; but I have to tell you, such a request is rare."

Annalise got up and smiled weakly. "Thank you, Sister Mergriet for listening to me. I am sure I can walk now, and I really should be going." She started down the path again, straightening her shoulders, but she walked slowly and her limp seemed more pronounced. Annalise tried to walk without limping, but she could not.

Why was I made this way? So many times she had asked herself that question. She had always looked different, felt different. When she was small, she struggled to keep up with her younger brother as he ran down the lane. She was not barefoot, like the other children, but stumbled along in the special shoes the shoemaker had fashioned for her. Sometimes neighbor children taunted her, calling her "cripple."

The midwife told her mother that when she pulled Annalise into the world feet first, the leg that was first tugged on ended up longer. "It is all right, Annalise," her mother would console her when the tears came after the taunting. "That is the way God made you, and no mother ever had a more devoted or helpful daughter."

"I must accept, and not question the will of God," Annalise sighed and murmured to herself. "But will these women even consider taking in someone like me? Jesus has already granted me one miracle. I cannot expect another."

It was at mass one Sunday almost three years earlier that the miracle happened. Annalise was lifted off her feet during the elevation of the host. Often she was caught up in the mystery of the Eucharist but that day, her twelfth birthday, was different. When the priest lifted the consecrated host, Annalise's thin arms, of their own will, curved upward. She rose up until she was on tiptoe, lifted as Christ's body was broken in two, lifted until she was floating at least a clog's height above the stone floor of the old church. Warmth flowed through her and she felt sustained by Jesus' love. Then, ever so gently, her feet touched the floor again, first one, then the other, the shorter one. She looked around, but no one, not even her brother, standing right next to her, noticed this miracle. The faces of the parishioners were expressionless as they waited for the mass to finish, so they could go home to a warm fire and their midday meal.

After mass Annalise as usual began to trail behind her family on the way home. Then she tried hard to walk faster, and at last caught up to her mother.

"Mama, didn't you see me on tiptoe during the mass?"

"Yes dear, I saw you trying to see better what was going on up at the altar. I've seen you do that before." Slowing her pace, she put an arm around her daughter.

Annalise decided to say nothing about the miracle God had bestowed upon her. That moment when she was lifted up by Jesus' grace was brief, but it <u>had</u> happened and she would never be the same. Never before had Annalise felt singled out, though some muttered that Satan had singled her out. They said that surely a messenger from the evil one had touched her, and that was why she limped.

More and more as the months passed, she felt called to enter a nunnery and devote her life to Christ. But convents were for the wealthy, those of the nobility and the upper classes, so she did not mention her desire to her parents. Yet often, while she swept the floor or scrubbed clothes, she imagined herself in a nun's habit, devoutly kneeling. One night, long after she and her brother had climbed into the big bed in the corner where all slept together, she heard her parents discussing her.

"Yes, Nicolas is learning a trade. But what about Annalise?" her mother spoke softly. "We have little money for a dowry, and besides, what man would want a wife who is crippled, and thus might not make a capable housewife?"

"Aye, and who might have difficulty carrying a child. I fear no man will accept her. She can spend her youth working here, but what will happen to her when we are gone?"

They had only confirmed what Annalise already knew: her days would be spent working in this one-room house, with no hope of becoming a religious. She pulled an edge of the frayed quilt up to her chin, and brushed away her tears. When all was quiet, she turned over and tried to sleep.

Annalise lifted her head and shook her dress, the cool autumn breeze helping to rid her clothes of the remaining dust from her fall. She tugged at her hose and managed to pull them up and tie them on, using the attached yarn string. Thankfully there was no one about. She walked slowly but determinedly down the path to the main building. She had put on her best clothes and her one pair of hose before leaving home, and had slipped quietly away while her mother was bent over her sewing. Straightening, she knocked at the door, trembling in both anticipation and fear. She stuttered as she announced herself, but managed a smile when she recognized the sister who greeted her.

"Ah—I am—Annalise de Kegel."

"Come in, come in." I remember meeting you in the shop on gold needle street. I am so glad you are here, Annalise. The grand mistress is in her receiving room, talking with a new student and her mother. You can wait for her down the hall there, where you see the chairs."

Annalise sat quietly, but her courage failed her more and more with each passing moment. How could she think she might be invited to live in such a place? The chair she sat in was cushioned in moss green wool as soft as velvet, and the tapestry hanging on the wall opposite was woven in glowing reds, purples and blues. It depicted the disciples gathered around Jesus, all with haloes embroidered in gold thread. She could not imagine passing by such a beautiful sight every day. At last, the grand mistress' door opened.

Annalise got to her feet unsteadily as a tall woman said farewell to a child and her mother, who was smiling and holding the little girl's hand. Trying her best not to limp, Annalise stepped forward and curtseyed to the woman, who while dressed like the other beguines she had seen, was clearly apart, with an authoritative presence about her. Yet her smile was welcoming.

"Curtseying is not necessary here. I am Sister Beatrice. Do come in." The grand mistress settled Annalise in a chair close by the large trestle table, and seated herself in a similar chair behind it. Gently she probed her with questions about her family, and what had brought her here. Annalise responded by telling the beguine mistress about the amazing experience that had convinced her she should give her life to Christ.

".... In truth, Sister Beatrice, I want to be a nun, to spend my life in prayer and adoration of Jesus, and go to mass every day. But I know that is not possible." For the first time she had revealed her secret—that Jesus had chosen her for a different life. But she had also confessed that she was not sure how she was meant to serve him. Was it possible that this place was where she was meant to be?

Beatrice sat back in her chair and waited, hands in her lap, as if she had unlimited time to speak with this young woman. The vision she had described sounded to the grand mistress like the dream of a child, not a message from Jesus. She would come to regret her dismissal of Annalise's vision.

"Can you tell me what it means to be a beguine, and if it is possible for me to become one?" Annalise ventured at last.

"We sometimes call ourselves 'sisters between,'" Beatrice began, "because we live a life that is halfway between that of a nun, and of a devout laywoman with a home and family. And, we try to live an apostolic life."

"An apostolic life? Like Jesus? Is that what you mean?"

"Not exactly, Annalise. For us, the apostolic life requires the careful use of what we have, so that we can support ourselves and care for those in need."

Then Beatrice leaned forward, her voice low and almost musical. "Our beguine school has a fine reputation in the community, and teaching supports us and our mission to feed the poor." For the first time, Annalise noticed the sounds of children outside, calling back and forth, and loosened her clenched hands. She pushed a strand of hair that had fallen in her face back into its braid.

"Every morning and evening we gather in the chapel for prayer. But for us, prayer and work are inseparable; our devotion to God is something we practice every day in the work we do." Beatrice took a deep breath that sounded almost like a sigh.

"Finally, we vow to live a chaste life behind these walls," Beatrice added. "We only go into town for good reason, and in the company of another sister."

"I—I am not sure how I could serve this community, Sister Beatrice." Now Annalise's voice was almost a whisper. "I cannot teach; I have not the learning for it. I spend my days cooking and cleaning for my family, and praying." Annalise held her breath, anticipating dismissal.

"All of us serve God in our own way Annalise," Beatrice responded. "I understand that your parents depend on your help, so we will have to see what we can do for you. But for now, we will show you our school and our chapel, and the kitchen where we prepare our meals and bread for the poor." Beatrice knew that it would be difficult to find work in the begijnhof for someone like Annalise, but there was something about her...

Celie knocked softly on the door, as if she had been summoned.

Some weeks later, Beatrice stood as Annalise's parents entered the receiving room, and led them to the two chairs placed before her desk. They were dressed much like other parents seeking to place their children in the beguine school. Her mother wore her best wool dress, with sleeves she had embroidered herself, and decorated hairpins held her linen cap and wimple in place. Her father was dressed in a well-worn but freshly pressed tunic and his best hose. But their hands told the story of their working lives—her mother's fingers stippled with tiny pinpricks, her father's permanently stained with paint smears, the colors blended together into a purplish brown.

"Thank you for inviting us, Grand Mistress Beatrice." Annalise's father sat straight in his chair and spoke quietly. "Our Annalise is most devout, as she perhaps has told you, and she would like very much to join your community. But we have little to provide in the way of a dowry for her—a chair for her room and a trunk to hold her clothes. Her mother can sew all of the clothes and bed linens she might need. And we can provide her a small, a very small monthly allowance." He cleared his throat and looked at his wife. "You should also know that my wife is not in robust health, and might on occasion need the nursing care Annalise has provided her when she cannot care for herself."

"I understand your concerns. As for the dowry, sometimes a generous patron will provide funds for just such a purpose. And of course I would allow Annalise to come to you if illness struck and her nursing care was required.

"Tell me, has she explained how we decide if this is the right place for her?" The parents nodded, but looked uncertain, so Beatrice smiled graciously and provided her usual explanation of beguine life, including the ritual for admission of a proposed member. Then she rose from her chair to indicate the end of the visit.

"Grand Mistress Beatrice, we apologize for keeping you, but we have one more question." Annalise's father rose also, but somewhat hesitantly. "It is about Annalise's safety, should you admit her. We have heard that someone, perhaps a thief, tried to break into one of the rooms occupied by a sister. Can you assure us that our daughter would be safe here?"

Beatrice sat down hard in her chair, her face flushed red and her hands trembling. Surely by now the whole town knew that something dreadful had occurred at the begijnhof that night. Yet until this moment no one had faced her directly and asked for an explanation of those events. Now these parents, who wanted only to provide a secure future for their fragile daughter and accede to her wish to become a religious, had confronted her.

Why, why had she not prepared herself for this question? She was the leader of a group of women who had chosen a controversial way of life, living by rules they had made for themselves, and thus inviting judgment, even condemnation. Beatrice stammered through a brief explanation of what had happened when the intruder came, not mentioning that Mergriet had been wounded, or that he had tried to assault Sister Clare.

"We have hired a night watchman to patrol our wall at night. As I am sure you are aware, these times of poor crops and unrest have brought more and more desperate country people into Sint Joric to seek refuge and look for work." The words tumbled from her lips without her usual forethought. "I can assure you that we are doing everything we can to make sure our community is safe, and that it... remains safe." The de Kegels nodded, and finally Beatrice ushered them to the door and bid them farewell, smiling weakly. She turned and began to pace the receiving room. At last she sat at her desk, and bent over a list of supplies needed from the town.

"Sister Beatrice, Sister Beatrice!" Sister Celie rushed in, forgetting to tap on the door. "It's the gatekeeper; he says he needs to speak with you and no one else."

Beatrice made her way to the front gate, shivering as the cold wind whipped her skirt. The gatekeeper, his rough work pants, shirt, and cap neat as always, greeted her with an air of importance and led her out the front gate and along the street, staying close by the begijnhof wall. He stopped at the indentation where the begijnhof wall met the town wall.

"You see, Grand Mistress, see that rough place here, where there's a stone missing? See the small pieces of stone on the ground there? The night watchman pointed it out to me, said someone could use that hollow place to step on and maybe pull himself up high enough to get over the wall."

When Beatrice returned to the begijnhof, it was to her little house, to lie down with a cool cloth on her forehead. She must find the money to repair that wall, and soon.

That night Annalise, unable to sleep, limped to the window of the family's home and pushed open the heavy shutter. She turned her face to the stars. Could they be heaven's windows? Could God look down at her from those windows and hear her prayers imploring Jesus to help her become a beguine? The night was unusually still as she leaned her head out of the window. But at last the night watchman's call, the creaking of a nearby shutter, and the sound of footsteps in the street brought her to her senses.

Witches and devils disguised as animals of every sort prowled at night, and the night air carried disease; she knew that. Quickly, Annalise pushed the shutter closed, and made her way back to the big bedstead where her mother and father, and her brother, lay sleeping. She settled under the covers and rubbed her chilled feet together. She couldn't imagine leaving her family and living at the beginhof. And perhaps it was wrong to wish for such a thing. Yet in her dream that night she saw the beguines in their simple habits walking to the small chapel. And she was there, one of them.

62

CHAPTER SIX

ergriet watched for a moment as Annalise limped along the path toward the main building and her meeting with the grand mistress. Then she turned her back on that building she had thought of as home, and walked stiffly toward Beatrice's townhouse, her heavy satchel slung over her shoulder. Again she touched the scrape the satchel's strap had left on her cheek when she pulled it off the donkey, then looked at her soiled hands, rough like the surface of the dark loaves of bread she used to make. Slowing her walk to a "beguines' pace" she smiled to herself. How difficult it had been to learn to slow down. Before entering the begijnhof, she had always walked at a brisk pace, always been in a hurry. Now she stopped, and aided by the strong breeze, shook the dirt out of her skirt, then resumed her slow pace and stopped at the far end of a row of six townhouses.

Aunt Beatrice's words at their last meeting came to mind: "And when you return, if we decide you should remain here, I wonder if perhaps you might like to move into my house. It is small, yet really more than I need. There is a room on the upper floor that we could make into a bedroom for you."

Mergriet had been quite aware that the invitation was a command she could not refuse. She felt a pang of resentment, but tried to push it aside, along with the thoughts of all that had brought her here.

Beatrice's house was the smallest in the row, its width measured by one window and a plain door. A window box with a few fall flowers, bent by the wind, was the façade's only adornment. Mergriet set down her bag, took off her wimple and her coat, shook both vigorously, then replaced them and knocked at the door.

Ingrid raised her eyebrows at the sight of Mergriet's clothes, but her lined face with its perpetually down-turned mouth softened into a smile. Mergriet had been her favorite of all the mistress' pupils. She was always laughing and ready for fun.

"Sister Mergriet, here, let me take that bag for you. We have your room upstairs all ready. Do come in." Ingrid led the way to the sitting room and Mergriet followed, suddenly aware that she was trembling from exhaustion.

It was as she had imagined: she would not return to her old room in the main building, not even for one night. But neither would she be turned away from the begijnhof, and with that thought relief washed over her. For a moment she felt cleansed. Then Ingrid's voice broke into her musing, and she stammered a reply.

"Yes, thank you Ingrid, an infusion of bergamot, and bread with honey, what a treat that would be." Mergriet managed a smile. "But first I must rest." She climbed the stairs and turned into a room with its door ajar. The small window afforded a view of the begijnhof wall and the town's rooftops. Her own bed, with her favorite quilt folded on it, took up much of one wall; her clothes chest with a candlestick upon it was placed next to it. In the opposite corner her armchair sat with a small table beside it, and on the adjacent wall her beguine habits, obviously freshly ironed, hung on a row of pegs. Rushes scented with rosemary had been strewn on the floor. She felt welcomed.

Closing the door, she stepped out of her clothes, leaving them in a heap on the floor. She bathed as best she could with the basin of water, bit of soap and worn cloth left for her on the table; Ingrid must have seen her coming. Finally she put on a clean shift and climbed into bed—her own bed, just in a different place, she reminded herself and then slipped into sleep, only faintly aware of boots thumping in the hall....

...and her father striding into the parlor, where she was usually summoned to hear a list of her latest misdeeds. She jumped to her feet with trepidation. But this day he spoke of inquiries he had made about a suitable husband for her.

"No, father! I do not wish to marry, not ever." Mergriet's voice was strident, sounding much like his. She turned away so he would not see the fear in her face at the thought of a man's sexual demands and the continual pregnancies her mother had suffered. She waited, but the expected roar of anger did not come. Instead, there was silence.

"Would you rather go into Sint Anne's? I suppose I might be able to pull some strings and get you in there." Hans voice was low as he pursed his lips and looked down at his large hands and scuffed boots. He knew his brusque manner had alienated some of the powerful men in Sint Joric, both clergy and laymen, and it was likely he might not get the assistance needed to gain his daughter's admission to the nunnery.

"No, Papa! I do not wish to be a nun, and certainly not a cloistered one." Mergriet turned back to face her father, hugging her elbows tightly, chilled at the thought of the nearby convent of the Sisters of Saint Anne. Then she burst into tears and ran to her room. Weeks later the two met in the parlor again.

"Papa, I would like become a beguine like Aunt Bea." Mergriet spoke first, her head high and her body tense, waiting for the expected opposition. But Hans only frowned and stroked his short beard.

"You will bring no honor to this family by becoming a beguine," he grumbled, but ultimately gave his permission, with the hope that his sister would resist accepting her.... Mergriet stirred, squinting against the light in this strange room; she had become accustomed to sleeping on an abbey floor, in a haystack full of squeaking mice, or with bedbugs in a peasant's loft. Now she wanted only to stay here in her comfortable bed and not face the grand mistress at all. Better yet, to go home. But where was home? She slept again.

"My sisters, I am pleased to announce that the weak place in our begijnhof wall has been repaired with new stone and mortar," Beatrice announced in chapel the following morning. "And all the work was paid for by the town fathers, so there was no cost to us." She smiled, and her beguine sisters nodded with satisfaction. They seemed unaware of the announcement's connection to the invader who had scaled that wall, so completely had they pushed the events of that night out of their minds.

Even Mergriet failed to grasp the significance of Beatrice's words. She was still feeling the effects of the long journey home from Chartres, her back stiff and sore and her legs aching. Kneeling on the stone floor was especially painful, and she found it difficult to focus on the prayers that followed.

A group of her sisters surrounded her after chapel, urging her to walk with them up the path to the school. "We have missed your baking, Sister Mergriet. Those wonderful crusty loaves of bread, and the warm buns with honey on special occasions." They were eager to hear of her adventures as a pilgrim, and she forgot her aching back as she began describing her journey.

"Well, as you know, I joined a group of Cistercian tertiaries on a pilgrimage to Chartres Cathedral. The tertiaries live in tiny huts attached to the walls of the abbey, rather like limpets clinging to the canals' walls, or so one of them told me." Her listeners smiled at the image. "The tertiaries wear plain habits much like ours, and we all had goatskin pouches filled with thin ale tied round our waists." And Mergriet demonstrated how she had looked with a heavy pouch dangling from her waistline. The sisters giggled: they had missed Mergriet's diversions.

"Father Matthias accompanied us, his tummy as round as his tonsure." Mergriet used her hands to mimic the priest's shape, and at this the sisters burst into laughter. "And my cousin Pieter, who is a Cistercian lay brother, went along as well for additional protection, or so he said.

"We traveled from Sint Joric to Ghent and were joined there by more pilgrims, from Ghent and the nearby towns. Leaving Ghent we traveled on to Paris, where we stayed at the Cistercian hospice and visited the Cathedral of Notre Dame." The beguines drew in their breath as they listened to Mergriet's description of the cathedral's cavernous gloom, of tall stained-glass windows that illustrated Old Testament stories in glorious color, and of side chapels larger than their own begijnhof chapel.

"Paris was like a dream world. Countless streets of shops selling food such as I've never seen before: snails still in their shells, tiny smoked fish that people ate head, tail and all, and carts selling sweets made to look like all sorts of animals. And a side street we peeked into was lined with cloth merchants selling all manner of fabrics, some that even looked like woven gold." The beguines audibly sucked in their breath in amazement. Mergriet paused to clear her throat. "And the smells! Some wonderful, sweet or pungent, and some…" Here, she wrinkled up her nose and everyone smiled knowingly, well acquainted with the smell of waste water running down the middle of the streets in parts of Sint Joric.

"The crowds were made up of people from all over Christendom, with faces from pale white like ours to a rich, dark brown, and every shade in between. The wealthy were wearing silk and velvet, of course; but there were plenty of ordinary folk, too. Oh, and there were street entertainers and vendors dressed in marvelous costumes, rather like the ones actors wear in the morality plays we sometimes see in our town square on holy days."

It was past time for the sisters to begin their work. More stories could wait until evening, when they often gathered around the fireplace in the dining room after supper. That was the best time for storytelling. When the others had left, Clare came up to Mergriet.

"I—I regret I am so late in thanking you for what you did for me on that awful night, Sister Mergriet. You risked your life defending me from that—that horrible man. You were very brave."

"I—I didn't see the knife at first, Sister Clare. When I saw him bending over you, I was so angry I just struck him as hard as I could." They looked at each other, the one slender and fair, the other solid and plain. Clare thanked Mergriet again and then hurried up the path to the schoolroom.

Mergriet made her way to the kitchen, relieved to be alone at last. She would tell more stories of her journey in the days to come; of following the pilgrim's way through lush, green fields dotted with clumps of trees and small hamlets whose inhabitants, duty-bound to provide for pilgrims, gave them food and shelter. The bedraggled, half-starved peasants at first refused the coins offered as payment, but many later accepted them with thanks. And Mergriet tried to convey the beauty of Chartres Cathedral, rising out of the mown fields like a mirage floating over a golden sea.

But she did not speak of the wariness of the Cistercian women, who stared at her, perhaps wondering why she had joined them so precipitously. And she could not speak of Sister Jana, the one friend she had made among them. The two had ridden side by side for much of the journey; Mergriet red-faced and freckled, her short legs sticking out from her donkey's side and Jana, thin and pale and obviously fragile, riding sidesaddle. They had shared their stories.

"Why did you decide to go on pilgrimage, Sister Jana?" Mergriet asked one warm afternoon, as she waved away the gnats. Jana seemed to lack strength for such an arduous journey.

"I am most devoted to the Virgin Mary, patroness of Chartres Cathedral. Since childhood I have dreamed of making this journey, and since becoming a Cistercian tertiary I have prayed for this day every day. And here I am." Looking around her, Jana laughed softly, but her laugh turned into a cough and she covered her mouth with a handkerchief.

"And you, Sister Mergriet, why did you decide to join us?" Jana spoke after a brief pause.

"I love traveling, seeing new places." There was silence, while Mergriet gathered her thoughts. She felt safe in a friendship that she knew would end with the pilgrimage, and free to tell the truth about herself. "I—I came very close to breaking one of my vows as a beguine. The grand mistress suggested that I go on this pilgrimage and pray that I might find both the path to forgiveness, and help in deciding if life as a beguine is my true calling."

Jana was shocked but at the same time pleased that Sister Mergriet had spoken so openly about her failings. This woman who laughed as she helped unload the donkeys and feed them, and appeared to find enjoyment in everything around her, had come on a pilgrimage to seek healing. Just as she herself had, though of a different kind.

"I am honored, Sister Mergriet, that you would share with me this burden you carry that no one else can see." Mergriet would always remember her words.

On the evening before they were due to arrive at Chartres, the Cistercians and another small group, both with animals that had slowed their pace due to minor injuries, stopped at a tiny hamlet strung out along the pilgrims' way. They were offered the loft of a barn to sleep in; it was the only large space available. Thick with hay, it smelled strongly of the apples stored below. Their hosts had just come in, tired and sweating, carrying more baskets of apples. Yet they wiped their hands on their rough work clothes and prepared a meal of warmed-over gruel with a few brown lumps of gristly meat floating in it, coarse bread, and spotted windfall apples. Sister Jana, her shoulders sagging with fatigue, was urged by Father Matthias to eat freely of the gruel, but the cauldrons were empty by the time Mergriet came in from helping with the donkeys. She was content with a large hunk of dark bread and two of the windfall apples, juicy and sweet, still warm from the sun.

The next day the Cistercian group fell still further behind the large groups of pilgrims from Flanders and Paris, as one after another of the women dismounted and ran into the bushes to relieve themselves. Many were suffering from diarrhea and some were feverish as well. Jana was shaking with fever and could take no food, only sips from her precious pouch of spring water.

Curiously, Mergriet and a few others remained untouched by illness. No one knew why, but Mergriet overheard a group of the Cistercian tertiaries discussing this anomaly as she and Jana rode behind them.

"Why should the beguine be spared this sickness when we are so afflicted?" one sister's discomfort spilled over into complaint. "She isn't one of us. And she has never told us why she asked to come on this pilgrimage."

"But Father Matthias and Brother Pieter and others are also well. Indeed, Father Matthias is fit enough to fast for two weeks without anyone noticing," another replied. The sisters listening smiled, easing the tension. "And Brother Pieter, well, he looks like a wraith all of the time. As for me, I am thankful that I have felt unwell only briefly." This came from a younger Cistercian, known for her health and strength.

One of the more pious sisters spoke up. "Perhaps the beguine wanted to be part of this pilgrimage because her sins are so grievous that she can no longer bear the burden of them, and she is seeking absolution from the Virgin of Chartres." There was a brief silence, and then the sisters returned to the usual complaints about food, lodging, and the lateness of the hour.

It was almost dark and turning cold when they reached the village of Chartres. Silently the pilgrims crossed the bridge over the River Eure, passed through the south gate close by a massive watchtower in the town wall, and wound their way through the streets to their lodging at an inn adjacent to the cathedral plaza. The cathedral's towers soared above them and disappeared into the night sky.

Father Matthias took those who were most ill to the crypt beneath the cathedral's sanctuary. An infirmary there provided bedding—thin pallets stuffed with straw, laid on stone benches lining the walls. Nursing sisters tended the sick and injured. Mergriet insisted on staying there with Jana, and Father Matthias, exhausted, rubbed his forehead with a grimy hand and nodded his approval.

She heaved herself up on the stone bench and sat all night holding Jana's hand. The cavernous space was damp and musty, lit only by a few candles; and the odor of yarrow, angelica, and bergamot the bedding exuded could not outweigh the smell of illness, decay, and unwashed bodies. Several times she nodded off in the midst of prayers for Jana: only once was the heavy silence broken by a hospice sister bringing broth. Mergriet helped Jana sip it whenever she woke, and bathed her face with cool water from a small basin the sister had provided.

But the once smiling young woman clearly was fading away, just as her own mother had. Mergriet's head drooped, and she slept. She dreamed she was struggling against heavy ropes binding her to one of the slabs of stone, and awoke just before dawn, cramped and sweating. Before she even touched Jana's hand, Mergriet knew she was gone.

Why had she, so laden with sin, survived and Sister Jana, who seemed so innocent, had not? Her sobbing finally brought one of the hospice sisters, and after a time Father Matthias led her away so the sisters could prepare the body for burial.

"We all know the risks a journey such as this entails. Sister Jana was a good Christian, a faithful member of our community, and eager to make this pilgrimage. She did see the cathedral, if just for a moment. We mourn her, but take solace knowing that she died in the company of saints." Father Matthias' voice was steady as he spoke to his charges, gathered together in the inn's main room. "Tomorrow morning she will be buried in a graveyard nearby. Her pilgrimage on earth is finished, but her life in Christ has just begun." The Cistercian sisters nodded dutifully but Mergriet stared impassively at the hard-packed earth of the inn's floor. "This afternoon I will listen to your confessions, and then we will celebrate a mass in memory of Sister Jana at one of the side altars in the cathedral."

When her turn came and she knelt before Father Matthias, Mergriet confessed everything. Her attraction to Sister Clare, and the guilt that tugged at her always. Her fear that she would be banished from the begijnhof community upon her return.

"But Father, Sister Jana really was a sister to me. We were true friends of the…the best kind, and that was all." Mergriet's face was wet and her hands were shaking by the time she had finished speaking. Father Matthias frowned and smoothed his thinning hair. No act of contrition could lift the burden the young woman was carrying, of that he was sure. He was silent for a long time. Finally, he gave her absolution, but tasked her with walking the cathedral's labyrinth.

"To walk the labyrinth is to make a pilgrimage to the Holy Land. Some say that the distance traveled through the labyrinth equals the walk Jesus himself made from Jerusalem to Golgotha, where he was crucified. Others say the journey through the labyrinth symbolizes our journey through life, which leads to the world of the dead and from there to Paradise." Mergriet had tried to focus on his words but found herself for the moment drained of faith, and the images he drew made little sense to her. Still, the last words he spoke stayed with her. "You have a chance to start again in this life, Sister Mergriet. Such an opportunity is rare. Do not falter, nor forget your good fortune."

The following morning was sunny, but cool and windy. The sisters held their coats close to keep them from billowing as they stood at the gravesite in a cemetery overlooking the town. Father Matthias' white robe had by now dulled to a dirty gray, and the strong breeze simply added more dust. Following the burial Mergriet, her eyes red from weeping and from the blowing dust, walked back to the plaza in front of the cathedral, and shielded her face with the hood of her coat. She looked up at the rose window, flanked by its two massive towers. The figure of Christ was at the window's center, surrounded by radiating circles of brilliant glass: it was as if the circles were dancing around him….

A few days later, a group of beguines gathered around the fireplace after supper, warming their hands with mugs of mint infusion. Mergriet spoke again about Chartres Cathedral. She told the sisters of the cathedral's stained glass windows, brilliant jewels streaming color, the dust on the floor from the feet of uncountable pilgrims rising to meet the colors swirling from above.

Father Matthias had "read" the Bible stories depicted in the beautiful glass panels: Noah and the building of the ark, with the animals in two's; Mary Magdalene, wiping Jesus' feet with her hair, and present at his crucifixion; and the story of the Good Samaritan. The beguines nodded and smiled at this story, one of their favorites.

But Mergriet did not tell her sisters about her journey through the labyrinth. The wind had pressed her against the massive door of the west portal that morning after Sister Jana's burial, and it was all she could do to open it far enough to slip inside. In the nave's center she saw a group of shadowy figures staring down at the floor, and moving in a slow circle. She had hardly noticed them the day before until Father Matthias pointed them out. She saw that some were on their knees, their garments sweeping the labyrinth clear of dust and dirt. Father Matthias told her that those traveling on their knees were most likely penitents seeking forgiveness for their sins. Mergriet felt herself to be one of those, and so had come this morning dressed in her heaviest leggings, her knees padded with strips of cloth she had found piled in a corner at the inn. Trudging to the labyrinth's opening, she waited her turn to begin. At last a space opened up, and she knelt and began sliding forward on her knees, wrapping her habit and her cloak tightly about her so that she and others would not trip on them.

The wind was howling now, and voices that might have been a distraction were reduced to a murmur. She shuffled through the labyrinth, following the winding pattern that led her toward its center, then away. She paused frequently to pray to the Virgin Mary that she might be freed from all the sins that weighted her down. The storm was raging outside and the cathedral had darkened, its windows dim. But for Mergriet the labyrinth had taken on a warm glow, and she was determined to journey to its heart. At last she reached the copper medallion at its center, and fell into a crouch facing the high altar, frozen in place. The pilgrim ready to enter behind her waited patiently.

"O holy God, Jesus Christ, have mercy on me, a sinner!" She touched her forehead to the stone floor, repeating the words over and over. Suddenly she was no longer cold and cramped, but was suffused in warmth. She was able to pray more fervently than ever before in her life. Was this the love of God that the beguine mystics described? That experience of the comfort and presence of God that could free one from the depths of despair? The pain of her sins faded away, and she felt embraced in love. The face that filled her heart and mind was that of the Jesus standing over the south portal of the cathedral, wrought in stone, but painted so beautifully that he seemed alive. Jesus, welcoming her

71

with outstretched arms, forgiving her. Jesus as teacher, loving father, God; the Jesus the beguines worshiped.

Mergriet finally retraced her path through the labyrinth. Her knees ached but she continued, reached the mouth of the labyrinth, and moved out of the circle. She struggled to her feet, then stumbled and fell. As she sat, and then slowly got up, she saw blood on her knees and limped to the side of the nave, leaning against one of its massive pillars. Then she felt Father Matthias' hand on her shoulder.

"You must go back to the inn and rest." Reluctantly Mergriet obeyed, and left the cathedral by the south door. Turning, she again looked up at Jesus, with his hand upraised. In that moment she felt the grace and mercy and forgiveness of God in a way she feared she never would again.

Mergriet walked back to Beatrice's house that night after the story-telling, her shawl pulled tight around her, trying to remember the journey home from Chartres. She had felt sad and lonely because Jana was not there, riding beside her. The wind had seemed to follow the group of Cistercians back to Sint Joric, pushing them along as it was pushing her now.

She climbed the stairs quietly and went to bed, and immediately fell asleep. She dreamed that she was in the big kitchen, the place where she had felt most at home when she first visited the begijnhof. She had entered by way of the covered pathway from the main building. The fireplace was huge, and Mergriet was immediately drawn to its warmth. If it were empty, she thought, you could walk into it, stretch out your arms, and not touch the walls on either side. She ran her hands over the massive, well-worn table that filled the center of the room, and marveled at the size of the large, open cupboard that held big cooking pots and an uncounted number of wooden bowls for pottage.

She smelled something delicious simmering in the big kettles hung over the fire. This was the place where she'd always felt at home. One of the sisters had come in to tell her that her bread was becoming so famous that the townspeople were grumbling, wondering why such fine bread was given to the poor when they had to spend their hard-earned money for loaves not half as brown and crusty.

When Mergriet awoke, she felt safe and warm. She stretched, sat up and looked around at the familiar furnishings from her old room. She was in her own bed, snug under the quilt her mother had made for her. Again Father Matthias' words came to her: "You have a chance to start again." This room, this place was where she would begin. She got up, and carefully placed the quilt at the end of the bed.

CHAPTER SEVEN

The best part of Clare's day was her time in the classroom each morning. The children played outside for a short time after chapel and then one of the sisters would lift her hand, the signal for them to run to the schoolhouse. Clare and several other teachers shared a large, bright room where the youngest students were learning to read and write in Flemish, and to do simple arithmetic. They were well-behaved in class— nothing less would be tolerated here. Most of all Clare enjoyed reading to the children, and among the books on the shelf along one wall were tales of knights and dragons, as well as simply told Bible stories. Each day she found time to sit on a low stool, gather her group around her, and read at least one story.

One of the children, a very small boy named Jan, always contrived to kneel close beside her. He would push back his thick, dark hair and lean forward when the book was one illustrated with pen-and-ink drawings. His delight in the stories she read was contagious, and Clare responded by trying to mimic the voices of the characters in the stories to help bring them to life.

After lessons and the main meal at midday, Jan would slip his hand in hers as the children proceeded from the dining room to the play area under the chestnut trees. That contact pierced Clare's loneliness: here was someone who sought her company. She responded by asking Jan about his life at home.

"I live with my father. He is a lawyer and sometimes has to travel, and when he comes home he always brings me a present," Jan announced. "Nona brings me to school each day." And Jan proceeded to name the other people who lived in his house. All appeared to be servants—there was no mention of a mother, or of sisters and brothers.

One morning as Clare was greeting the day students at the begijnhof gate, she noticed a man dressed in the new shortened tunic that fell only to mid-calf. It was finely cut and of a rich, dark material. Then she saw Jan at his side, seizing his hand and tugging him forward.

"Come and meet my papa, Sister Clare!" he called to her, and before she knew it Clare was standing before the tall, elegant figure.

"My name is Michiel von Lede," he greeted her and bowed. "Jan's nanny—that is, Nona, his companion," he corrected himself, noticing the boy's frown, "is ill this morning, so I decided to accompany him to school and meet the Sister Clare I have heard so much about. I did not expect someone so young."

Clare blushed and drew herself up to what she hoped was a dignified posture. Her cap and wimple covered her hair, but as usual the morning breeze had teased a few wispy blonde curls from their confinement, and they framed her face.

"Good morning, Mijnheer von Lede. I am pleased to say that Jan is learning very quickly." She spoke with what she hoped was an air of pro-fessionalism. "He can already read simple sentences and his handwriting is improving every day." Jan smiled, wriggling with pleasure at her praise.

"I brought Jan to the beguines because while he is a very friendly child, he has had little contact with other children. And your school has a repu-tation both for academic excellence and for your patience and gentleness with the children. Some of the brothers' discipline can be rather...harsh. Jan needs discipline, as do all children, but I find a strong word or two suffices. He has never been disciplined physically."

"Nor shall he be here, I can assure you." Clare spoke firmly. "We teach Christian love, and we try to treat one another accordingly." There was an awkward silence, and Clare took Jan's hand, her own a bit clammy. "We must go. It is almost time for morning prayers. It was a pleasure to meet you, Mijnheer von Lede."

As they hurried down the path to the chapel, Jan turned back to wave to his father, and Clare found herself taking a long look at Michiel, who was smiling at his son. How different he looks when he smiles, almost young, she thought, and quite handsome, with hair as dark as Jan's. She realized that her mouth had curved into a smile too. Clare pulled open the heavy door just as the chapel bell rang, and Jan stumbled into a run in his hurry to join the other children.

The sound of the bell faded away and the sisters and day students stood silently, waiting for the boarding students to arrive. Finally, Sister

Elisabetta pulled open the door and led them to their places. After the opening song of praise died away, Beatrice murmured to Sister Clare, who turned and hurried out of the chapel. Beatrice stepped forward and knelt, and the sisters and children got down on their knees, all wondering why Sister Celie, who always accompanied the children to chapel, was absent.

Clare ran the short distance to the main building and once inside, rushed up the stairs to Sister Celie's room on the top floor. She found Celie lying on her cot, her quilt barely up to her shoulders. Her eyes were closed and her breathing shallow. Her room, across from the children's dormitory, was furnished sparely; just a battered wooden box for a clothes trunk and a stool next to the cot. Two well-worn habits hung on pegs on the wall, but her prayer beads were splayed on the floor beside her cot.

"Sister Celie, what has happened? Can you speak to me?" Celie opened her eyes, framed by a web of wrinkles.

"Oh yes, I can speak."

Clare knelt on the floor and leaned closer to better hear her voice, which was scarcely more than a whisper. "But there is this heavy stone lying on my chest, and I cannot seem to get up."

"Please, Sister, do not move." Clare ran to the dormitory room to find a pillow. When she returned she knelt again, gently lifted Celie's head and slipped the pillow under it. Her frail body seemed as light as the pillow, and her white hair, unbound, was wispy and thin against her pink scalp. Beatrice had mentioned to Clare and others, who had nodded agreement, that she had seen warning signs lately: Celie's voice was softer, her steps slower, and her slight frame bent more and more. Yet she still deemed it her duty to greet everyone who came to the main door with a broad smile, unaware or uncaring that many of her teeth were now missing.

Celie had been at the begijnhof far longer than any other sister. She had come when she was very young, twelve or thirteen Clare thought, but she really did not know. Celie never talked about her past life as some other sisters did. After helping her to the chamber pot, and giving her a sip from the remains of a now cold mint infusion in a mug next to her bed, Clare sat quietly by her cot. Her breathing was even, but when questioned, Celie murmured that the pressure on her chest had not lessened. In spite of her effort not to appear anxious, Clare's hands were in constant motion, smoothing the coverlet, then her own habit; she could not keep them still.

Finally, to Clare's great relief, Beatrice arrived, and she related to the grand mistress all she had done since arriving at Celie's bedside. Beatrice first prayed for healing for Celie, leaning close so she could hear every word. Then she straightened and raised her voice.

"Sister Celie, I am going to ask one of the brothers from the hospital to come and visit you. I know Brother Lucas has healing hands." Beatrice spoke firmly and ignored Celie's frown. "And now I am going to see about making a broth to give you strength. I have noticed that you have not been eating much lately." Beatrice asked Clare to sit with Celie until another of the sisters arrived, and Clare took Celie's hand in hers, murmuring assent..

Breakfast was long over but the smell of fresh-baked bread still filled the kitchen with a yeasty fragrance when Beatrice reached it. Briefly she explained what had happened. "And it is time for that fat old rooster to go," she said to the sisters beginning to prepare the midday meal. "Let us make a clear broth for Sister Celie, and put the rest of him in today's pottage. Please call me when the broth is ready; I will take it to her."

Beatrice then hurried to the beguine school, where the sisters were helping the children get ready for the morning's lessons, and asked for two sisters willing to seek out Brother Lucas and ask for his help. Clare begged to go, and Beatrice quickly dispatched her and Elisabetta to the hospice in town, then went back to check on Celie. She was asleep and breathing evenly, a good sign. Beatrice fell to her knees in prayer.

Clare and Elisabetta, both always eager for an opportunity to leave the begijnhof, made their way to the hospice near the edge of town where the seriously ill and travelers in need could find rest and care. They found Brother Lucas there and he listened closely to their description of Celie's symptoms. He thought a moment, and then carefully wrote down the restoratives needed.

"You should grind the dried herbs and roots into a powder. Sister Celie is to drink, twice daily, two generous pinches of the powder dissolved in boiled water, then cooled to lukewarm. She must rest in bed as much as possible. I will come and see her as soon as I am able." The beguines thanked him profusely. "Better that you pray for your sister's recovery; there is no need to thank me." But the Cistercian acknowledged their thanks with a nod and a smile.

The sisters left the apothecary with the prescription and started back to the begijnhof. As they approached the main square in the middle of town, it began to rain and the two stepped up their pace and pulled their wimples forward to shield their faces. They rounded a corner and Clare, slightly ahead, bumped into a man coming toward her.

"I am sorry, sir. Please excuse me for stumbling against you."

"Sister Clare, is that you?" Clare pulled at her wimple and stepped backward. It was Jan's father.

"Mijnheer von Lede, indeed it is I and this is Sister Elisabetta. Both beguines acknowledged him with a slight curtsey, and Michiel bowed low. "Sister, Mijnheer von Lede is Jan's father, and Jan is one of my students. Clare could not bring herself to look at Elisabetta; instead she addressed Michiel. "Sir, we must not tarry; one of our sisters is ill and we have with us a remedy that may be of help her."

"Of course, you must be on your way. But could I walk with you and shield you from the rain?" And with that, Michiel managed to place himself next to Clare. He took off his coat to shield her from the rain and stretched it out to Elisabetta, who leaned inward, straining to listen to their conversation, as she was a bit hard of hearing. When Clare asked after his family, he told her he was a widower, and had been for some time. She was just beginning to learn more about him when they arrived at the begijnhof gate.

"Thank you for your company, sisters, and I hope your ailing sister returns to good health." Michiel bowed low, looked into Clare's eyes, and swiftly strode away. Elisabetta had missed nothing; indeed she had both felt and seen their mutual attraction.

A week later, Celie was still confined to her room, though unwillingly. Brother Lucas visited her and left another remedy which eased her discomfort, in spite of her complaint of its bitter taste. Her face had more color, her appetite had increased, and the strength of her protests indicated that she was indeed improving.

"But," Brother Lucas spoke to Beatrice calmly as he was leaving, "she is very old; we should not be surprised by something like this. Perhaps it is her time to go to God."

A week later, as Clare, cramped from sitting for so long on the stool beside her bed, got up to leave, Celie spoke softly. "Sister Clare, do you think the grand mistress might find time for a visit?"

"I am sure she will come as soon as she can, dear Sister."

Beatrice hurried up to the tiny room, feeling guilty that she had visited less often as Celie's condition improved. She found her sitting on the stool by her bed, hands quiet in her lap. Celie assured Beatrice that she was feeling well, and then straightened her shoulders.

"I think it is time for me to tell my story, Sister Beatrice, and I think you are the one who should hear it."

"I would be honored to hear about your family and what brought your here, Sister Celie, but only if you feel sure you want to tell me."

"It is time." Celie repeated firmly. "I think I am at peace with my beginning; it is the ending that matters now, and I—I think I am at peace with

Jesus, too." Beatrice brought a chair from the dormitory, settled Celie in it, and sat down on the stool, ignoring her protests that the grand mistress should have the chair. Celie leaned back in the chair with a little sigh and spoke, her voice quavering a little.

"Sister Beatrice, when I came here I had never even heard of Jesus." Beatrice tried not to show her surprise. "Growing up, I remember darkness and gloom more than anything. The lane we lived in was narrow and dank; our house was almost always dark because there was no money for candles, and most of the time we kept the shutters closed against the cold. It was a one-room hut, and there was never enough to eat." Celie studied her gnarled fingers and shifted in her chair. "I can't remember much about my mother; maybe I have deliberately wiped away my memories of her. There were many births, I remember that, but few babies lived beyond a few months. I was the oldest child and only two others had survived, both boys. My mother took in washing, carrying water from the pump at the end of the lane. She hung the clothes to dry on a rope strung between the rafters, so the room was always damp, and water sometimes dripped on our heads.

"My father drank up the little money he made doing odd jobs. He was a violent man and drink only made him more so. He beat all of us at the slightest offense, or just because he was angry at something, anything. Naturally, none of us went to school or to church or anywhere except out in the streets to beg. We rarely bathed, and then only sponged down with cold water, and so we smelled bad and I was ashamed to go outside. But sometimes we were forced to take to the streets to beg for food. The passersby, well-dressed and sometimes plump, seemed like people from another world.

"We all slept in one bed without our clothes in winter, to keep warmer under our thin quilts; and I usually slept beside my mother. One night when I was about twelve, my father pushed my mother aside and tried to force himself on me. The room was dark and cold; the fire had long since gone out. I tried to fight him and I pleaded with my mother, who was heavy with child again, to help me but he kicked her and she turned away from me and pulled the bedclothes over her head." Beatrice saw a tear fall on Celie's lap, but she kept silent.

"My father was rolling on top of me, and I was frantic, feeling him pushing his—himself against me. Somehow I found the strength to wriggle out from under him, scramble out of the bed, and run out into the street. I didn't even try to shut the door, and I heard my father roaring and my mother crying as I ran naked into an alley nearby.

78

"I hid behind a pile of garbage in the dark alley, shaking with cold, afraid that a shade from the devil, or a band of dogs might attack me. When the first light of dawn came, I saw a rat's tail in the debris, just hanging there, limp. A movement, then a big crow appeared, and walked towards me carrying the dead rat. I cried out, and he looked at me with his one yellow eye, then flew away silently on his big, black wings. Everyone knows crows are harbingers of death." Celie shuddered. "I shook with such a fear I've never had since.

"When I heard the bang of our door and the clumping of my father's rag-wrapped shoes I crept to the house, afraid that someone would see me naked, but thanks be to God there was no one in the lane. Once inside, I dressed and gathered up my few belongings. No one spoke to me. My brothers were in a corner fighting over a crust of bread. My mother turned away from me and did not speak. It was as if I wasn't there a'tall, and so I turned my back to her. But she must have thrust some bread inside the small bundle I had made. I hated her for failing me when I needed her help. I hated them all! My only thought was to get away, as far away as I could, before my father came home.

"I made my way toward the town gate, and when I stopped for a moment to rest I looked around and saw the begijnhof wall, and the chapel spire rising above it. I thought it must be a hospital or a monastery, though I didn't really know what those words meant.

"For some reason, I thought I might get help from someone inside that wall, and I was so desperate that I swung the heavy knocker at the gate with all the strength I had, crying for help. When the gatekeeper pulled the gate open, I begged him for a little food."

Suddenly, Celie's wonderful smile lit her face. "I was taken to the grand mistress, Sister Clarissa it was then. I begged her to let me stay there, told her I would scrub floors, do laundry, anything for food.

" 'We all work here,' she answered. 'But before we talk any more, let us give you a bath and some food.'

"I was taken to the kitchen, a wonder to me, such a big, warm room, and full of light. A large tub was dragged out and hot water from the kettle hanging over the fire was poured into it. I was scrubbed from head to toe, lice and their eggs scrubbed out of my hair. I wept from pain or relief, I don't know which. My clothes were taken away and a fresh, clean shift was dropped over my head, and for the first time in my life I wore something like a real dress, not just rags. My hair was so matted that tears ran down my cheeks while one of the sisters combed it, so she ended up cutting the snarls out. I was a sight!" Celie laughed, but her voice quavered. "Then

I was set before the fire and given a bowl of pottage and a spoon. Awkwardly I began to eat, never having used a spoon before. Soon I couldn't keep my eyes open and I was led off to a dormitory room and put to bed."

"Please, Sister Celie, rest a moment," Beatrice interrupted, concerned that Celie was tiring herself. Celie frowned, but sat back in her chair and was silent for a few minutes. Then she leaned forward.

"I am fine Sister Beatrice; please let me go on." Beatrice nodded assent. "When I woke up, I thought I must have dreamt it all. But someone had covered me with a quilt and I was warm, so warm I wanted to stay in that cot forever. Then one of the sisters came and said that the grand mistress wanted to speak with me. She had brought a simple dress and I slipped it on over my shift; it came down to my feet. Then she led me to the receiving room.

"The grand mistress told me about the beguines in a very simple way, saying they were women who taught children and fed the poor. I told her that I had no learning, but was willing to do any work if they would only let me stay. I said I had left home after a beating, and she asked no questions.

" 'We will let you stay until you and I together decide what you should do next,' Sister Clarissa told me. And I have been here ever since. Here I learned how different the world could be from the one I knew. A world of love and caring, plenty of food, a warm bed. Light from the sun by day, shining through windows of glass! Candles to light our way in the dark. And I learned about God and Jesus." Celie paused for a moment. "I became a pupil in our school and learned to read and write and do simple sums. In the afternoon, I went to work in the kitchen or in the garden. I loved being outside in the fresh air and hearing the birds, and digging in the earth and making things grow.

"One morning, after I had been here several years, I was helping to pass out bread to the poor folk waiting outside our gate, when my heart jumped so strongly in my breast that I thought I might fall down. There was my mother, bent over, her clothes in tatters, with a small boy clinging to her skirt. She looked up and saw me, but did not recognize me, her own daughter. I did not stop to think how different I must look from the ragged child who had left her years earlier. I simply placed the bread in her arms and turned away. I was ashamed that I had not greeted her, but I did not want the sisters to know that this poor beggar was my mother.

"And then one day a long time after that, when I was in town shopping with one of the sisters, I found an excuse to walk down the lane where I once lived. Our tiny hut was no longer there—just a charred black pile where it had burned to the ground.

"All these years, I have carried with me the guilt and shame of denying my mother and abandoning my family. I believe Jesus has forgiven me, but I cannot forgive myself for not speaking to my mother when she came here, for not making any effort to find my family." And Celie brushed away the tears that had run down her cheeks.

Beatrice looked down at her lap, plucked at her habit, and straightened her shoulders. She was determined not to let her own tears fall.

"And this is the most important part," Celie continued. "As I said, I loved helping in the kitchen and the garden, but when I became too old for that work I began my most important work, the work that Jesus truly called me to do. You see, I came to realize that there might be other girls, or even women, who needed to escape from…an unbearable life such as mine was when I came here. What if they came to the gate and were just given bread and turned away as I had turned away from my own mother? How would the sisters be able to tell who needed refuge? I would know. I could tell."

"Did—did that ever happen?" Beatrice could not keep herself from asking.

"Yes, once a child came alone, but she was starving and close to death. We could not save her." Celie paused and looked away, again wiping tears from her eyes.

"So please understand, Sister Beatrice, why I need to get back to my work of greeting everyone who comes here for bread, lest someone like me be turned away."

Again Beatrice bowed her head for a moment to hide her own tears. "Well, I do understand why you feel the need to get back to work. We will put a chair by the front door so you need not stand, and always at least one of us will be there with you. When a stranger is among the poor who come to our door, someone we are not used to seeing, and you think that person needs the kind of help you did, please bring her right to me. You know Jesus' story of the Good Samaritan?" Celie nodded and smiled the smile that had greeted so many over the years. "We should all be Samaritans, and you have shown me what that means. Thank you, Sister, for telling me your story." Beatrice rose, and held out her hand.

"Come, I know just the right chair for you." And the two women, one tall and straight, one small and stooped, left the room together.

CHAPTER EIGHT

The wind blew in from the North Sea, and the harvested fields, divided only by canals, lay supine as it passed over them. The town walls were but a minor impediment; the wind swept over them and raced down the narrow streets, weaving and turning corners. It soughed down chimneys and moaned through every crack in doors and shutters. It slipped over the walls into the town-within-the-town, and there found a door unlatched, caught its edge and pushed it open with one great gust. As the wind whirled through the small sanctuary a full moon emerged from the clouds gliding across it, shone through the glass windows, and lit the figure of Christ on the triptych behind the altar. The gold halo crowning his head glowed.

A gray-clad figure, dark yet ethereal, suddenly rose up before the altar, gave a loud cry and slumped to the stone floor. The wind rattled the panes of glass and sought entrance around the window frames, but finding none, contented itself with banging the heavy door against the outside wall. The figure on the floor heard nothing and did not stir.

Beatrice had gone to bed late and was awakened suddenly by a loud noise. Was it her front door banging in a gust of wind? No, it was further away than that, perhaps something in the town. She drew the covers closely around her, trying to ignore that heavy, thudding sound. At last she fell into a restless sleep. She woke early, the eastern sky the color of wet slate. The wind had quieted somewhat, but she could still hear the occasional dull clunk of what sounded like a door or a gate banging.

Reluctantly she got up, knowing she would sleep no more, and dressed quickly, pulling on her heavy clogs and her coat. She slipped quietly out of her house, closing the door firmly behind her. No need to disturb anyone else. The day was cloudy and windy; she shivered, and wrapped the coat tightly around her.

Inside the rows of townhouses hugging the begijnhof wall were the chapel and the infirmary: both were sheltered from the buffeting of the wind by large shrubs, and all seemed quiet there. But as Beatrice reached the graveyard, she heard the banging sound again, and knew it must be coming from the chapel. When she reached the entrance, she saw that the heavy door was ajar, leaning against the outside wall.

She entered the chapel, and secured the door behind her. Peering through the dim light, she saw what appeared to be a twisted pile of gray cloth on the stone floor. She hurried down the marble aisle, knowing what it must be. The body was stretched out on the floor in front of the altar, face downward, arms outstretched. Beatrice, her head pounding, got down on her knees and carefully uncovered the hooded face. It was Annalise. She did not stir.

Gently Beatrice tucked one of Annalise's arms under her body, and then slowly turned her over. Surely she must be dead. But perhaps her spirit had not yet left her body. Annalise's face was pale and her body cold, yet her chest appeared to be rising and falling slightly but steadily. There was a large bruise on her forehead and one side of her face was scraped raw. Beatrice quickly removed her coat and covered Annalise, tucking the coat around her. I must get help, she thought and immediately Mergriet came to mind. She was strong, and probably already in the kitchen since she was in charge of the bread-making and usually rose with the dawn. Quickly Beatrice left the chapel and headed for the begijnhof kitchen.

"Mergriet, did you not hear that banging noise?" Beatrice came up behind Mergriet as she was sliding a large tray of loaves of bread into the big bread oven outside the kitchen door. Beatrice had spoken loudly, but Mergriet shut the oven door before answering.

"I have been here for some time and have heard nothing but the wind. But I make a good deal of noise myself." Mergriet stalked into the kitchen and immediately shifted a tray of rising bread to the large worktable near the door. And in truth, Mergriet had to raise her voice to be heard over the sounds of the fire crackling in the fireplace and the thud of the pan as she set it on the table. She waited for Beatrice to tell her what had brought her to the kitchen at such an early hour.

"Come quickly, Sister, I need your help. Sister Annalise is lying on the floor of the chapel as cold as the dead, yet still breathing. I need you to help me carry her to the infirmary." Beatrice turned back to the door and Mergriet followed, wiping her hands on her apron as she flung it aside. As they hurried to the chapel, Mergriet frowned; she could not help but hope that Sister Ida, who helped with the baking, would get to the bread oven before the loaves burned.

Bracing open the chapel door with a large stone kept for that purpose, the two women found Annalise's coat, then carefully lifted the limp form and wrapped the coat tightly around her. They also found a thick pad of cloth, like a kneeling pad, beneath her and they scooped that up too. Beatrice, shivering with cold, retrieved her own coat. Slowly and awkwardly the two women carried Annalise to the infirmary and lifted the latch on the door.

They placed her on one of the cots in the main room, reserved for the injured or ill. Mergriet remembered when she herself had been helped into bed there, her arm throbbing. It seemed long ago now. Beatrice covered Annalise with warm quilts, and soon her cheeks began to turn pink.

"There is nothing more I can do here, Sister Beatrice. I must get back to the bread oven, lest the loaves burn." Mergriet hurried away and Beatrice pulled a chair to the side of the bed and sat quietly, praying that Annalise would stir. At last she opened her eyes and struggled to sit up. Beatrice leaned over the bed to support her. Somewhat dazed, Annalise looked around her.

"Sister Beatrice, what am I doing in the infirmary?" She rubbed her forehead. "I feel perfectly fine, except for this headache. And my face hurts." She put her hand to her cheek. "How did I get here?"

"I found you in the chapel just before dawn, lying on the floor in front of the altar. Do you remember why you were there at such an hour?" Beatrice queried gently as she slipped another pillow behind Annalise's head. The room was quiet except for the sound of the wind sighing outside the window. Annalise lay back against the pillows, and spoke softly.

"I went to the chapel last night to pray. I can pray in my room, but I feel so much closer to Jesus in the chapel. And I know that we are expected to remain in our rooms once we have said good-night, but I—" Annalise's throat tightened and her voice was strained. Beatrice poured a mug of well water from the jar nearby, and lifted her up so she could take a sip. "Ah, thank you, Sister. I—my head is so heavy." Beatrice eased her back down on the pillows.

"You see, there is not enough time for prayer during the day, at least not time enough for me. I would like to spend all day in prayer, but I know that is not possible. So I have been returning to the chapel after evening prayers. Kneeling is difficult for me, and kneeling on the stone floor for a long time mostly on my 'good' leg is painful, and the pain distracts me from my prayers. So I found some old cloths and sewed them together to make a kneeler, with one side thicker to support my other leg." And Annalise pointed to the worn pad Beatrice had laid at the foot of her cot.

"Last night, after I got to the chapel a great wind came up, and I was afraid to go out in it so I stayed much longer than usual, praying on my kneeler. Then suddenly bright light shone on the triptych, on the figure of Jesus, and I could feel him looking <u>right at me</u>. Tiny sparkling lights surrounded him and he was beckoning to me; truly he was, Sister Beatrice. I got up and moved toward the altar. It was like the miracle that happed to me at Sint Agustin's long ago, when I felt caught up in Jesus' love and my feet left the floor. I had wanted so much for Jesus to lift me up again—and he did.

"Sister Beatrice, I have seen people look at me with pity, or fear, or even disgust. Only Jesus sees me as I truly am. There are times when I see him everywhere. Times when I despair of losing his love. But last night I saw him again.

"You, Sister, and my family, have given me this chance to devote my life to him, to seek his grace, and to make that search an offering, however small. I want to open my heart and soul to God, to Jesus, and prayer is the only path I know. Prayer is all I have to give."

By now Annalise was weeping openly, her frail body shaking. "Please, Sister Beatrice, grant me the chance to devote my whole life to God. I feel that the Almighty is reaching out to me and I cannot turn away." Finally, all was quiet. Beatrice rose and paced the room, her hands gripping her elbows. Then she sat down by Annalise's bedside again and stroked her hand.

"Well, I think you should rest here today, and not try to get up unless one of the sisters is here to help you." Beatrice held up her hand as Annalise began to protest, and Annalise bent her head in assent. "I will see that a heated brick is placed in your bed to warm you." Beatrice rose and began to walk away but at the sound of Annalise's voice, she stopped.

"Sister Beatrice? Are the stars windows that God uses to look down on us from heaven? Could it be that the bright light and the loud noise during storms are signs that He is throwing open his door to us?" Beatrice could not bear to hear that pleading voice any longer. She opened the infirmary door, and turned. "Please Sister Annalise, please try to sleep."

"Sister Marie, I need your advice." Beatrice gripped her mug tightly. "It's about Sister Annalise." It was late afternoon, and Beatrice and Marie were seated in front of the small fireplace in Beatrice's parlor, watching the rain beat against the window and warming their hands on hot mugs of an infusion of mint and chamomile. The small table nearby held a plate with two thick slices of bread, spread lightly with honey.

"This must be serious, Sister, if you are offering honey with bread, albeit day-old bread." They both laughed, and then Beatrice pressed her lips together, took a deep breath, and placed her mug on the table. "Sister Annalise fell and scraped her face, as I told you, but that is not the whole story." And Beatrice recounted what had happened in the chapel.

"As you know, I persuaded one of our patrons to provide the money needed for Sister Annalise's dowry. And I pressed the 'wise ones' to acquiesce in asking her to join us. Unlike Sister Elisabetta, I think it is a good thing to have some sisters here who do not come from well-to-do families. But I may have made a mistake."

"A mistake? How so?"

"Annalise really belongs in a nunnery; she said that was her wish the first time I spoke with her." Beatrice sighed audibly. "She felt such a strong desire to spend more time in prayer that she deliberately broke one of our rules, and went to the chapel at night. And now she claims to have had this—this 'vision.' Sister Marie, in spite of her disobedience, I feel obliged to accommodate her, and allow her more prayer time. Also, she has asked me several times if we could have mass in our chapel more often. How can I answer her? What should I do?"

"Well, I do not think Annalise is alone in wishing for more than the occasional mass. I believe most, if not all of the women of this community would like to attend mass in our own chapel more often, perhaps even on a weekly basis." Marie paused and took a sip from her mug and a large bite of the sticky bread. "Why not ask the sisters how they feel about the matter? As to her wish for more prayer time, I think it is within your purview as grand mistress to grant Sister Annalise as much prayer time as you think is necessary for—" Marie hesitated, and frowned, "for her soul's health. And then just inform the 'wise ones' of your decision."

Beatrice sat back in her chair. The ache in her stomach had lessened. "Talking with you always helps me with problems that seem insurmountable, Sister Marie." The two smiled at each other, but Marie's smile was a bit tentative. When they had finished their infusion, she rose, put on her hooded coat, and left for her own house.

Beatrice spent so much time praying on the prie-dieu in her little bedroom that she felt the need to pad it with a cushion. Were there beguines who spent their lives as contemplatives? Who gave themselves over to prayer as a means of serving God and their community? She knew that many other beguine communities existed; indeed, one of the begijnhof's patronesses had told her of a begijnhof in Liege that numbered almost one thousand women. One thousand! By that measure, theirs was a very small group indeed, fewer than one hundred, though she rarely had need to count them. When a woman came for a trial period and seemed likely to join them, she looked for a spare room. Only then did she know exactly how many beguines lived in the Sint Joric begijnhof.

For the first time, Beatrice wished she could speak with beguines from other communities. But did numbers, or what other beguines did, matter? Was not each community free to make its own rules? She decided to talk to Sister Celie; perhaps she could remember a beguine here at Sint Joric who had spent her life in prayer.

Several days later, Beatrice invited Celie to come to her house and share a hot drink. A cold, damp wind was blowing when she arrived. It seeped through tiny cracks around the warped window frame in Beatrice's small parlor, so the two sat close to the fire, wrapped in warm wool shawls. Celie was bent over her mug of mint infusion; Beatrice sat straight in her chair, staring into the flames.

"Sister Celie, you have been here far longer than any other beguine. Do you remember a beguine who ceased to work as a teacher, or to cook or work in the garden and instead gave her life over to prayer?" Pleased that the grand mistress had consulted her, Celie thought for a long time before answering Beatrice's question. At last she smiled and looked up at her.

"Yes, I do remember one sister, Sister Greete, her name was. She came here long ago; I think Sister Therese was the grand mistress then. At first, Sister Greete worked in the garden with me. She would pull weeds and she worked hard, but she had this look on her face like she was somewhere else. One day, I found her pulling up the parsnip shoots right along with the weeds." Celie's small frame shook as she laughed. "Then she started spending more and more time in her room, and finally she only left it for morning and evening prayer in chapel, for Bible study, and for meals. And the grand mistress even had to remind her to take a bath, when all of us could tell she needed one." Celie shook her head, still smiling.

"Some of the sisters complained that she never did any work, but the grand mistress would say she was doing God's work; praying for the sins of all of us in this community, and for the whole world. After a while, we just got used to her. And you know, she had a wonderful way about her, never put on airs or acted like she was special. But she <u>was</u> special. When she died, we all knew she went straight up to heaven."

"What a wonderful story, Sister." The two spent a pleasant hour chatting. Celie always knew what was going on inside the begijnhof walls, more than did Beatrice, who was content to sit back and wait for news to come to her.

Afer Celie left, Beatrice went back to her prie dieu with renewed zeal. She prayed for success in persuading Abbot Paulus to provide more frequent masses for the community, and for guidance in how best to persuade the community that Annalise should be granted more prayer time. Much more.

Several days later Beatrice sat at the desk in her receiving room. Bitter cold was now upon them. A fire burned brightly in the fireplace, yet she needed a heavy woolen shawl over her shoulders to keep out the chill, and an infusion with bitter yarrow to help her think. She knew why Grand Mistress Anna had arranged for a Cistercian priest to say mass at the begijnhof. It was not just because the beguines had long ago sought the protection of the Cistercian Order. It was also because they knew that even though Father Johan's parish included the begijnhof, he would have refused to come and say mass had he been asked, so great was his disapproval of their way of living. Rubbing her forehead, she pulled a sheet of parchment from the box nearby, dipped her pen in freshly prepared ink, and began writing.

"November, in the Year of our Lord 1333

Most Reverend Abbot,
I pray this finds you and your Brother Cistercians in good health. Please know that we continue to thank you in our daily prayers for the spiritual guidance and protection you have given us these many years. I am writing about a matter of great concern, which affects the health and well-being of the Sint Joric beguine community. . . .

Choosing her words carefully, Beatrice described the community's worship and prayer life. She wrote of the longing of the sisters for more frequent celebration of the Eucharist. Finally, she asked if Abbot Paulus would consider allowing one of his priests to make the journey to Sint Joric to celebrate mass more often, perhaps even weekly. Recognizing that this might be a burden for their community, she thanked him effusively for considering her request.

"...In closing, I pray that you can aid me in my efforts to provide my sister beguines with more frequent

celebration of the Holy Eucharist, which I believe
will enable all of us to better worship, teach, and serve.

I remain your most obedient servant,
Beatrice, Mistress of the Beguine
Community of Sint Joric

Beatrice felt as though she had bent over the sheet of parchment for hours. She signed the letter, wiped her hands on the cloth she had tucked in her sleeve, and stretched her arms over her head. Then, carefully rolling the letter, she tied it with a bit of fine ribbon and sealed the knot with wax. She placed the letter in a small sheepskin packet and prepared it for Brother Pieter, who had visited her the previous day. He would be leaving for the abbey in the morning, and had promised to stop again at the begijnhof and take the packet to the abbot.

Abbot Paulus was tall and so thin that when he strode through the abbey's cloister after matins in his white Cistercian habit, his brothers jokingly said he looked like a ghost. His lined face was dominated by a prominent forehead, dark eyebrows and a long, thin nose, giving him a stern expression that belied his normally genial disposition. He wore a full beard, now graying.

Walking to the window in his study, he looked over the abbey's fields and orchards, now only dark outlines in the morning fog. The abbey had been built as strong as a fortress, the windows narrow slits in gray stone. But there were welcoming places inside it, and this comfortable room was one of them. Paulus warmed his hands before the small fireplace and seated himself in one of the worn armchairs drawn up to it. He read again the petition from the grand mistress of the begijnhof in Sint Joric.

The Cistercians were a powerful force in the church; respected, tolerant, and devout, following the example of their founder, St. Bernard of Clairvaux. They chose to build their abbeys outside towns and cities, yet remained very well connected to what was going on in the world around them. Thus Paulus was aware of increasing criticism of the beguines of late, even from bishops in some dioceses. He knew that a petition had been written requesting that beguines be required to attend mass daily. He did not know whether the petition had been sent to Pope John.

Stroking his beard, Paulus sat back in his armchair. Perhaps a closer scrutiny of the beguines of Sint Joric was in order. He would indeed consult with the grand mistress, after he had spoken with the brother priest who visited the begijnhof.

"Father Matthias, welcome, I trust all goes well with you." Paulus waved Matthias to the other armchair close by the fireplace. "I am considering a new mission for you."

"A mission, Abbot Paulus?" Matthias straightened in his chair. Paulus smiled.

"Not like your pilgrimage to Chartres, dear brother, when you were a hen in charge of a flock of chicks." Both men laughed, Matthias somewhat uneasily. "No, this would be a mission with a far different purpose," Paulus went on, and explained that Matthias might be asked to make a weekly journey to Sint Joric to say mass for the beguines and speak with the grand mistress. He would spend the night in the small house the Cistercians kept in the town, and report to Paulus upon his return about the state of the community and its leader.

"You could help me to understand something of how that community of women lives, what their daily life is like. I do not know how much freedom they have or what their rules are. I am aware that they sometimes go into the town, but for what purposes? And does the grand mistress have to give her permission for such outings? I would ask you to be discreet, Father, but I have need to know these things. Can you be my eyes and ears in the begijnhof?"

"Yes, yes I can do that, and gladly. And I would be privileged to celebrate the mass with the beguine community. I will talk to the grand mistress and to the sisters when I have the opportunity. But Sir, I pray you will provide a companion for me on these journeys. The roads, as you know, continue to be dangerous. All these bands of men fighting for different lords, different masters...."

"Of course, of course you may take someone with you. I will send that restless Brother Pieter. He's a strapping lad, and always eager to travel. You'll have strong horses to see you there and back, and you must travel only during the daylight hours."

The beguines were delighted with the abbot's decision. But Beatrice felt the need to consult the "wise ones," and asked them to come to her reception room, warmed that day by morning sunshine.

"I know how pleased everyone is that our desire to attend mass each week has been granted; but as you know, this mid-week mass will interrupt both our bread-making and our teaching. However, Sister Mergriet and her helpers have agreed to rise even earlier on that morning, so that the bread is baked before mass. We will tell those who come to us for bread that on Wednesdays they should gather at the gate a bit later. And I think the children will not mind if their lessons are somewhat shorter on Wednesday mornings." The sisters smiled and nodded their approval.

Morning and evening prayers in the chapel went on as usual, the beguines continuing to sing their songs of praise in Flemish, blending their voices in polyphonic melody. The weekly mass on Wednesdays, with Father Matthias officiating, was chanted in Latin.

For Annalise, mass every week was a gift from God, a chance to feel Jesus' presence in the bread placed on her tongue. Still, she longed for more time to pray. She could not view her work in the kitchen and the garden as an offering to God, as Sister Beatrice had described it. She wanted to pray with her whole mind and heart fixed on God, on Jesus. She wanted to feel Christ lifting her up, as He had that day in Sint Agustin's, and on that night in the beguine chapel when the wind was howling.

CHAPTER NINE

The chestnut trees in the courtyard were past full bloom. Spent blossoms floated on the breeze, showering the beguines and the children as they passed into the bright sunshine beyond the begijnhof wall. At last the feast day of Corpus Christi had arrived. Juliana of Mt. Cornillion, who had lived for a time in a beguine community over a hundred years ago, had much to do with persuading the church to institute the feast of Corpus Christi. So for beguines the day had special meaning beyond that of celebrating the Eucharist as a holy day.

Beatrice had announced that Brother Matthias would officiate at a special mass in the beguine chapel that morning. Afterward, the beguines could attend the Corpus Christi procession in the town if they wished. Because the children were freed from lessons on Corpus Christi, the day students would not be present.

After mass in the chapel, and breakfast, the sisters gathered the children together, and each sister took the hand of one or two of them. They did not leave all at once, as that would attract too much attention. Rather, they left in groups of two or three sisters and their charges. Annalise was with the first group to leave. She was eager to arrive early at the street where the procession would pass by, so as to get the best possible view. Sister Elisabetta wanted to spend some time wandering the town, and was happy to accompany her. They took three children with them, Annalise clasping the hand of one of the older girls, who helped her maintain her balance in the crowd.

It was a glorious morning, with flowers blooming in pots everywhere and vendors calling out their wares, offering all manner of sweets in honor of the holy day. Everyone was out on the streets, since all work ceased during the Corpus Christi parade. The crowd was cheerful and convivial, many heading for the largest church in town, where the procession would begin.

"Let us make our way to the front, so the children can have a better view." Annalise urged Elisabetta forward and they managed to make their way to the edge of the street where the procession would pass by. Now Annalise would have an unfettered view of the beautiful monstrance and the large host placed inside it. The crowd was large, but she stubbornly resisted efforts by latecomers to press her back into the crowd. Elisabetta was surprised by Annalise's tenacity; she was usually so deferential.

Other beguines, holding tightly to the hands of the children in their care, were scattered in small groups up and down the street. Clare, with two other beguines and their charges, were several blocks away, closer to the church. She heard a familiar piping voice behind her, and turned. There was Jan reaching for her hand, and behind him, his father. She smiled and greeted them both.

"What a coincidence that we should happen to meet when the streets are so crowded. I am pleased to see you again, Mijnheer von Lede."

"And I you. Jan insisted that we come to this street corner: how prescient he was. Your presence makes this Corpus Christi day a truly memorable one." Michiel bowed and looked down into her blue eyes. Her habit could not completely conceal her slender figure and he moved as close to her as propriety would allow.

"Papa, Papa, I can't wait. When will the procession start?" Jan managed to wriggle between them, and took the hand of each.

"It has already started, son. It will be here soon." And Clare and Michiel continued their polite conversation. When the crowd pressed Michiel against Clare, she did not move away as she should have done. Rather, she straightened her wimple, looked up at him, and saw his eyes soften. A rush of feeling unlike anything she had felt before swept over her; a need that traveled down her body to that place she never allowed herself to touch. She had a sudden, fervent wish for this handsome man to put his arm around her. At that moment, someone in the crowd stumbled against them and Michiel encircled both her and Jan with his arm to steady them. Clare wished she could prolong that moment, but of course he took his arm away and carefully took a step away from her. She sighed involuntarily.

"Perhaps we could meet in the park next to the town hall and talk some day," Michiel spoke in a low voice. "Or somewhere else?"

"I wish that could be, but I am not allowed to leave the begijnhof alone."

"Not even if Jan is with you?"

"No, I must be in the company of another sister. But I will find a good reason to visit the town, and there will surely be a sister who wishes to come with me."

"God willing, the opportunity will come. Please let Jan know if such an occasion arises." Michiel smiled at her and then responded to Jan, who tugged at his arm, asking for sweets from the vendor who was making his way through the crowd, carrying a large basket. Clare also gave in to the pleas of the children in her care, and all sucked on sweets contentedly.

Father Johan, walking toward the church to take his place in the procession, had noticed the couple leaning toward one another, in spite of the children around them. A beguine, a fair young woman, in intimate conversation with a gentleman from one of the leading families of the town. How disgraceful, he thought. He vowed to speak to the Cistercian priest who visited the begijnhof when he next saw him. He doubted that the priest would hear of this incident from the beguine mistress. Just then, Johan heard the sound of the trumpets heralding the procession, and hurried to join it.

Annalise leaned forward as gilt-edged banners, held by acolytes representing the various parish churches, followed the trumpeters. Then the festive canopy, held aloft on four poles by prominent laymen, turned the corner. Finally the monstrance containing the large consecrated host could be seen, suspended under the canopy. Many in the crowd genuflected, some knelt, and passersby by stopped and stared. Even those who never went to church were attracted by the pageantry and color.

As the monstrance passed in front of her, Annalise saw a glow illumine it and tiny lights sparkle around it. Was it only the sun shining through the pale wafer? And could tiny stars gleam at midday? She saw again the glow on Jesus' halo in the chapel on that cold winter night, and she spontaneously raised her hands, saying, "My Lord, Jesus!" Others in the crowd murmured words of praise and sank to their knees. But then, fixing her eyes on the host, Annalise cried out loudly, "Lord Jesus—thy face!" Shuddering, she fell against Elisabetta, knocking them both to the ground.

A woman nearby exclaimed, "She says she saw Jesus' face!" and her words traveled through the crowd. Beatrice and Marie, hearing Annalise cry out, pushed through the crowd and knelt at her side. Her parents, well back in the crowd across the street and straining to see the monstrance, heard that familiar voice, followed by shouts from the crowd around her.

"Sister Annalise, Sister, can you hear me?" Beatrice put her mouth close to Annalise's ear, and tried to shield her from the press of people gathering around them. Elisabetta, unharmed and already on her feet, bent to help her. Annalise's face was pale, her body limp.

"It must have been a vision from God!" someone in the crowd shouted, and a number of people crossed themselves. Beatrice grasped Annalise's shoulders and with Elisabetta's help, raised her to a sitting position.

"We must get her to the infirmary as soon as we can." Beatrice kept her voice low. The two women managed to lift Annalise to her feet and half carried, half dragged her through an opening in the crowd. Marie gathered the children who had been in Annalise's and Elisabetta's care together with her own, and followed behind.

"There she is; that's the girl who had the vision. She's one of them, a beguine!" Someone in the crowd pointed at Annalise, and hearing those words, Beatrice stepped up her pace. Annalise's eyelids fluttered and she stumbled, trying to get both feet under her. With Beatrice's arm around her, she at last began to walk with her slow, characteristically uneven gait. Her head, which had drooped against her shoulder, straightened.

Looking around, Beatrice saw Father Johan in the procession, watching them with a frown so tight that his eyebrows looked like a black smear on his forehead. She felt a chill run down her back, though it was damp with perspiration. "Please, Sister Elisabetta, pass the word to our sisters that we should all return to the begijnhof."

Sister Elisabetta moved quietly through the crowd, stopping to speak to each group of beguines. By now the procession of priests had passed by, and the crowd was dispersing. The children were quite ready to return to the quiet of the begijnhof courtyard. The sun was hot and it had been difficult for them to see, or even to breathe freely with so many townsfolk pushing against them. After they had sipped cool well water from a flagon and eaten the special sweets prepared for them, the children were soon playing games and singing songs to celebrate the day.

For the beguines the day was no longer one to celebrate. They were worried about Annalise, and distressed by the unwanted attention she had brought them. Would her exhortations be forgotten by the morrow, or would the townspeople be reminded of her outburst every time they saw beguines in Sint Joric?

In his sermon the following Sunday Father Johan described Annalise's reaction to the monstrance paraded on Corpus Christi. "When that girl fixed her eyes on the monstrance with the bread of Christ in it, the forces of good and evil within her fought for her very soul!" His hand whipped downward. "She was caught in the devil's grip and flung to the ground." He shook his fist. "And she is a beguine, one of those women who live to themselves, beholden to no man, subject to the forces of evil. Women should know their place, and that place is in the home or in a nunnery, and nowhere else!" And the priest continued to rant against the beguines, while the congregation murmured to one another and shook their heads. They had heard his harangues against women, and beguines in particular, many times.

"Seems Father Johan manages to see the devil in everyone," one man said. Several couples close by him nodded appreciatively.

At the rear of the church, Willem de Belle stiffened on hearing the word "beguines." "What is he talking about?" he muttered, and shook his head. With all the new orders arriving at the warehouse, he had not had time to think about his mother, much less the beguine community. He listened more closely to Father Johan.

A few days later Beatrice received a note from her son, asking about Father Johan's sermon. Many of the sisters were distraught, having received similar inquiries about the priest's criticism of their community. Bent over the desk in her receiving room, Beatrice felt a nugget of fear clutch at her. Should she have seen this coming, this second vision or whatever it was that Sister Annalise experienced? She shook her head. There was no way she could have foreseen that something like this would happen.

"What shall we do, sisters? We cannot let whatever it is that grips Sister Annalise happen again in public." Beatrice paced in front of the elders seated before her in the receiving room after evening prayers. "Thanks be to God she seems to have recovered from this fall as quickly as she did from the first one." The wind rattled the window frame and made the candles waver and smoke in the chilly room, contributing to the beguines' unease.

After much discussion the "wise ones" decided that Annalise should not leave the safety of the begijnhof. And they proposed that for a time, none of the sisters should go into town. Thankfully, they had plenty of flour and other grains. Trips for sundries, thread and such, would just have to wait. Surely talk of the young beguine's vision would soon die down, other gossip would take its place and things would be as they were.

"But sisters, what if there is an urgent family need? My niece is pregnant; it is her first pregnancy, and she begged me to be at her side when the child is delivered. I promised I would be there to pray for her. When I am sent for, I must go!" Several other beguines spoke of serious family concerns. The elders agreed that the grand mistress could make exceptions in such cases.

After morning prayers the next day, Beatrice announced to all the sisters that they must not venture into town unless there was a family emergency. "I hope this restriction will be brief, sisters, and things will soon be as they were before." There was murmuring and some grumbling as the sisters left the chapel, but most agreed that after all, their work was here and their place was here.

Annalise limped up the path to the schoolroom as fast as she could, finally catching up to Clare. "I—I am sorry about the restrictions, Sister Clare. I know that it is because of me that we have been confined to the begijnhof." Clare's face reddened, knowing full well that Sister Annalise understood why she was so distressed at the restriction placed upon the beguines. How many other sisters had seen her so close to Mijnheer von Lede during the Corpus Christi procession?

"What happened to you just…happened, Sister. I am very glad that you were not badly hurt when you fell."

"Oh no, it was wonderful, Sister Clare; it was as if Christ's face were imprinted on the monstrance, though I know that seems impossible. But I saw it." Annalise's face took on a beatific look that appeared to put her in some special place no one else could see.

"I cannot imagine such a vision, Sister. You have a—a gift few can claim." Clare smiled in spite of herself; how could she not, when Annalise looked as though she had received the most wonderful treasure imaginable.

Clare's frustration that the grand mistress's decision meant she would not be able to meet with Mijnheer von Lede made him seem even more attractive. He was handsome: tall, his chest broad, his legs slim but sturdy, his hair and eyes dark, his clothes always elegant. She found herself thinking about him at meals, at night, even in chapel, and she wondered if he was thinking of her as well. Most of all, she did not want him to think she had forgotten their conversation about possibly meeting again. After morning prayers several days later, when she saw Jan ahead of her on the path, Clare hastened after him and caught up to him just as he reached the schoolhouse porch.

"Jan, I was going to talk with your father again some time soon, but I cannot leave the begijnhof now, nor for the foreseeable future." Clare spoke softly, but urgently. "Will you tell him for me that I regret I cannot meet him?"

"But why can't you?" Jan replied. "I think my father will be disappointed. I think he likes you. I know I do." And he smiled up at her.

"And I like you too, Jan, very much. It is hard to explain what has happened, but the grand mistress has asked that none of the sisters leave the begijnhof for the present. I just hope your father understands that…I am sorry I cannot be with him, but I hope to see him again one day."

"I will tell him so, Sister Clare." Jan's face reflected his delight in having been taken into Clare's confidence. He marched into the classroom ahead of her.

That evening Clare did not sit reading in her comfortable chair, and instead lay on her bed, brooding. She felt restless, dissatisfied, and wondered, as she had so often, why she had chosen to become a beguine. But what other choice had she? She missed her father and prayed for him daily, but she did not want to return home. A few days ago he had written that Marta was expecting a child, his joy evident in his words. She felt as if the door he had said would always be open to her had been closed, quietly but firmly.

As a teacher in the beguine school, Clare had gotten to know young children for the first time. She found that she loved teaching, and was good at it. Her patience and affection for the younger children had both surprised and uplifted her.

And if she had not become a beguine, she might never have met Michiel. Again thoughts of him came to her unbidden. What did she know about him? That he was a lawyer and a cultured man. Perhaps he shared her love of books. She imagined the two of them seated before a fire, reading together, as she and her father had done so often. The beguine sisters studied the Bible together, but it was not the same; there was not the closeness she had had with her father, the intimacy of sitting by the fire, sipping hot mulled wine and talking about science, philosophy, and history as well as the Bible. Could she find the same intimacy with Michiel? Could she really talk about books with him?

For the first time, Clare tried to imagine the possibility of marriage to Michiel, but then slid away from the idea, turning her thoughts back to the missed opportunity. Meeting Michiel would be impossible until Sister Beatrice again allowed trips into town. Until then she would be confined to the begijnhof. Confined. The word evoked guilty feelings. This was her home and her life now; she should not feel confined. But she did.

Clare turned on her side and stared out her window, now almost dark. Why was the night so much darker here than at her father's house? Perhaps it only seemed darker because of the silence. At home, nights were quiet compared to the noisy life of the streets by day, but the night watchman called out as he made his rounds, and there might be a dog barking, a child crying, or a couple arguing, their voices raised. Here, there were never rancorous voices or children fighting. Here the silence seemed absolute, and the watchman's voice far away.

In the moonlight one could at least see outlines, but many nights were cloudy and the dark enveloped everything. Occasionally the yelp of a wild animal out in the countryside pierced the air and then the darkness seemed menacing, but most of the time it was just there, separating the days, inviting sleep for some, but not for Clare.

Finally she gave up trying to sleep, sat up, and lit her beeswax candle. Sister Beatrice had given her books to read by beguines like Marguerite Porete. The famous beguine had written a book in which she declared that one's spiritual goal should be union with God, "having the same will as God…" and abandoning personal will. Marguerite had been executed as a heretic for continuing to circulate the book after she had been forbidden to do so.

Clare wrapped a quilt around her and opened a small book containing the beautiful Flemish poetry of the beguine Hadewijch:

> Love then causes more sorrows
> than there are stars in heaven.
> The number of these sorrows must be unspoken,
> the great weighty burdens remain unweighed…

How could a beguine know so much about love? Perhaps Hadewijch had been married. But Clare thought it was Jesus' love, and the love the Christian martyrs had for Jesus that Hadewijch was writing about, not what she imagined love for a man might be. Her thoughts were jumbled, unfocused. Continuing to brood, she closed her book and fell asleep.

She dreamed of an evening the previous spring, during a celebration of the spring solstice. It was still light when the sisters gathered in the dining hall after the children were in bed. All of the tables had been pushed to one side and the benches pulled into a roughly hexagonal shape, creating an intimate setting. The sisters seated themselves and Sister Marie began to pluck her lute. They sang in Flemish a simple song of Minne, God as love. Then a few of the younger sisters rose and began to dance to the music. Clare watched transfixed.

Then in her dream she rose and joined them, swaying to the music. The dancers moved in a circle, their arms extended overhead, moving gracefully back and forth, bending like saplings in a strong breeze. She, all of them, were wearing thin linen shifts, their breasts and hips outlined when they passed in front of the candlelight. Their hands were willow leaves that moved in gentle rhythm, yet never quite touched. At last, all curved their bodies toward the cross mounted on the far wall, arms extended and heads bowed in obeisance and love, and the dance was finished.

When Clare awoke the next morning, her arms were stretched over her head. An unfamiliar melody washed over her, but before she could capture it, it faded away.

Beatrice spent much time on the prie-dieu in her little bedroom, thinking and praying about Annalise's visions. Were there beguines who spent their lives as contemplatives? Who gave themselves over to prayer as a means of serving the community? Beatrice knew that other beguine communities existed; indeed, one of their patronesses had told her that the begijnhof in Liege counted almost one thousand women. One thousand! By that measure, theirs was a very small group, fewer than one hundred, though she seldom had reason to count them. For the first time, Beatrice wished she could communicate with other beguine communities. But did numbers matter, or what others did? Was not each community free to make its own rules? She decided to talk to Sister Celie; perhaps she could remember a beguine here at Sint Joric who had spent her life in prayer.

Pleased that the grand mistress had consulted her, Celie seated herself in the armchair in the grand mistress' receiving room, her feet barely touching the floor, and stared into the fire. After a long silence she turned toward Beatrice, smiling.

"Yes, I do remember one Sister, Greete, her name was. She came here long ago, when Sister Therese was the grand mistress, I think. At first, Sister Greete worked in the garden with me. She would pull weeds and she worked hard, but she had this odd look, like she was somewhere else. One day, I found her pulling up the turnips shoots right along with the weeds." Celie laughed, shaking her head. "Then she started spending more and more time in her room, and finally she only left it for prayers in chapel, Bible study, and meals. The grand mistress had to remind her to take a bath." Celie smiled and looked up at Beatrice.

"Some of the sisters complained that she never did any work, but the grand mistress would say she was doing God's work, praying for the sins of all of us and for the whole world. After a while, we just got used to her. And you know, she had a wonderful way about her, never put on airs or acted like she was special. But she <u>was</u> special. When she died, we all knew that she went straight up to heaven."

"What a wonderful story, Sister Celie." Gratified, Beatrice thanked Celie and helped her out of the big chair. That evening, she went back to her prie-dieu with renewed zeal.

"We need to talk about Sister Annalise." Beatrice stood before the "wise ones" in the receiving room after evening prayers several nights later. She began by describing, for the first time, how she had found Annalise unconscious in the chapel during the big winter storm, and what Annalise had told her.

The sisters, seated around the large table that served as the grand mistress' desk, had been sipping warm chamomile infusions. They immediately put down their mugs and listened closely to what the grand mistress was saying. Of course they had noticed Annalise's absence the day after the storm, and saw her face scratched and bruised when she appeared at chapel the following morning. But she had said nothing, and they had respected her privacy, though there was much conjecture. Most agreed that she had probably stumbled and taken a hard fall; after all, she was lame. Now they were being told that she had fallen after seeing a vision. Thus the Corpus Christi vision was not her first. But why had Jesus chosen to visit this frail young woman?

"I believe Sister Annalise truly feels set apart in a special relationship to Christ that enables her to see these visions she describes so vividly," Beatrice continued. "But this last experience occurred in public, and has focused unwanted attention on our community. For that reason, I am reluctant to allow her the same freedom the rest of us have. Or rather had, until our self-imposed isolation, which I hope will be brief. I wonder if we should consider confining her to the begijnhof indefinitely, unless her family has need of her help.

"In addition, I am proposing that we allow her to increase her prayer time, perhaps even let her move towards the life of a contemplative. It is clear to me that this is the life she envisions for herself, even though she has not expressed it in words. Ultimately, I believe she would like to stay within these walls, and never leave the begijnhof." There was quiet as the sisters looked at each other. Then the protests began.

"We are not a cloistered nunnery like St. Anne's. That is not our calling." Sister Lisbette, always forthright, spoke firmly and others nodded in agreement, clearly uncomfortable with the idea of a cloistered beguine.

"That is true; however, this kind of step has been taken before." And Beatrice repeated the story Celie had told her about Sister Greete of long ago.

"But what of Sister Annalise's parents?" Sister Elisabetta asked. "Is not her mother in need of her help at times? Would she be forbidden to see them?"

"I do not think we need go that far. There is no reason her parents could not visit her here on special occasions. And if there was an emergency she could go home, but I would choose carefully whom to send with her.

"Let us at least consider this idea of Annalise becoming more like a contemplative, and begin by allowing her more prayer time." The elders finally agreed after much discussion, but some were disturbed by the grand mistress' words. Was this God's will for their community? Or was it only the will of the grand mistress?

Elisabetta was most agitated. The following night, after evening prayers, she invited to her townhouse a number of the sisters she knew would listen to her views. Hers was the largest house in the community, and the sisters admired her fine furnishings as they sipped their infusions from fine china cups passed to them by her servant. The servant left, closing the door behind her, and Elisabetta set down her cup. She recounted the discussion of the elders, and the possible change in Annalise's status as a beguine. She began pacing up and down in front of her fireplace, where a small fire burned to ward off the evening chill.

"Is the grand mistress trying to change this community into something it was never meant to be? A place for poor women such as Sister Annalise who think they have visions of Christ, and so have earned the right to live here? I believe Grand Mistress Beatrice was unwise in pressing the elders to allow Annalise some kind of special status. She would no longer be a true beguine, working to sustain our community and providing for those less fortunate." Two of the beguines looked at each other, both with the same thought—everyone knew that much of Sister Elisabetta's "work" consisted of corresponding with her friends in town and thus keeping up with news and gossip, which she freely related to her beguine sisters.

One sister, who rarely voiced an opinion, spoke hesitantly. "I do not feel comfortable with the idea of a sister praying as if she were a nun, and not taking part in the community." Several others nodded their heads.

"But how can we deny her, if prayer is her vocation, and if it is God's will?" another sister ventured. Finally, after all had had their say, Elisabetta rose from her chair.

"For now, we can but wait and see what comes of this…this change that will affect all of us," Sister Elisabetta concluded, and the sisters left, continuing the conversation as they went to their own abodes, their candles flickering in the fading light.

CHAPTER TEN

On a clear day, before morning prayers, Mergriet greeted Beatrice with the news that the begijnhof's goats had escaped their enclosure. Boredom and warmer weather had made them increasingly mischievous, and having freed themselves, they had chewed and pushed through the hedge surrounding the kitchen garden and eaten the young bean plants and their swelling pods. How much damage a half-dozen goats could do in such a short time! The remaining small store of dried beans must be planted as quickly as possible, or else the harvest would not provide enough beans to dry for the winter months. Several of the younger beguines chased the goats and confined them before more damage could be done, while others hastily repaired the enclosure.

Thankfully, it was late spring, and almost time for the goats to go outside to graze on the town commons with the householders' animals. The fields outside the town walls were green with new shoots of millet and wild plants, and soon one of the beguines would meet the goatherd at the back gate each morning and transfer the frisky goats to his care.

The sisters had been confined to the beginhof for almost two months. There were increasing complaints about the diminishing supply of food staples and the sisters' inability to visit the shops for their own needs.

"Sister Beatrice, I need to go to the weekly market to buy barley for pottage and oats for bread making," Mergriet stated firmly. It was true; the kitchen stores of salt, oats and other foodstuffs were all but gone. Thankfully, the begijnhof had not lacked for bread; Mergriet's father had continued his delivery of flour. Hans' pledge, to supply all the flour the beguines needed for as long as he was alive, was her dowry and had become increasingly valuable as the price of grains continued to rise.

Beatrice asked the "wise ones" to come to her receiving room to discuss ending their sequestration. Sister Marie spoke up.

"Many of us need to visit the shoemaker to be measured for new shoes. Even the patches on the soles of my leather shoes have worn thin."

"And I, among others, need to buy some fabric, thread and needles, things of that sort." One of the "wise ones" who prided herself on always being well-groomed spoke up next. Unspoken was the desire of some of the wealthier elders to visit the soap-maker for their favorite scented soaps and the chandler for beeswax candles. Beatrice had discouraged delivery of such items to the begijnhof; she had not wished to draw attention to the beguines' self-imposed isolation.

"The freedom to leave these walls when necessary has always been a part of beguine life." Sister Elisabetta, her head high and her hands clasped in her lap, spoke firmly, and the others nodded. Beatrice bowed her head, nodding in acquiescence.

At morning prayers the next day, she announced that the sisters could once again go into town when necessary. They smiled at one another in relief: it was as if some invisible binding had been loosened. The begijnhof had become a cloister, and now they felt free, even if they seldom ventured outside its walls.

Beatrice sat back, a warm feeling flowing through her at the thought that now she and Mergriet could be present at Willem's wedding. The previous Sunday Father Johan had read the first of the banns for the marriage of Willem de Belle and Ilse Van der Erbe. It was a union that would join two prominent families of the town.

Beatrice understood her sisters' feelings, yet she was uneasy about the decision to end the sequestration. She sat at the window of her little parlor the next morning. How much little things can matter in our lives, she thought, looking at her patched shoes. How frugal are we, really. She smiled wryly, remembering the effusive welcome accorded townsfolk who had brought with them a gift of salt, sugar, even a jar of precious honey, when they came to the begijnhof seeking prayers for a family member who was ill.

The wedding day was clear and bright, and of course the bride was beautiful, her fine linen chemise covered by a tunic of pale blue silk, her mantle edged in delicate lace. For the last time her hair was unbound; it fell over her shoulders and was crowned by a narrow band of gold velvet, holding fast a small veil. Willem had his father's height and bulk, and his tunic of finest wool fitted smoothly over his broad shoulders. Father Johan, smiling, accepted Willem's generous gift for performing the ceremony.

106

Uncle Hans hosted the wedding feast at his house, which stood on a slight rise just outside Sint Joric's walls, with a view of the river and the countryside beyond. Sint Joric had become crowded as its cloth merchants and other businesses had grown. Thus, many wealthy families were now building walled homes outside the town walls; usually they were connected to the town through a door leading from their common wall into the town.

The parlor doors of Hans' house led to a porch and a large garden behind the house, where spring flowers bloomed in carefully tended beds. Stone paths had been laid to take advantage of the view, and Mergriet walked down the one with the best view over the fields. She wished she could go to the country on a horse-drawn cart, as she had so many years ago. One of her young cousins ran up, offering her a sweetened bun on a plate, and Mergriet accepted it with a smile and a bow, and turned back to the house.

Hans was a generous host and liked to demonstrate his increasing prosperity at family gatherings. There were joints of meat of every kind; plates piled high with bread and butter, jam and honey to spread upon them; sweetmeats of all sorts; and Hans' best wine, with mild ale for the children. His new wife directed the servants, who were hurrying back and forth to the kitchen, replenishing the long tables on the porch where the guests sat feasting. After all were sated, the children climbed down from the benches to play, and Willem and Ilse went from table to table, greeting all of their guests. Then Willem came over to Beatrice, a glass of wine in his hand.

"I am so pleased, Mother, to be living in my own home again."

"And Ilse, is she content to live there?"

"Yes, she is pleased with the new furnishings I have added. In fact, she chose most of them. And I have moved my belongings out of the warehouse loft, and found someone to keep an eye on things there."

"Ah, that is good news. Does your new hire seem reliable?" Beatrice found conversing with her son awkward at times.

"Well, I took a chance, but he seems an honest country lad. I found him sleeping in a pile of straw behind the warehouse one morning. He was half starved, and begged me for any kind of work. He cares for the animals, and can make simple repairs to harnesses and wagons. Now he is sleeping in the loft, and I give him a few coins for food, for which he is most grateful. But he is a bit odd; he wears a large cap of some sort of cheap wool, never takes it off. I think it's because he has an ugly scar on one side of his face, though it's no more disfiguring than pox scars.

"I don't plan to keep him too long; he has no learning and a thick country accent, and so is little help with customers. Oddly, when I told him about the bread you provide at the begijnhof each morning he turned white as milk, and replied that he would not consider going there. Perhaps it was pride, but it seemed strange to me that someone in his circumstances would not take bread freely offered."

"Yes, that is strange.... what a beautiful day for your wedding, Willem, and Hans has outdone himself, don't you agree?" Beatrice turned toward the river and quickly changed the subject. She reached toward her face to brush away a fluttering moth and realized that her hand was trembling.

Could the man Willem described have been the intruder who attacked Sister Clare? Surely not. Surely that wretched man had left Sint Joric the next morning as soon as the town gates were opened. But Mergriet had mentioned a large scar on the intruder's face. And why else would he be afraid to go near the begijnhof? She did not hear a word Willem said in reply to her attempt at conversation. Days later she was still asking herself whether she should have questioned him further, but she decided to do nothing.

The following week Clare spoke to the grand mistress and received permission to go into town, taking Celie with her, as both needed to be measured by the cobbler for new shoes. Beatrice agreed with Clare's suggestion that it would be a good idea for them to stop in the Sint Agustin churchyard to give Celie a chance to rest before going on to the cobbler's.

After school the next day, Clare talked with Jan and asked him to tell his father that she would be at Sint Agustin's porch, three days hence, in the afternoon. Jan frowned, puzzled. "But why would he want to know that?"

"Do you not remember that he asked me to meet him once before but I was not able to go? Now I can. But this must be a secret between us, Jan."

"Oh, I love secrets. Is the secret in the church? Can I come with you?"

"No, there is nothing secret in Sint Agustin's Church. The secret is that I may spend a little time talking with your father: that is all. Can you keep my secret?"

"Of course I can," Jan assured her, standing tall and attempting to look responsible. "I will not tell even Joachim, my best friend. But what about my afternoon story?" He frowned. Clare smiled down at him.

"On that day, Sister Marie will be there to help you with the story you and I have been reading together. I will not be gone long."

That night Clare did not light her candle when she went to her room. She put on an old shift and lay on her bed in the darkness, thinking of Michiel. What if he was not able, or willing to meet her? She refused to consider that possibility. She had pressed her best gray-brown habit that afternoon, being very careful not to scorch it, and hung it carefully.

How would she explain Michiel's presence to Sister Celie? What if Jan forgot his promise and told someone about her assignation? Clare tossed and turned and fell into a restless sleep.

Misty clouds filtered the sunlight as Clare met Celie when the midday meal was over, but the day was warm and they decided to leave their coats behind. Clare felt she looked unremarkable, even plain, dressed in her beguine habit, in spite of her fine linen cap and wimple. She remembered a time when heads turned as she walked by in a dress of soft lavender wool, her hand on her father's arm. Now it was Celie's hand holding her arm as they walked up the path to the begijnhof gate. The gatekeeper closed the gate behind them, touching his cap respectfully.

Sister Celie walked so very slowly, but Clare patiently matched her pace, and at last they reached Sint Agustin, only a few blocks away. Clare saw Michiel strolling through the church's graveyard. He turned and swiftly walked to the church steps.

"Sister Celie, this is Mijnheer von Lede, little Jan's father." Celie turned and looked up at the tall figure whose face at that moment was a blur.

"I am pleased to meet you, Mijnheer."

"It is my pleasure also." And Michiel bowed low.

"Sister, would you like to sit on the bench here by the porch?" Clare asked. Celie sank down gratefully, so tired after the brief walk that she was shaking.

"Perhaps Mijnheer von Lede and I will take a short walk through the graveyard while we discuss Jan's progress." Clare had to speak loudly. Celie nodded, smiling.

The path through the church's graveyard was well-worn, and the trees that lined it were old, their branches bent low. Noise from the nearby town square barely penetrated the deep shade. Clare and Michiel were careful not to touch one another, lest this appear to be more than a casual conversation. And indeed, it began that way. They spoke of Jan, how well he was reading and the friends he had made, and Clare smiled as she described his eagerness to learn and his pride when he had mastered a new word or an arithmetic problem.

"The beguine school is a godsend for him; he has been making friends for the first time," Michiel commented. "At home he sees only adults, and his governess is very protective of him. She is his nanny, really, though I must be careful not to use that word in front of him. Jan's mother died when he was an infant and he is lonely at times, especially when I am away.

He has no brothers or sisters and just a few cousins, all of whom are considerably older than he. When I prepare for a journey to Ghent he clings to me, and he flings himself at me when I come home again." Michiel paused.

"And…I confess, at times I am lonely, too. I have…often thought of marrying again, but I have never made the effort, or wanted to…until now." Michiel looked down at Clare and she responded calmly, her voice steady.

"As for me, my father did not insist that I marry, and I was content with his company; but when he married again my life changed, and I—I did not wish to continue living at home. So I became a beguine. However, lately I have had some doubts about my decision…about my calling." In truth, Clare was not sure that she had ever had a "calling."

"And have you taken a vow to remain a beguine always?" Michiel asked the question hesitantly, then quickly continued. "Obviously you are not cloistered as are the nuns of St. Anne's convent, but I know nothing about your obligation to your community." Clare paused, and when she replied, Michiel realized he had been holding his breath.

"Oh no, our vows are not necessarily lifelong, though most who enter the community remain there," she responded softly. "We take a vow of chastity, frugality, and service to the poor; but we are to free to leave if we wish."

They came to a bench under a large willow tree and Michiel brushed it off so Clare could sit down. Then he sat beside her, the willow's cascading branches forming a curtain that almost hid them from view. He reached for her hand, and Clare felt a thrill, then a pang of guilt. She did not pull away, but she knew very well this kind of contact was forbidden. Even if she were still living in her father's house, such behavior would be viewed as shocking. And she had taken a vow of chastity.

She rose from the bench and the two walked back toward the church. They heard the sound of voices and saw that Father Johan had come out of his church, and was speaking with Sister Celie. At once the couple moved farther apart and again spoke of Jan and his progress in school.

But Johan had already seen them walking so close together that you could not see daylight between them. Later, he sat in his tiny office and pulled out an almost clean sheet of parchment. It was time to write to Bishop Christophe and ask for an audience. The bishop should know that the beguines living in this parish were not obeying the pope's strictures, nor were they living the chaste lives they themselves had pledged to uphold.

"Well, now, please read that first paragraph once more." Clare straightened, and tried to listen closely as Jan read the paragraph without hesitation. Her mind wandered to the meeting with Michiel; then she caught herself, wondering if the other sisters noticed how easily distracted she was these days. Was she paying too much attention to Jan and not enough to the other children in her group? She started guiltily, as if someone were reading her thoughts. She noticed with relief the other sisters and their charges leaving the large, bright room where the younger children had their lessons. At last it was time for the midday meal.

"I have noticed that the children in your group are a bit restless these days, Sister Clare. They are some of the youngest; do you think the lessons are too difficult for them?" Clare and the grand mistress walked together to evening prayers, the sun sinking slowly behind the begijnhof wall in the lengthening day.

"Ah, no...no, Sister Beatrice, they are in fact doing very well."

"You teach with such enthusiasm; perhaps that is why they are a bit boisterous at times." Beatrice probed gently, knowing the problem was not with the children.

Clare finally broke the silence. "Sister Beatrice...ah, could I come to your reception room and talk with you privately? At your convenience, of course."

"Shall we have an infusion together at my house, instead? That is a more private place. Come tomorrow, when you have finished teaching for the day."

A strong breeze whipped Clare's habit around her as she walked slowly down the path to Sister Beatrice's small house the next afternoon. How simple and unassuming it looked, compared to some of the other townhouses in the begijnhof. Sister Beatrice herself sometimes appeared unassuming as well—but her eyes miss nothing, Clare thought. There was no use trying to hide the truth from her. She knocked gently on the door, and it opened almost immediately.

"Do come in, Sister Clare. Sister Mergriet is asleep upstairs. She rises so early to start the bread rising that she needs to rest in the afternoon. I guarantee you complete confidence: Sister Mergriet sleeps like the dead, just as she did when she was a babe." Clare nodded, recalling that Sister Mergriet was Sister Beatrice's niece, though there was no family resemblance. The house was quiet. She listened for the sounds of a maidservant; she had heard that Sister Beatrice had an elderly maid living with her, but there was no sign of her.

"Let us sit in the sunroom; that is what I call it, and fortunately it is a sunny day." Beatrice was smiling. "I have prepared a mint infusion with just a touch of lavender. I think it is a soothing drink, don't you?" Clare was led into a small, inviting room with two padded armchairs at the window, and several smaller chairs grouped near the fireplace on an adjacent wall. A few lumps of glowing coal warmed the hearth. Beatrice poured the infusion, and both sat down near the fire.

"I asked for this time, Sister Beatrice, because I think you should know that I have become…ah, friendly with Jan's father, Mijnheer von Lede. I first met him at the begijnhof, when little Jan pulled him over to meet me one morning. But I have met him thrice on trips into town, though of course I was always with another sister. The first two times were purely by chance: once when Sister Elisabetta and I went to the hospice for a potion for Sister Celie; and then during the Corpus Christi procession, when Jan saw me with two of my little students and tugged his father over to be with us." Clare did not mention that Michiel had put his arm around her. She reached for the cup of mint infusion on the low table nearby, careful to keep her hand steady. "I confess that I am very attracted to him, and he to me, I believe." She had trouble meeting Beatrice's gaze.

"I see." Beatrice broke the silence and leaned forward. She had heard of those encounters, but had been provided no details. Gossip flourished behind the begijnhof walls and she imagined that there was little the sisters did, whether in the begijnhof or in town, that escaped her notice. Sister Clare had continued unburdening herself.

"…so you see, Sister, the third encounter was deliberate. Perhaps you remember that Sister Celie and I went into town to be measured for new shoes that day?" Beatrice nodded. "Well, Mijnheer von Lede and I had arranged to meet at Sint Agustin's." Clare described their meeting as a walk through the graveyard, leaving out their intimate conversation, their clasped hands, and then Father Johan's untimely appearance.

"Since then, I find myself unable to focus on my tasks, as you noticed; my discipline of the children is uneven, and I begin to doubt my commitment to my work, even to this place. I do not know what to do, whether I should return to my father's house, what my future should be."

"As always, I urge you to take all this to Jesus in prayer—"

"I have been praying, but I feel further from Jesus than ever, and I…" Clare blushed, realizing that she had interrupted the grand mistress. "Forgive me, Sister Beatrice. Please continue."

"We strive to be filled with the love of Jesus when we take our vows as beguines. Many people outside this community think that we leave ordinary feelings at the begijnhof gate; that desire and the need for physical…

completion, for example, simply vanish. We know better. It is perfectly natural that you might become attracted to Jan's father, Sister Clare, and nothing to be ashamed of. He is well-educated, of good family, a loving parent. What you do about your feelings is up to you, of course. But I must counsel restraint; any expression of affection in public will bring condemnation not just on you, but also on our community." Remembering the meeting in the churchyard Clare's face reddened, and she bowed her head so the beguine mistress would not see the blush suffusing her face.

"Please, prayerfully consider your future here, Sister Clare. You are free to leave, of course, but if you make that choice, I hope it is one you will not regret. I will keep you in my prayers, as I do all of the sisters. Is there anything more I can do to be of help?"

"I—I would like so much for my father to meet Mijnheer von Lede, but I do not know where or how that could come about. Could you help me arrange such a meeting?"

"Let me think about it, and I will see what can be done. We will talk again."

CHAPTER ELEVEN

Bishop Christophe leaned back in his chair, his rotund figure straining against the fine black silk of his cassock, his feet resting on a footstool covered in magenta velvet. His cap, the same magenta color, anchored the wispy strands of hair on his nearly bald head. Christophe was overly fond of the color magenta; he considered it the purple of royalty. He shifted in his chair. His feet pained him. The wretched gout plagued him almost constantly. After all, the palace was also a fortress and its thick walls helped keep it always damp and cold.

The library, containing some twenty volumes inherited from his predecessor and a shelf stacked with parchment scrolls, was the bishop's preferred reception room. For one thing, the fireplace drew exceptionally well, and the tapestries lining the north wall helped keep the space warm. Christophe reached for some papers on his desk. It was time to prepare himself for his meeting with this…Father Johan, from Sint Agustin's. He hoped to find a way to make this difficulty with the beguines of Sint Joric go away, and quickly.

The Council of Vienne's decrees regarding the beguines' status had been confusing, contradictory, really. Christophe slowly shook his head, rubbing the back of his neck where his stiff collar met the silken cassock. The Council first prohibited the beguines' way of life, but then allowed them to continue, preferably in communities. Then in the Lord's Year 1318, Pope John issued a papal bull, a ruling that urged bishops to continue their efforts to look for "heretical beliefs" among beguines, but repeated the Council's exception for those beguines who upheld the church's teachings. Finally, the pope had denied approval of the beguines as a religious order.

Christophe sighed and pushed the documents away. As far as he was concerned, the less said about the beguines, the better, but he knew this Father Johan would not share his view. Brushing the crumbs from his cassock, he finished his mulled wine, straightened his pectoral cross and ordered his servant to summon the priest from Sint Joric.

"Thank you so much for granting me an audience, My Lord Bishop." Father Johan strode into the bishop's chamber, then immediately slowed his pace and reverently knelt down on one knee to kiss the episcopal ring. He was wearing his best cassock and the cross that had been presented to him at his ordination, but still felt unkempt in the bishop's presence.

"Of course, of course. We always welcome visits from our priests. We hope things are going well in your parish."

"My parishioners are bearing up well in spite of last year's drought, and attendance is up at mass, My Lord Bishop. But I am concerned about one group. You did receive my message concerning the beguines?"

"Yes, yes, we read it with great interest. Your concerns seem to be with the behavior of just a few of the women, not with the entire community, is that not so? You should know that so far we have conducted an inquiry only when formal charges are made against a beguine community as a whole." Johan's face stiffened.

"Most priests in my diocese allow the grand mistress herself to handle individual offenses brought to her attention, either by promptly expelling any sister found guilty of breaking her vows, or by taking appropriate measures against lesser infractions of the community's rule." Christophe leaned forward, his eyebrows raised. "Tell me, Father Johan, have you spoken to the grand mistress about your concerns?"

"Ah, no, My Lord Bishop. I have not." Johan, nervous, chewed on the inside of his lip. "May I speak plainly?"

"Of course. We appreciate forthright communication, Father Johan." Christophe winced as he shifted his feet, his stern expression somewhat belying his words.

"I confess that I find the beguines' way of life offensive in principal. As I am sure you know, My Lord Bishop, each individual beguine community establishes its own rules. So far as I have been able to determine, there is no overarching rule such as recognized orders have. Thus, I have no guarantee that the 'vows' these women set for themselves could not be altered to exonerate behavior that I know to be wrong." Johan's carefully prepared words sounded weak even to his own ears, and he wished the bishop would invite him to take a seat. He feared this would be a brief audience.

"We appreciate the fervor with which you presented your objections in the missive you sent us." The bishop stroked his sparse beard, reflecting that the priest was indeed the firebrand described to him. "However, we assumed you would present yourself here after having had some contact with the beguine community, and having made an effort to resolve the situation on your own. You seem to have little knowledge of the community or the vows those women take, Father Johan." He raised his voice.

"Thus, we would like you first to question the grand mistress in a straightforward manner about your concerns. Then, we advise you to try to resolve your differences with her handling of the specific incidents you described in your letter. If you are unable to do so, you may write us again and we will consider conducting an investigation of the entire community--that is, if we deem it necessary."

Clearly this was a dismissal and Johan bowed, thanked the bishop for granting him an audience, and left the chamber. He was vastly disappointed. He had hoped that the bishop's inquisitors would swoop down on the begijnhof and catch those women unawares, with no time to prepare a defense. How naïve he had been, and how like the church to work its will so as to make problems go away without confronting them. Johan's hands were clenched and his jaw tight as he walked back to his spare lodgings, just a bed above a rough-hewn tavern in a muddy lane on the city's outskirts. He seated himself on a bench in the tavern and asked for a mug of strong ale and a hunk of bread.

He took a big gulp of the ale, then his head drooped and his shoulders sagged. Now he would have to face the grand mistress himself, with little hope that the bishop would take any action at all. The van Belle woman was clever, and would seek support from her allies in the town and from the Cistercians, who supposedly were keeping a watchful eye on that "community of women." Johan shook his head. Women: they were foreign to him, to be avoided whenever possible.

His mother was the only woman he'd ever been close to, and that was when he was young. When he thought of her at all, he pictured her face as she stood by impassively during the frequent beatings his drunken father gave him. One year the winter fever swept both his parents away. His older sister managed to find work as a maid. She said to Johan coolly, with a look that reminded him of his mother, that he would have to fend for himself. But no one had work for a scrawny boy of nine. If the local priest had not taken him to the monastery nearby, he probably would have starved. The monks fed him, schooled him, and set him on his path to the priesthood. Preaching was what he did best; he knew that. He shook his head.

What was it that St. Thomas Aquinas had said? Something about how women existed for only two reasons: to assist procreation and to provide food and drink for men. Oh, and caring for any children they might bear. He nodded his head in agreement with this logic as he drained the last of his ale and got to his feet. It was time to change his clothes, retrieve his aging horse from the stable, and head back to Sint Joric.

The sanctuary of Sint Agustin was almost as gray as the day outside when Father Johan rose to deliver his homily the following Sunday. "I have had an audience with our bishop, Bishop Christophe." Johan's eyes glittered in anticipation as he leaned over the pulpit. All whispering ceased, but the congregation shuffled their feet as they stood on the dusty stone floor. "I told him of your devotion to the church, and of Sint Agustin's stature among the churches here. He sends his blessing and may visit St. Joric in the spring. But, I also had to inform Bishop Christophe of some unfortunate incidents that have occurred lately."

People muttered to each other, waiting as Johan paused for effect, and wondering what he was talking about. Surely not the woman whose husband beat her as she ran down the street, loudly accusing her of looking lasciviously at another man. Or the landlord who dumped a penniless family out into the cold, throwing their few possessions after them. And there had been several robberies in the parish lately. But their priest would not speak of such common occurrences to the bishop, would he?

"The beguines who live behind those walls," Johan's voice rose as he pointed in the general direction of the begijnhof. "They belong to this parish, yet they have disgraced us all! Women who take vows of chastity, yet feel free to walk hand in hand with unattached men in the churchyard outside our doors! Or who shriek about visions on a public street. And I can do nothing. Nothing." Johan's voice fell, his shoulders slumped and he shook his head. No one in the congregation moved; all were listening intently, some with hand cupped to ear so as not to miss a word.

"They live by their own rules, not by the rules of the church, and not keeping in their place as the Bible commands women to do. I had no choice but to inform the bishop about their misdeeds. I am to speak to those women about their misbehavior, and I pray that they will reform and repent. But you, faithful followers of the Word, you can help." Johan's voice rose as a child began whining and was shushed immediately.

"You can watch these beguines when they stroll through our streets and come into your shops. You can observe their behavior and see for yourselves if they are the chaste religious they claim to be." Johan began pointing to individual parishioners. "If you choose to send your daughters to that begijnhof school, listen to what they say when they come home. Are they being encouraged to become beguines themselves? Is that what you want for them, to be without husbands, and living with these strange women?" Johan paused for effect.

Some of the women straightened, feeling as though they were under attack. Their mood appeared indignant and anxious, rather than fearful. Men stamped their feet on the stone floor to warm them, turned to each other and exchanged views. Some were dismayed at the priest's accusations, others just curious.

"Are not those women the ones who give bread to the poor every day?" one said.

"Yes, and I hear it's better tasting bread than the bakery on my street sells."

"And how would you know; have you been sneakin' in the line to get free bread?" His neighbor jabbed him. Laughter followed this remark, and unease turned to amusement.

"They look like magpies, the way they dress, all gray and black with white here an' there. But they're always polite and quiet," the man added, after his wife prodded him.

"My daughter has learned more from the beguines about manners and housekeeping than my mother taught me, and she reads and writes as well as I do now." A thrifty housewife spoke up, not bothering to whisper. "She begged me to let her go to their school one more year, said they would teach her fine sewing and some Latin as well. And they do not charge any more than the brothers do."

Johan frowned; clearly he was losing their attention. He raised his voice. "I will wait to hear any reports from you. And now, let us pray." The service continued with the usual shuffling of feet as the congregation muttered the prayers and the mass began.

After the service Johan left his vestments in the sacristy and walked to his tiny rectory next door. He settled himself in the one comfortable chair in his small parlor, and called to the old woman who came in by the day to prepare his meals and sweep.

"Bring me some of that ale, Gerte. And some bread and cheese." As always Johan fasted faithfully before mass, but then was so hungry that he could not wait for the Sunday pottage, with its small piece of meat or fish, that he knew would be coming later. He cut a piece of the hard cheese, broke off a hunk of bread and then washed them both down with a draft of ale. He stretched out his legs and stared at his worn boots and his cassock, no longer crisp and black, but faded to a dull grayish color from many washings, and frayed at the hem.

He had heard some of his parishioners' comments during and after mass. He knew the beguines were tolerated by most, and favored by some. In any case, he had to fulfill the bishop's request to meet with the grand mistress. The thought of meeting with the leader of those women made him both exceedingly uneasy and ashamed to acknowledge such weakness. Shrugging his shoulders, he looked down at the little doughy balls of bread his hands had made, and swept them to the floor. He had no intention of going into that begijnhof. Mistress van Belle would have to come here.

Johan's parlor had been swept, and the one window of oiled parchment cleaned for the first time in over a year. But cleaning failed to improve the appearance of the room's meager furnishings, and the hazy light from the window only served to emphasize its shabbiness.

"Mistress van Belle, come in." Johan would not address that woman as "Sister" and certainly not as "Grand Mistress"; that would be an admission that the beguines were a community of religious. He left the parlor door open, as was proper, and noticed that another beguine was waiting outside.

"Sit down, please." Johan motioned to a straight chair placed uncomfortably close to his own, due to the room's small size, and seated himself. "There have been a number of complaints about the behavior of some of your members." He paused, and fingered the plain cross on his chest.

Beatrice entered, but remained standing. She said nothing. Willem had come to the begijnhof and with his usual probity had given her a full account of the priest's accusations, speaking almost in a whisper, distress evident in his voice. She had tried to hide her dismay at the news that Father Johan had visited the bishop expressly to complain about their community. Nor did she reveal to Willem that she had been unaware that Sister Clare and Mijnheer von Lede had been holding hands in Sint Agustin's churchyard. Beatrice was sure that poor half-blind Sister Celie had seen nothing of their assignation, or she would have been informed immediately.

She had decided that she would make no attempt to refute Father Johan's accusations. He himself had witnessed each of the "complaints," of that she was sure, and would attempt to draw her into a discussion of her sisters' alleged wrongdoings by describing in detail every gesture, every word, every action that offended him.

Beatrice had witnessed only Annalise's "vision"—she still did not know how else to think of it—and had been summoned so abruptly by Father Johan that she had not had the opportunity to speak at length with Sister Annalise, nor to confront Sister Clare about the details of her meeting in the churchyard with Mijnheer von Lede. Yet she dared not delay this meeting. She looked at the scarred table and chairs, trying not to show her impatience as she waited for Father Johan to continue. At last he broke the silence.

"At the Corpus Christi procession, one of your members pointed to the monstrance and then shrieked and fell to the ground, in the grip of some kind of demon. Another 'sister' was observed having a private conversation with a gentleman as they viewed the same procession." Johan tallied each offense with a thrust of his fingers. "On still another occasion, two of your beguine sisters came to Sint Agustin, and one of them was seen in the churchyard arm in arm with a man. Their relationship quite obviously was not, ah, platonic." His face reddened at the thought.

Beatrice pressed her lips together. Finally she spoke.

"I will certainly consider what you have said, Father Johan." She straightened her shoulders and turned to leave.

"Have you nothing to say in defense of your community?" Johan raised his voice. Her demeanor was haughty; that upper-class superiority that made him feel as though becoming a priest had gained him little in status.

"Nothing, Father." The door closed behind her.

Johan's mouth twisted wryly; he was pleased at the beguine mistress' refusal to speak. He had made the effort the bishop had asked of him, and had heard no denial of his accusations. Perhaps now he would get what he most wanted, a chance to face this woman in front of the bishop and openly confront her. Mistress Van Belle and the beguines would be disgraced by his accusations, whether proven or not.

Marie had been waiting patiently near the doorway of the small rectory, and greeted the grand mistress with an inquiring glance. Beatrice shook her head, and the two walked back to the begijnhof in silence. A sharp pain had begun at the back of Beatrice's skull and spread around to the front, squeezing it in a tight grip. It was as if her entire head were held in a vise. The reputation of the beguines, their livelihood, perhaps their very existence was at stake, and she felt helpless and at fault.

For the first time since she had become grand mistress, Beatrice doubted her ability to lead the community. She was sure that some of her sisters had known about Sister Clare's assignation with Jan's father at Sint Agustin. Why had no one told her? Was she too distant? Had they noticed that she spent most of her free time with the children rather than with them? Her hands fumbled as she pulled the bell at the begijnhof gate. Murmuring a greeting to the gatekeeper, Beatrice walked with Marie up the path to the main building.

"Thank you for coming with me, Sister Marie. I feel your support even when you're out of sight. But I must rest before evening prayers." Beatrice managed a faint smile, and then turned down the path toward her house.

She walked past the chapel and the infirmary until she reached her door, then slowly climbed the stairs to her bedroom. A cool cloth on her forehead and some time to think; that was what she needed. She heard water swishing in a basin; it was Ingrid behind her on the stairs.

~~~

Abbot Paulus and Brother Huygen made the journey to Bishop Christophe's palace peering through a steady drizzle. Pressed by his brother monks, Paulus had brought with him young Huygen, a large, silent man of imposing size and strength.

Paulus had been surprised by Christophe's invitation, but accepted readily; he had been a long time inside the abbey's walls, and welcomed the chance to visit an old friend. The bishop was a reliable source for the latest news about the church, from Rome to the Hebrides. But the abbot's brow was furrowed as the two rode up to the palace gate. He was unable to shake a premonition from a dream he had had the previous night; of mud that caught and held him in its grip, mud that splashed on his white habit and onto his traveling companion, mud that was everywhere.... He jerked himself back to the present, straightened his shoulders, and asked Brother Huygen to pull the bell-rope at the imposing gate to the bishop's see. The two were passed through its well-kept grounds and thence to the carved wood doors of the palace. As they dismounted, Huygen tried to hide his awe at the grandeur of their surroundings. A stable boy led their horses away.

Christophe, in his black silk cassock and purple bishop's cap greeted Paulus in the large entrance hall, then signaled to a servant to escort him to his room. After bathing his face and hands in the large basin of warm water provided, Paulus changed into a clean habit and his damp and dusty clothes were whisked away. Outside his door another servant bowed, waiting to escort him to Christophe's library. Though modest in size, it was furnished with several tall chairs covered in magenta brocade and placed near the small fireplace. Paulus felt somewhat uncomfortable in such sumptuous surroundings. A stiff breeze had cleared the afternoon sky, and sunlight fell on the desk in front of the window and on a richly patterned carpet covering the open space in the middle of the room.

"I am so glad you found the time to come, Paulus. We seldom see one another now, but I remember fondly the time we spent together when we were students in Paris all those years ago. I regret I have seen so little of you since you left to join the Cistercians."

"My Lord Bishop, it is good to see you again. You must come visit us at the abbey, though I cannot begin to offer the accommodations you have so generously provided me here. The brothers and I would be honored by your presence."

"Ah, thank you for the kind invitation." A servant appeared with refreshments, and soon the two were sipping mulled wine and chatting about old times. Paulus refused the proffered sweetened cakes, but Christophe reached for another, then dismissed the servant and broached the subject of the beguines.

"I understand that you have established a close relationship with the beguine community in Sint Joric. Are they rather like a third order of Cistercians now?"

"Far from it." Paulus chuckled at Christophe's sly joke. "It is true, however, that we have increased our visits there, and are sending a brother priest almost weekly to say mass. We accepted that responsibility…partly as a result of the Council of Vienne. But no, they are by no means under our control, as are our third order sisters who live in huts up against the abbey wall and spend much of their time in prayer for us all.

"Beguines, as you know, are a very independent group of women, and completely self-governing. The beguines in Sint Joric, like most in Flanders, live in an enclosed community; in some ways, that makes it easier for the church to keep abreast of their doings. Forgive me for going over what I know is old ground, Christophe. However, we do not monitor their comings and goings. How could we from such a distance?"

"Of course, of course that would be impossible. But…would not Father Johan, as their parish priest, have been the logical person to take on that responsibility?"

"Yes, but his relationship with the community is not an amicable one, and so we Cistercians stepped into the breach, as it were," Paulus explained, though he was quite certain the bishop was aware of the situation. "The Cistercian Order was one of the monastic orders which had…agreed, shall we say? to provide a degree of protection, if not control, of a nearby beguine community. But only when requested by the sisters. The abbot shifted in his chair, feeling more and more uneasy, uncertain as to where the conversation was headed.

"How very obliging of you." Christophe leaned forward and poured them both more wine. He paused, reluctant to continue. "Well, it has come to my attention that a few of the beguines of Sint Joric may have engaged in some…questionable behavior. Have you received any such reports?"

Paulus straightened, his wine glass trembling slightly. "Indeed not; I am surprised, quite frankly." There, it was out in the open: no sweetened wine could smooth over the real reason for this invitation. "The beguines of Sint Joric teach many of the daughters of the well-to-do, and even some of the noble families send their young daughters there for instruction. Their grand mistress appears to be a woman of wisdom and probity, and she is from an old, established family of burghers in the town. She would, I believe, do all in her power to uphold the reputation of her community. I would have expected her to take swift action against any beguine who had not assiduously kept her vows. I will certainly take this up with Brother Matthias, the priest who now visits the begijnhof weekly."

"Please, Paulus, do not be distressed. Father Johan is the source of my information, and indeed he does disapprove of the beguines and their way of life. He may well have exaggerated the occurrences he described to me." And Christophe recounted Father Johan's description of what he observed at the Corpus Christi procession.

"I only wished to know if you had received any similar complaints from another source. Obviously, you have not. But now, let us put this matter aside, and have another glass of wine."

Paulus managed a smile and tried to compose himself. If the allegations were true, not only might the beguines come under scrutiny, but also his role as their protector. He felt a chill, in spite of the warm fire.

The men turned to other matters, and tried to return to reminiscence, but Paulus felt a gloom now hung over his visit, and try as he might he could not lift it, nor push it away. In fact, it was like that dark mud in his dream, oozing everywhere. A few days later, as soon as good manners allowed, Paulus thanked the bishop for his hospitality and he and Huygen left for the abbey. Thanks be to God, their journey home was uneventful.

CHAPTER TWELVE

Sunlight streamed through the long slit of window in the abbot's study and lay on the floor like a bright white ribbon. The small fire lit earlier was now ashes, having done its work of driving the damp from the room.

"Good morning, Abbot Paulus. Our prayers for your safe return have been answered, and for that we are all grateful." Matthias had no idea why he had been summoned, but hoped it would not involve a mission like the one to Chartres.

"Thank you, Brother. I have no doubt that the prayers of the community helped shield us from danger. Now, please sit down." Paulus waved Matthias toward one of his two wood armchairs, their seats worn smooth, and seated himself in the other.

"The day promises to be a pleasant one; I shall not keep you long, as I know you would like to be outside in the gardens. But I think you should know about a conversation I had with Bishop Christophe." As Paulus recounted the bishop's concerns about the behavior of some of the beguine sisters, Matthias' face turned from its normal pink to bright red, and he began dabbing at the perspiration on his forehead with a scrap of cloth pulled from his sleeve.. Finally Paulus finished, and looked at him inquiringly.

"Father, visiting the begijnhof has been a privilege." Matthias leaned forward in his chair and spoke slowly. "The beguines never fail to express their gratitude for my celebration of the Eucharist, and I feel honored to serve them. Always, I have a conversation with the grand mistress after the midday meal, and she has never voiced a concern about the behavior of her sisters. I see them at their daily tasks in the begijnhof: teaching, giving loaves of bread to the poor, working in their garden. But I have never encountered any of the beguines in Sint Joric itself, so I confess I have no direct knowledge of their actions there." Matthias sat back, breathing heavily, and paused to mop his forehead again.

"However, Father Johan did speak to me about the sister at the Corpus Christi procession who was rendered insensible by some sort of vision. He seemed affronted by what happened, but I would hesitate to call the young woman's affliction misbehavior, Abbot Paulus." Matthias' face mirrored his sincerity and earnestness.

Paulus nodded in agreement. Somewhat encouraged, Matthias straightened and went on. "Father Johan also spoke of witnessing what he considered inappropriate behavior exhibited by a beguine and a gentleman of some standing in the town—the incidents you described to me. But, as you acknowledged, the priest bears considerable animosity for the beguine community, and I—I simply discounted much of what he said." By now Matthias was sweating profusely. Paulus sat back and busied himself with placing his wooden cross, banded with silver, exactly in the center of his white robe while he waited for Matthias to collect himself.

"I agree with your assessment of Father Johan, Brother." Paulus' voice was somber. "His antipathy for the beguines could very well be clouding his judgment. Nevertheless, he has taken his complaints to Bishop Christophe, and the bishop may perceive that we have failed to provide adequate stewardship of the sisters." At this, Matthias slumped and bowed his head. After a long silence he spoke, his voice almost a whisper.

"Father Paulus, forgive me. I see now that I have failed in my duty. I simply assumed all was well at the begijnhof—perhaps because I wanted it to be so—and thus I did not confront the grand mistress about the possible misbehavior of her sisters after Father Johan recounted those incidents to me."

"Father Matthias, it was natural for you to assume all was well with the community in the absence of evidence to the contrary." Paulus' slight frown belied his words. "But Grand Mistress Beatrice should have advised you of the incidents I spoke about. That is, assuming she was aware of them." That thought had just occurred to Paulus while he was speaking. "We must remember that the beguine communities guard their reputation assiduously; for that reason she may have deliberately withheld information that might reflect poorly on her or her sisters." When problems pressed on him, Paulus felt his body bend under them. He straightened and sat back in his chair.

"I must speak to the Grand Mistress before this business goes any further. I think I will ask her to come here. My presence at the begijnhof would simply draw further attention to this whole matter." The silence that followed was interrupted only by the twittering of small birds on the window sill outside. Finally, Matthias spoke.

"Tell me, Father Paulus, why you entrust such important matters to my care. There are brothers far more able to handle such responsibility." Matthias' voice was low, almost tremulous. Paulus stood, and looking down at him, placed a hand on his shoulder. "Ah, my brother, you are both trustworthy and discreet, qualities I prize greatly. Come, let us go for a stroll in the cloister and enjoy this beautiful morning."

~~~

Annalise was shaking as she recounted to the grand mistress the news she had just received. Her mother was gravely ill and was asking for her.

"Of course, you must go immediately. Gather up your things, Sister, and I will find someone to accompany you."

Whom could she send but Mergriet? From her very first visit to the begijnhof, Annalise had seemed more at ease with Mergriet than with any of the other sisters. How unlike they were: the one pale, slow-moving, and quiet; the other animated, always in motion, eager to join in any conversation. Yet they appeared to enjoy each other's company. Annalise would need someone to sustain her when she faced her mother's suffering. Mergriet should go with her.

"Please take Annalise home so she can be with her mother. "But you will stay very close to Sister Annalise, Grietje." Beatrice's voice was stern in spite of her use of Mergriet's childhood name. "Only when someone dependable is there and you can safely leave her, should the two of you leave to buy medicine for her mother and whatever the family needs in the way of food." And Beatrice handed Mergriet a small purse. "Again, do not let her out of your sight while you are in town."

"Of course, Aunt Bea. I will be as close as if we were wearing the same apron." The family joke made them both smile in spite of their mutual unease.

"I've brought an infusion of hyssop sweetened with honey to ease your cough, Mother. I'm going to heat it for you now." Annalise spoke firmly; for the first time she had taken the role of caregiver. Her arrival had seemed to rouse her mother, but her voice was hoarse and her face flushed.

"I'm so glad you're here," was all her mother managed to say before she began coughing. She took a few sips of the infusion, then sat back and closed her eyes. Annalise covered her mother's hand with her own and leaned over her.

"Mother, don't you think you would be more comfortable in bed?" she spoke softly. Her mother nodded and Annalise settled her in the large bed, and propped her up on pillows to ease her breathing. From time to time her mother would cough uncontrollably, and Annalise would sponge her face with a cool cloth. Mergriet busied herself by tidying the room and sweeping the floor.

The one-room house was just as Annalise remembered it. Its one large window was open and sunshine poured in, illuminating a glazed, rust-red pot in the center of the large table by the fireplace. It was a family treasure and usually held preserved fruit, such as pear honey; but when Annalise lifted the lid and looked inside, she found it empty.

The empty jar reminded Annalise of a journey the family had made to an orchard years ago. Together with neighbors, her parents had rented a large cart and a sturdy donkey, and as soon as the sun was up, they set out for a pear orchard that the family at the end of the street had recommended; the farmer was one of their cousins. Each family brought a basket and helped the farmer pick his bumper crop, paying him only a few coins for the pears they heaped in their own baskets. Annalise and her brother Jon were encouraged to wipe off the windfalls, brush away any bees, and eat as much of the fruit as they wanted. How wonderful the pears had tasted, warmed by the sun! Pear juice ran down her chin, and when she finished eating she had to wipe her sticky face and hands to keep the bees away.

When the families returned, most went home to store their pears in a cool place until market day. But Annalise's parents worked at making pear honey far into the long twilight. The pears were peeled and cored, then crushed in their largest pot and sweetened with precious honey they had bought from the farmer. The fruit was so sweet that very little honey was needed, but it thickened the mixture and was thought to help preserve it as well.

Their door and the window shutters were thrown wide open and the smell of cooking fruit wafted down the street on the evening breeze. Soon neighbors stopped by to chat. Her parents took turns stoking the fire and stirring the mixture to keep it from sticking, their linen work clothes soaked with sweat. Annalise fanned them, content to watch the children, who began a game of tag, running, falling, laughing, until it was dark and time for bed. Next morning the preserves, thick and rich, were ready for sale. After Annalise's mother scooped out a generous amount for their own use, they made ready to carry the heavy pot, and the ladle, to the street market.

A knock on the door jerked Annalise out of her daydream. It was the upstairs neighbor, who was both their landlady and a distant relative, asking if there was anything she could do to help.

"Mother is asleep. Perhaps we could go to the market while she sleeps, and buy food and some medicinal herbs. The stalls may be closed by the time my father and brother get home from work." The plump woman in a worn linen shift and thin wool dress, her sleeves pushed up, nodded and promptly sat down on a stool beside the bed, pulled a sock from a bag tied at her waist, and began knitting.

"You two go on, she'll be fine with me here."

On this sunny market day the square was crowded, and the two beguines drew little attention as they made their purchases. Mergriet bought a sack of barley and another of oat meal, Annalise a small bag of salt and a larger one of dried fruit. At the herbalist's stall they bought ingredients for a poultice to ease congestion. As they were leaving the market, an elderly man wearing a torn shirt and pants tied up with a tattered cord suddenly blocked their way.

"Excuse us, please. We must be on our way." Mergriet frowned and squared her shoulders as she stepped back. Annalise, beside her, held her purchases tightly to her chest.

"Wait, wait just a minute, don' be in such a hurry. Ain't you the one who screamed that she saw Jesus at that Corpus Christi parade?" The man pointed to Annalise, his voice loud and his breath heavy with ale as he leaned toward her. Shoppers on their way to the market stalls paused and turned their heads to see what was going on.

"I <u>did</u> see Jesus, that is, I had a vision. I saw his face in the monstrance as it passed by me." Annalise's voice was firm, her head held high.

"What is it with you—ah, beguines? Are you somethin' special, that you can see things the rest of us poor mortals don't?" Some of the shoppers stopped to listen.

Annalise's figure crumpled, and she shrank away from the man as he staggered closer. "I—I—" Her hands shook and she dropped the bag of salt, then quickly bent to pick it up, lest any of the precious grains be lost. Mergriet put down her sacks of grain and stepped forward, her fists clenched and her voice strident.

"Yes, old man, we beguines <u>are</u> special, if you mean that we live differently from other townsfolk. Our begijnhof was built long ago, and we live together behind its walls. But we do not withdraw from the world as

129

do the cloistered nuns of Sint Anne's. We serve the Lord and the people of Sint Joric by feeding the poor, and we support ourselves by teaching children. We live a simple life of prayer, worship, and service to others. The kind of life Jesus called us <u>all</u> to live." She paused, realizing that her voice had been rising, and more and more people were stopping to listen.

"What are you, lady, s-some kind of preacher?" The drunk pressed forward.

"I was not preaching. I was just answering your question." Mergriet lowered her voice and tried to speak more calmly.

"Sounds like preachin' to me. Maybe you oughta get yourself a pulpit." The man laughed at his own wit.

"Sir, give us leave to pass." Mergriet spoke firmly and the man gave way, stumbling backward, a smirk on his face. By this time a small crowd had gathered around them.

"Come, Sister Annalise. We must be on our way." Mergriet picked up the sacks of grain, and as the two women tried to press through the crowd they crossed the path of a laborer in worn work clothes, his large cap tilted over his face. He raised his head as he pushed past a heavyset woman blocking his way, and Mergriet glimpsed a puckered scar marring his face; then he disappeared into the crowd.

For months after the attack on Sister Clare, Mergriet had seen that face in her dreams, but finally, the nightmares had ceased. Now she found herself perspiring heavily, though there was a cool breeze. Her shift clung to her body, and she felt as though her habit was smothering her. Was the man she had seen truly the one who had attacked Sister Clare, or was she just imagining it was he?

Mergriet looked around and reached for Annalise's hand; it was cool, and grasped hers firmly. Now Annalise was leading her out of the crowd. "And I am supposed to be the protector," Mergriet murmured. At last they were away from the clamor of the market and on their way back to the de Kegel home.

They were greeted at the door by Annalise's father, who had come home from work early, worried about his wife's condition. He had found her sitting up in bed, sipping the infusion Annalise had made, and eating a piece of bread. Their landlady had declared that she was sweating off the fever, and after helping her into a clean, dry shift had gone back upstairs, well satisfied with her ministrations.

Annalise steeped the dried herbs she and Mergriet had bought in a small kettle of boiling water, and prepared a poultice to be applied to her mother's chest when she lay back again. Yet she was uneasy. She wanted to be sure her mother was improving before returning to the begijnhof, and implored Mergriet to let her stay behind.

Mergriet remembered her promise to the grand mistress. She took Annalise aside, and the sisters sat on two stools near the fireplace. Mergriet lowered her voice.

"Sister, the grand mistress wanted us to travel together to and from the beginhof. It would be difficult for me to stay the night, yet I—"

"I know what you are thinking—that if left alone with Mother, I will go out into the streets and have another vision and bring more unwanted attention to my sisters. But I promise you that I will not leave this house. I will stay busy caring for my mother and praying for her. My father can buy whatever food we need. And he will escort me back to the beginhof when we are sure that Mother is out of danger." Annalise was adamant, and Mergriet finally assented.

Nevertheless, she was uneasy. What if Annalise had another seizure? Yet she felt she had no choice except to go back to the begijnhof and explain to Sister Beatrice what had happened. Annalise's father escorted her, and she thanked him profusely. Then she went straight to the grand mistress' receiving room.

"Yes, yes, Sister, I understand. You would have had to sleep in the same room with two men unrelated to you." Beatrice sighed. "Returning here was the right decision." Then Mergriet recounted her altercation with the drunken vagrant, and how he had accused her of preaching.

"...But I was not preaching, Sister Beatrice. He wanted to know what we beguines are about, and so I told him. I might have raised my voice, but..." and with that Mergriet's face flushed. "By the time I had finished there was a—a group of townsfolk listening to me. And I'm sure the word will get back to Father Johan. He might even have been at the market; he seems to be keeping track of every beguine who goes to town."

"As to Annalise's visions, Sister Mergriet: I have talked to your aunt, to my aged aunt, and a female cousin of your Uncle Gerard's. Several of them advised me that some women, when young, may experience ecstatic visions such as Annalise does. However, the visions usually fade as they grow older." Beatrice tried to hide her unease about Mergriet's latest mishap with a change of subject. Mergriet was silent, hands in her lap, chewing on her lower lip, a habit from childhood. At last she looked up and spoke in an intense but uncharacteristically soft voice.

"Sister Beatrice, I have dreams, not visions, but they are always of seductive women beckoning to me, like 'Minne,' the demanding lady; and I am always the faithful knight. The women are dancing away from me, or

131

playing a harp, but always beckoning, beckoning." Mergriet had bitten her lip until it bled.

"Grietje, as you said, dreams are not visions; but perhaps your dreams, too, will fade away as you grow older. I know you tire of hearing this—"

"I know, I know, but prayer has not helped, Sister. I have taken your advice and I do pray, but now I ask God to help me keep my feelings deep inside, and not let them show. That is the most that I can do." Mergriet rose and left the room, sucking on her sore lip.

Annalise could not sleep that night. Her mother's occasional cough, her father's snoring, her brother tugging at the coverlet, and all the creaking noises of the old building made sleep impossible. She missed her room at the begijnhof: the sturdy bed her father had made for her, with its straw mattress and its cover of old quilts; her trunk, with a wooden candlestick on top; the prayer beads hung on the wall over her bed. Sleeping in her own bed was a luxury she had become accustomed to. She wanted to go home, and for the first time, she realized that the begijnhof <u>was</u> her home.

Finally she got up and went to the window. The shutters were open to the night breeze; it felt cool against her face, but also brought the familiar odor of decaying refuse. She stroked the two plaits of hair that lay against her shift and as always, that helped calm her. High in the sky shone an almost full moon, and she could see little creatures flitting across the faraway white orb, too far away to harm her. But the moonlight could not fully penetrate this old neighborhood of two-story houses, and certainly not their street, a mere dirt track only a few steps wide.

Suddenly, an animal ran down the street, pitch-black and almost invisible in the dark, its cry splitting the night calm. A black cat, one of the minions of Satan! Annalise stumbled back and limped to the big bed. She knelt beside it and pressed her forehead into the worn quilt she had folded back when she had boldly gone to the window.

"Our Father..." she recited the paternoster, and prayed for her family, and most especially for her mother. She vowed to keep her promise to Sister Mergriet, and not leave the house. Finally, she prayed that some day she might be allowed to spend the rest of her life in prayer, and she thought of the begijnhof chapel, where she felt closest to God.

Some days later Father Johan left Sint Agustin's in his usual hurry, striding down a short lane that led to the street that was known by everyone as "the begijnhof street". Head down, hands clasped behind his back, he turned the corner and slammed into Father Matthias, who had just left the begijnhof after his weekly visit.

"I say, man, watch yourself." Johan stepped back, recognized Matthias, and apologized perfunctorily, his disdain for the priest evident in his voice.

"You visit that place almost every week, don't you, Father?" Johan nodded toward the begijnhof wall. "Have you Cistercians no power to control those women? I have made you aware of my concerns about their behavior before; and now, just the other day, one of my parishioners told me a beguine was 'preaching to a crowd in the market square.' You know that such behavior is forbidden." Johan blocked Matthias' path, determined to have a confrontation with the mild-mannered Cistercian.

Matthias drew himself up, clutched his missal to his chest, and took a deep breath. He had had enough of trying to pacify this strident priest.

"The answer to your question, Father Johan, is that indeed we Cistercians have agreed to provide a degree of oversight and assistance to the beguine community here. To that end, I visit the begijnhof to say mass, and to speak with the grand mistress and any of the other sisters who wish to consult me. But I am <u>not</u> here to spy on them. And I do <u>not</u> follow them and take note of their comings and goings when they leave the begijnhof walls, as you seem to do. Good day, Father." And Matthias strode away, leaving Johan looking after him and rubbing his jaw, his eyebrows raised in disbelief that the amiable Cistercian had dared to reprove him.

CHAPTER THIRTEEN

eatrice was afraid, and her fear had twisted into a knot deep inside her that had grown until she was weighted down by it. She felt inadequate to the task before her and all her prayers for guidance had been unanswered.

It was nightfall, and she sat by the window of her house, her body slumped against her chair. Both door and window were open to catch the evening breeze, stirring the air at the close of an unseasonably warm day.

She pulled off her cap, tucked loose strands of hair back into her braid, and wiped her face and neck with a cloth from the small pouch at her waist. Then she lifted the abbot's letter from the small table beside her, turned to focus the fading light on the parchment, and read it again.

Abbot Paulus began by stating that it had been over a year since he had visited the begijnhof. Then, for the first time, he asked that she travel to the Cistercian abbey to meet with him there. Always before he had come to Sint Joric, celebrated the Eucharist in the beguine chapel, stayed for the midday meal, and then spoken privately with her in the receiving room. The parchment quivered slightly in her hands. Beatrice gripped it more firmly.

The request that she visit the abbey was of course a thinly disguised order. The abbot no doubt had heard of Father Johan's vindictive sermons against the beguines, reiterating their "misbehaviors." And, most assuredly, Father Matthias had relayed the latest news, that a beguine was seen "preaching to a crowd near the market square."

Much needed rain had brought a welcome quiet to the countryside, the abbot wrote, and the hope of a better harvest this year had lessened unrest. Farmers heading to market meant increased traffic on the roads, providing more security for travelers.

Abbot Paulus closed his letter by informing Beatrice that her nephew, Brother Pieter, and Brother Huygen, the abbot's aide, would soon be arriving in Sint Joric. They would wait upon her and accompany her on her journey. The monks would provide steady, gentle mounts with well-padded saddles suitable for ladies, and whatever else she deemed necessary to make the trip as comfortable as possible. And of course she was expected to bring another sister with her. Beatrice rolled the parchment paper carefully and tied it with a thin leather cord.

The small group left the begijnhof on a warm, overcast morning a few weeks later. The Cistercians' dull white robes flowed down their mounts' backs, the sisters' dark habits blended into their horses' dun-colored sides, and behind them a donkey pulled a small cart. The tableau was evidence enough that this was a harmless group of religious.

The two-wheeled cart had a square wooden bed and sturdy sides. The women's belongings were carefully packed in a satchel tucked in one corner, and next to them were the provisions their escorts had brought for the journey. For the midday meal the brothers had provided a jug of ale, a loaf of crusty bread, a large hunk of cheese carefully wrapped in oiled cloth, and dried fruit. For their Cistercian brothers, they brought items the monks could not provide for themselves; in this case, several well-wrapped bolts of cloth for new habits and, Pieter confided to Beatrice, a round of particularly fine French cheese that Abbot Paulus had ordered as a treat for everyone.

Beatrice had decided to bring Sister Ida with her on the journey. The young sister was from one of the hamlets not far from Sint Joric and had accepted the invitation with alacrity, in spite of the grand mistress' warnings about the uncertainties of traveling outside the town walls.

"Sister Beatrice, I'm so pleased you asked me to accompany you to the abbey. When I was a child I could see it, looking like a toy castle far away over the fields. I pretended it was the castle of a princess and I was she, waiting for my knight to come home from battle." Ida's youth and enthusiasm made Beatrice smile in spite of herself.

"I've been warned about the dangers around me since I was old enough to walk," Ida continued. "I've heard the pounding of hooves, the yelling of men on horseback, have grabbed my little brother and run inside the house with my family; all of us waiting, listening.....But they say times are better now. And I am not afraid."

Ida rode with ease, glancing often at the grand mistress riding beside her, who was clearly uncomfortable. She had persuaded Beatrice that riding astride would be the most secure position for a journey over farm roads that spring rains had surely turned to muddy pathways. Beatrice held the reins firmly with one hand while constantly twitching at her long overskirt with the other, to make sure that her skirt covered her ankles. All the while she was wishing she was back with her sisters in the begijnhof.

Black-and-white magpies called over the fields, and a pair boldly swooped down close by the riders to feast on early ground berries at the roadside. The young beguine squared her shoulders and sat up straight and Beatrice copied her, breathing in the clean air. She loosened her grip on the reins, freeing one hand to wave away the tiny insects that had formed a cloud around the riders' faces. Beatrice relaxed a little, even smiled, remembering the schoolroom on gold needle street and a small child exclaiming at a magpie's call, "That's the big bird with the fancy coat on!"

Inevitably Beatrice's thoughts returned to the string of events that had put her on this road to the Cistercian abbey. Again she listed them in her mind as her patient horse plodded along behind Brother Huygen's more powerful animal.

It had been more than a year since Sister Annalise's vision in the chapel during that late winter windstorm. The following spring, her very public vision during Corpus Christi had stirred up the townsfolk. The result of that miracle—or apparition—had caused a controversy within the beguine community that continued to this day. Some sisters still remained uneasy about allowing Sister Annalise to move toward a life devoted exclusively to prayer. They insisted that beguines were meant to be a community working and worshiping together, as the early Christians had.

Most distressing to Beatrice was that she seemed to have been the last beguine to hear of Sister Clare conversing with her suitor openly on the streets of Sint Joric. Even worse, on another occasion she was seen walking arm in arm with him in the churchyard of Sint Agustin! The ensuing scandal, made public by Father Johan, had left Sister Clare unable to face either her father or her future.

In truth, Sister Clare had never had a vocation for beguine life. The "wise ones," including Beatrice, suspected that from the beginning. But Sister Elisabetta had spoken fervently on her behalf: she wanted Sister Clare, in her beguine habit, to provide proof certain to the townsfolk that a woman clearly of the upper class had chosen beguine life.

"Brother Pieter, isn't that the abbey wall in the distance?" Ida's voice startled Beatrice and she gripped her horse's reins so tightly that the animal jerked its head up, snorting loudly.

"Nay, Sister, we've covered but half the distance by now," Pieter answered as he rode up and quickly calmed Beatrice's mount. She vowed to pay attention to the task at hand, but soon continued her silent enumeration of the events that had resulted in this uncomfortable journey to the abbey.

When poor Annalise was accosted in the marketplace, Sister Mergriet, dear Grietje, bravely defended both her sister beguine and the community. Her reward was being accused of preaching in public. Beatrice tried to offer her comfort and support, but Mergriet went down on her knees, just as she had done when she was a schoolgirl admitting her latest misdeed. Beatrice had floated her hands above Mergriet's head, not touching her, dreading what might come.

"Sister Beatrice, I—I am still having forbidden thoughts and those dreams of young women in silky gowns, parading…"

"Stop, Sister, say no more, please." Beatrice's voice suddenly constricted, and became a whisper. "This—this confession should not be made to me; it should be made to a priest."

"But who would hear my confession without immediately condemning me?" Mergriet's voice was hoarse, and she began a terrible weeping that sounded more like groaning. Beatrice had no answer. Finally, she had simply laid her hands on Mergriet's head.

Beatrice's horse, hearing a faint rumble of thunder, flipped its ears back, then forward. Finally aware that her horse was falling behind, Beatrice tangled one hand in the reins and tugged on them slightly. The horse briskly stepped up its pace to close the distance between it and Brother Huygen's mount. Beatrice was tired and uncomfortable after riding for so long and straightening her back no longer helped. She bent her head, hunched her shoulders, and began muttering under her breath:

"Father Johan sees beguines as women who are warped, twisted out of shape, and so would cast us out of Sint Joric. But a fine piece of wood that twists a bit when drying can still be made part of a sturdy table, perhaps more beautiful for its uniqueness. Why can he not see us as worthy, and honor our way of life as the Cistercian brothers do?" Beatrice leaned forward in the saddle, trying to ease her cramped legs, and her horse responded by again picking up its pace. A light rain had begun to fall.

~~~

Sister Elisabetta had become a beguine because of her contentious-ness. She had not been able to find a single family member, not even the son who had inherited her house, willing to provide her a home after her husband's death. Humiliated by her family's rejection, she had come to the begijnhof, but her reputation had preceded her. She had been admitted only after Grand Mistress Anna's warning that she must humble herself and make Christian charity her foremost duty. At that time some of the sisters, shaking their heads, had whispered that the large dowry she pro-vided must have been a decisive factor.

On the day of Sister Beatrice's departure, Elisabetta sat thinking of that evening long ago, just before the intruder's attack. She had been chatting with a sister who had returned from town that afternoon, bringing the latest news. Reluctant to return to her home after dark, she decided to spend the night in a vacant room in the dormitory. Having gotten up to use the chamber pot, she had heard a noise close by the room she was staying in. Tiptoeing to the door, she had peeked out just in time to see a gray-white shadow become a stocky form in a shift, walking quietly down the hall toward her. Softly she closed her door and got into bed. She knew that only one beguine had that shape—and that red hair. And that Sister Mergriet was the first to come to Sister Clare's aid. But Elisabetta also knew by now that it was best to keep some things to herself.

Sister Marie led evening prayers, and after her final prayer for the grand mistress' safety and of those with her, Elisabetta quietly invited the remaining "wise ones" to her spacious parlor. Afternoon showers had not cooled the air, and both door and windows were wide open to the sisters walking down the path in the long twilight. Elisabetta poured a fragrant infusion of mint with a bit of lavender into the delicate cups her servant had placed on a large table. Small sweetened buns from a bakery in town were arranged on a polished silver plate. The sisters sat, grateful for the padded chairs, and waited for their steaming cups to cool. Soon the long days would be filled with summer work: shelling and then drying beans on broad trays, and fruits on racks; making preserves; and sewing tears in well-worn habits in the long evening light. But now there was time just to talk.

Marie smiled and chatted with the others but kept thinking of Beatrice, knowing that the grand mistress dreaded facing the abbot for what might be termed an "inquisition". She shuddered at the thought. At least young Ida was with her; thinking of how the new beguine loved being with chil-dren, especially the youngest ones, made Marie smile. Sara passed the sweets once more, and then Elisabetta waved her hand.

"Thank you, Sara; I will not need anything more this evening." When Sara had left the room Elisabetta leaned forward. She spoke in a firm, measured voice, the corners of her mouth turning up slightly. The elders knew her well: she had gathered them for more than just idle chatter.

"I am distressed, sisters, so naturally I wished to share my concerns with you. I revere the beguine way of life as much as anyone here and I want the best for all in this community. But I believe that some of the decisions our grand mistress has made have cost us greatly."

The sisters shifted uneasily in their chairs, avoiding one another's glances. This sounded far more serious than Elisabetta's usual complaints: about townsfolk who failed to greet beguines with the respect due them, or the gatekeeper forgetting to doff his cap respectfully when she returned from town, or a younger beguine not being sufficiently deferential to her elders.

"You may remember that I questioned Sister Beatrice's wish to admit Sister Annalise to the beguine community. As you know, she was only fifteen when she arrived, and she came from a family with very limited means. In fact, she began her initial visit with few clothes or other necessities."

"One of our patronesses soon provided all Sister Annalise needed, and most adequately as I recall, Sister Elisabetta." The oldest beguine present spoke up, her voice quavering slightly and her veined hands picking at the nubs in her thin summer habit.

"Yes sister, that is true, and her dowry was provided as well." Frowning slightly at the interruption, Elisabetta continued.

"Beyond her youth and her lack of resources there is her...instability; or perhaps I should say her fragility, which Sister Beatrice evidently did not perceive when she recommended so strongly that Sister Annalise be admitted to the community. Granted, her behavior during her trial period seemed acceptable, but perhaps that was because the child hardly spoke to anyone, so how could we get to know her?" Taking a sip of her infusion, Elisabetta looked at her sisters appraisingly. Only Marie, usually the first to smile and smooth over an uncomfortable moment, held the older woman's glance. But she said nothing.

"As I see it, poor Annalise is just an example of a much greater problem for this community, one that I believe we elders, including our grand mistress of course, should have discussed long before now. Is it possible that not all of our sisters feel...free to confide in Grand Mistress Beatrice when certain problems arise involving beguines outside these walls? And so she has not always been informed immediately of the...questionable behavior of certain beguines when they go into town?"

Marie studied the pattern of mint leaves in the bottom of her cup. What could she say in her friend's defense? True, the door to Sister Beatrice's receiving room was kept open, but her free time was most often spent with the children. Some of our best conversations have taken place on that bench under the chestnut trees, watching the children play, Marie thought. But I welcome the occasional need to go to town and feel part of its goings-on, if only for a short time. Sister Beatrice used to accompany me on occasion. Now, she rarely leaves the begijnhof.

Elisabetta leaned back in her chair. "Sisters, what can we do to help our grand mistress? To help all of us regain our status in the community?" There was silence. Some of the sisters fingered their prayer beads, others simply sat, expectantly. At last, Marie cleared her throat and spoke softly, looking from one to the other.

"Abbot Paulus is a wise and thoughtful leader of his Cistercian brothers, and he and our grand mistress have met together many times. Perhaps we should simply wait: wait until Sister Beatrice returns and tells us what he had to say." Several of the sisters nodded, relieved, and Marie said no more. She was tired, ready to go to her room and her private prayers. Looking around at the others, she could see her fatigue reflected in their faces. Then the faint rumble of thunder in the distance drew their attention.

Sister Elisabetta rose, and brushed the crumbs from her shift. "Sisters, the rain may soon be upon us. Let us pray before we leave one another, especially for the safe travel of our grand mistress and Sister Ida." Together they murmured their favorite verses from Psalm 121:

> "The Lord himself watches over you;
> the Lord is your shade at your right hand,
> So that the sun shall not strike you by day,
> nor the moon by night.
> The Lord shall preserve you from all evil;
> it is he who shall keep you safe.
> The Lord shall watch over your going out and your coming in,
> from this time forth for evermore."

The beguines quickly gathered up their cups and placed them on the table by the door, thanking Elisabetta for her hospitality. Under the thickening clouds there were still faint streaks of light, just enough to light their way if they hurried. Each took the arm of another; the path was smooth, but the possibility of a misstep, and a fall that could result in a serious injury, was a fear buried deep in all of them. Such a fall could mean going to live in the "waiting room." That was what the sisters called the large room on the upper floor of the infirmary. It was where sisters would reside when they could no longer walk with a cane, or with the help of a steadying arm, to chapel or to meals. From their beds they could listen for the sound of their sisters singing as the chapel doors opened after morning and evening prayers. But they would remain in the nursing sisters' care until they were called to God.

No one spoke as they made their way home, but many pondered Elisabetta's criticism of the grand mistress. Some of the oldest felt that by God's grace they, like Sister Elisabetta, had survived into a time of wisdom; and they should honor her and listen to her. And they had agreed with much of what she had said.

Others distanced themselves from the inevitable disagreements that arose when a large body of women, many elderly, tried to live by the beguine rule. These sought inward quiet and serenity as they aged, and strove to accept calmly the will of others.

All the sisters were relieved when they finally reached their beds.

CHAPTER FOURTEEN

"Ahhhh!" Beatrice cried out against the pain. She had slipped on leaves slick with rain and had fallen hard on the shallow bank, her shoulder striking a large stone. She managed to lift her head, and reached toward a broken branch poking through her linen overskirt, but the effort left her exhausted and dizzy. She laid her head down on the muddy ground and closed her eyes.

The travelers had stopped briefly near a copse of shrubs and tall grass so all could relieve themselves. Then they would have a brief meal before continuing their journey. Hearing Beatrice's cry, Huygen put down the bread he had been unwrapping and rushed down the bank to her side.

"Sister, can you tell me where the pain is? Do not try to move, just speak if you can."

"It is my shoulder"—Beatrice waved her free hand over her left side, pinned against the ground by her own weight, "and my—my leg." her voice was faint.

"Let me go to her, please." Ida was watching from the path. Without waiting for permission, she clutched her overskirt, and stepped carefully down the bank. She knelt next to Beatrice, untangled the branch caught in her skirt, and at the sound of Pieter's voice, looked up.

"We need to move on!" Pieter had spotted several figures far away over the fields, impossible to identify at that distance. He had stopped on the road a short distance away from the others, had watered and fed the animals, and was keeping watch while they calmly munched the wispy grasses on the verge.

"Help me, Brother." Huygen called. "Bring the cart here. Sister Beatrice has fallen." Pieter yanked up the mule's bridle, and brought animal and cart as close to the place where Beatrice lay as the muddy bank would allow. He looked down, a lump in his throat.

Huygen was hauling one of the bolts of wool from the cart, his teeth clenched with the effort. He spoke with his usual calm. "We can slip a length of this heavy wool under Sister Beatrice and lift her into the cart." Pieter grabbed the bolt and steadied it as Huygen unrolled a long piece of the tightly woven wool, cut through the selvage with his knife, and tore the cloth off the roll.

"How is she?" Pieter called to Sister Ida.

"There is a small cut and some long scratches on her leg; but thankfully, little blood. The front of her shoulder feels swollen, and she is in considerable pain." Ida brushed the debris from the cut and dribbled a little water over it and the scratches. She tore a piece from Beatrice's shift and bound the cut, then wrapped the overskirt tightly around her legs. Huygen and Pieter doubled the piece of fabric, laid it next to Beatrice, and lifted her onto it as gently as possible. Beatrice groaned, her eyelids fluttered, and her body went limp.

"Sister! Sister!" Ida called softly to Beatrice, but there was no response. The men lined the bed of the cart with padding from her saddle, eased the bundle that was Beatrice into it, and tucked more fabric around her.

Huygen shielded his eyes and looked across the field toward the figures Pieter had seen, and sighed with relief. They were just a family group, headed out to work in the fields. He turned back to the road. "Come, we must get Mistress Beatrice to the abbey as quickly as possible."

Beatrice regained consciousness soon after she was placed in the cart, but moaned softly with every jolt of the now heavily laden cart, and did not speak. Ida rode beside her, watching over the grand mistress as best she could. Finally the abbey loomed over the sodden fields. It looked more like a fortress than a monastery, its crenellated stone walls unbroken except for the slits, which appeared to be windows, placed high above the ground and a heavy wooden gate below, faced with iron studs.

"Greetings!" Abbot Paulus smiled, welcoming the rain-soaked travelers as the gate swung open. Then he saw Beatrice lying in the cart, her face the color of the dull white fabric covering her. "What has happened?" he exclaimed. Huygen explained as he led the mule to the abbey's small infirmary at one end of the chapter house.

Paulus tried to reassure Ida as he helped her down from her mount. "One of our brothers has been trained in the healing arts; perhaps he can use his skills to ease the grand mistress' pain." Ida described Beatrice's fall as they entered the infirmary; behind them Huygen and Pieter quickly transferred Beatrice from the cart to a pallet and carried her to the sickroom. A single window provided dim light, revealing a room furnished with several cots, a chair, and a small table. A thin, elderly monk with a few wisps of white hair above his leathery brown face appeared from the shadows, nodded in greeting, and listened as Sister Ida described Beatrice's fall.

"Place her on the cot there by the window," the monk spoke firmly, and Pieter and Huygen obeyed. "I am Brother Denis, Sister Beatrice. Can you hear me?" The monk leaned over Beatrice and spoke quietly but clearly. She looked up at him but did not answer. Then Brother Denis carefully began to remove her clothes, until she was left lying only in her wet, muddied shift. It was plastered to her body like a second skin; she appeared as if naked and began to shiver.

"I will get a clean shift for her," Ida spoke up. Abbot Paulus nodded, and Ida followed him from the room.

Flustered by the sight of a woman all but unclothed, Denis hurriedly left the room, soon returning with a basin of water and several coverlets. He set the basin on the table and loosely tucked one of the coverlets around her body, but did not undress her completely. Instead, he gently lifted the injured leg, peeled the wet cloth away from the scratches, and uncovered the tear in the flesh of her thigh. As he washed away the dried blood and bits of bark that still clung to the wound, fresh blood appeared, but he could see that the cut was not deep. He was securing a strip of linen around the bandage he had placed over it when Ida returned.

"I wish to stay here with Sister Beatrice, Brother Denis." Ida spoke firmly, lifting her chin.

"Of course, Sister. I have cleaned the cut and put some healing ointment on it. I will return later and examine her to see if there are other injuries. Keep her warmly covered, and give her sips of our sweet well water when she wakes." Again Brother Denis left the room.

Ida finished undressing Beatrice, wiping her clean with the damp cloth he had placed on the table nearby. It was then that she noticed the swelling in Beatrice's left shoulder. It looked odd; the arm did not seem to fit into the shoulder as it should. When Ida tried to pull the clean shift over Beatrice's head, she cried out, and shook her head from side to side. But Ida could not leave her naked; she was still shivering and needed to be warmly covered. So she persisted, and eased the shift over Beatrice's head. When she tried to lift her left arm gently and place it into the sleeve, Beatrice cried out in pain.

"Do not touch my arm, please, Sister! The pain is unbearable." So Ida carefully laid the injured arm close to her body, and slipped the other arm into its sleeve. Then she slowly tugged the shift down until it covered Beatrice down to her ankles, and tucked the threadbare quilts the brother had left closely around her.

"Sister, what has happened to me?" Beatrice murmured.

"You fell, Sister Beatrice, and injured your leg and your shoulder. We brought you here to the infirmary at the abbey, and Brother Denis is caring for you. He seems a kind and gentle man."

"Ah, I am glad you are here with me, Sister. But I am so tired. Could I have something to drink?" Ida lifted her head so she could drink deeply from the mug of water the monk had placed on the table nearby. Wincing, Beatrice lay back, but was soon asleep.

Sunshine poured through the narrow window in the abbot's study, providing just enough heat to dispel the early morning damp. Beatrice's left arm was in a sling, and bound to her side with strips of heavy cloth. She sat in a thinly padded chair and sipped from the cup of mint infusion placed on a small table close to her free hand.

"I really am quite comfortable, Abbot Paulus." She tried to speak with conviction, but though Brother Denis' ministrations had soothed the burning pain in her leg, her left shoulder ached almost intolerably. Two days ago, Denis, with Pieter's help, had wrenched her arm and shoulder back into place; she had cried out in spite of herself and then wept from the pain. Now she simply tried not to move, and not to clench her teeth when the pain came. She just wanted this meeting to be over.

Paulus, sitting in a chair next to her, leaned toward her. "To be sure, there are matters we need to discuss, Mistress Beatrice, but they can wait until you have completely recovered." Paulus had observed how stiffly she walked to the chair, and how carefully she turned her body when she lifted the cup to her lips.

"I would like at least to begin our conversation now, Abbot Paulus. I have been away many days and I must get back to the begijnhof; there is much of import that awaits me there. And my sisters must wonder what has happened to me." Beatrice's voice was soft, and quavered slightly.

"Mistress Beatrice, I can send Brother Pieter to Sint Joric this very morning. He will explain to your beguine sisters what has transpired and try to allay their distress at your continued absence."

"Ah, how very kind of you. And could Brother Pieter possibly carry a note to them? It will take me only a few moments to write." Beatrice leaned forward, eager for an opportunity to communicate with her sisters, however briefly, and thankful that her writing hand was free.

"Certainly. The small room you came through is my office. Let me show you." Paulus gently helped Beatrice to her feet, and led her back into his anteroom, where a table with pen, ink, and paper was tucked into a corner. The room was indeed small, and lined with shelves that climbed up to the ceiling. Beatrice had not noticed them earlier; she had been fixed only on walking steadily. Now she stood amazed: the shelves were filled with books, more books than she had ever seen in one place. Paulus eased her into the straight chair at the table. "Please, help yourself to pen and paper and take all the time you need."

Back in his study, Paulus rested his chin on tented fingers. He had seldom encountered such a strong-willed and brave woman. He smiled wryly; in fact, he could not remember the last time he'd had need to speak to any woman at length.

A short time later, Beatrice placed a small roll of parchment paper in his hands. "Thank you, Abbot Paulus," she said as, feeling a bit dizzy, she carefully lowered herself into the padded chair. For the first time, she felt old.

"Of course, Sister." He tucked the note in his sleeve. "We can talk for a time now, and then continue later, after you have rested." He pulled on a cord near the window and a bell sounded a clear, low note. Soon a lay brother appeared. He listened to Paulus' instructions, accepted the parchment, bowed to them both and left, his sandals flapping softly on the stone floor.

"Father Matthias has always had high praise for your leadership, Mistress Beatrice," Paulus began. He leaned forward, and the silver bands in the cross on his chest glowed so brightly that Beatrice had to look away. She felt as though a spell had been cast upon her. She shivered, and looking up into the abbot's face saw not his usual benign expression, but a piercing gaze fixed upon her. Slightly dizzy, she struggled to listen to what he was saying. "...since he has been visiting the begijnhof almost weekly these past months I felt, or rather I assumed that all was well there. Clearly, I was mistaken." Beatrice looked up, but said nothing. Then she bent her head and drained her cup, breathing in the last faint odor of mint.

"The bishop instructed Father Johan to discuss his concerns with you. Did he tell you that he complained to the bishop about the beguines of Sint Joric?"

"No, Abbot Paulus, we did not speak of his visit to the bishop. But I was...ah, made aware of his sermon describing that visit."

"I see. Did Father Johan speak to you regarding the behavior of some of your beguine sisters when they visited Sint Joric?"

"Yes, he spoke to me at some length, and I said I would consider his complaints." Beatrice spoke reluctantly, pressing her lips together just as she had when she spoke to Father Johan.

"And did you discuss with him the events in question?"

"No, Abbot Paulus, I did not." Beatrice looked down at her left hand, immobilized in the sling. Paulus sat back in his chair and exhaled audibly, his lips pursed in frustration. Not only was the beguine mistress not forthcoming, but the friction between her and Father Johan was quite evident in her voice. Thus it was left to him to settle the dispute and make clear to Grand Mistress Beatrice her responsibility for the actions of her beguine sisters.

"This is what Bishop Christophe told me," he began. "In instances he knew of where an individual beguine was found to have broken a rule of the community, discipline of that sister was left to the grand mistress. Thus, he instructed me to discuss with you the complaints against your community, and to make clear to you that it is your duty, as grand mistress, to discipline your sisters when they do not conform to the rules they have chosen to uphold." Paulus looked at Beatrice expectantly. "Now, tell me how your community has fared since my last visit."

Beatrice felt as if she had been struck. She tried to sit up straight, but the pain stopped her. Heretofore, she had seen the abbot as a kindly mentor. On his infrequent visits he had patiently listened as she recounted the details of life behind the begijnhof walls: their income from teaching, supplemented by the occasional donation or bequest; the success, or lack thereof, of their large garden and small pear orchard; and their bread-making, the bread shared with the poor who came to them daily. She had spoken with pride of their school's reputation.

Beatrice bent her head and touched her face. It felt stiff, like a mask, her cheeks hot to the touch. She thought of the painted faces of puppets in the mime shows presented in the town square on holy days. Did her face look like that?

The abbot's dictum was what she had both feared and expected: the resolution of the complaints against her beguine sisters had been laid upon her. As Grand Mistress, she was responsible for punishing them for whatever "misdeeds" had occurred. Again she tried to straighten up, and again the pain in her shoulder prevented her.

As Beatrice saw it, Abbot Paulus' directive interfered with her authority as grand mistress. She counseled her sisters, cautioned them, even warned them on occasion, but she had always stopped short of delivering punishment. To punish them was to treat them like children, and she saw that as both belittling and disparaging. She could not do it. She tried to speak, to explain her view, but her throat was too dry. No words would come.

Paulus rubbed his forehead and then broke the silence. "Mistress Beatrice, you oversee a community of women who have chosen a different, even a controversial way of life. Thus, when your sisters leave the begijn-hof, their actions are examined even more closely than those of ordinary women, at least by some. Do you not agree?" The abbot's gray eyes, fixed on her face, reflected his manner, now cool and distant.

"I...know that some in the community seek to find fault with us." Beatrice swallowed, trying to coax some moisture into her mouth. She knew her voice sounded weak. "But I think most in Sint Joric are tolerant, if not supportive of us, and recognize the good we do." She met Paulus' gaze, and tried to keep her voice firm.

"I am sure that is so. Nevertheless, I should think you would urge your sisters to avoid attracting attention when they go outside the begijnhof walls. Instead, at least three of them appear to have done just the oppo-site—stirred up the townspeople and become the subject of gossip. Yet you apparently have taken no action against them for doing so."

Paulus had raised his voice, and to calm himself he stood and began pacing back and forth in the small room, hands clasped behind him. This woman was speaking as if she were his equal. He had expected submission and obedience, not defiance.

Beatrice looked at the narrow slit of window where a tiny brown bird was pecking insistently at something on the stone sill. In a moment it flew away, yet she remained, a captive in this fortress inhabited by men in white robes. Unbidden, the words of one of the psalms of David flowed over her: "If I take the wings of the morning and settle at the farthest limits of the sea, even there your hand shall lead me, and your right hand shall hold me fast." How comforting those words were. Surely God would take her hand, and not abandon her or her sisters for the transgressions of so few.

"Could I have some water, please, Abbot Paulus? He nodded and pulled the cord, and soon a mug of cool water appeared at her side. Beatrice slowly sipped the water and then continued, her voice restored. "I have spoken at length to each of the three sisters whom Father Johan has accused of misbehavior, Abbot Paulus.

"Sister Annalise truly believes she saw the face of Jesus on the host in the monstrance paraded through Sint Joric on Corpus Christi. I was there, a little way down the street from her, and I heard her call out Jesus' name. Those close by her appeared astonished, but not offended by her behavior, as far as I could tell. Then a woman shouted something about a vision; the word was passed from one to another, and some of the people became agitated. I saw Sister Annalise fall, and I pushed through the crowd to get to her. She had fainted, and all I wanted at that moment was to get her safely back to the begijnhof and away from public view." Beatrice paused, and Paulus nodded approvingly.

149

"But how could I deny that she saw Jesus? I do not know what she saw in that monstrance, Abbot Paulus, but I am in awe of Sister Annalise's faith. It never occurred to me to rebuke her." Beatrice collected herself and then continued, her voice almost a whisper, as though she were conveying a secret.

"Abbot Paulus, what Sister Annalise most wanted was to become a nun, but she knew her family had neither the means nor the status to gain her entrance to a nunnery. So she came to us, and I have promised her that she can stay with us. I will keep—"

"I understand completely why you saw no need to discipline Sister Annalise, Mistress Beatrice." Paulus stood, interrupting her and thus keeping her from openly defying him. "But now, let us prepare for the midday meal. We can meet again later, in the afternoon." He helped her out of her chair, and she followed him back through the anteroom.

Long tables filled the abbey's refectory, a rectangular room with tall windows that on one long side looked out on the cloister with its neatly clipped beds of herbs, some already in flower. The other side of the room opened onto an arched walkway; Beatrice and Ida had been led along it, and seated at the end of a table near the door.

The brothers sat at benches pulled up to the tables, and ate silently while an elderly monk on a dais at the far end of the room read from scripture. Beatrice picked at the simple meal of bread and a vegetable pottage, while Ida ate heartily. Both were uncomfortably aware of surreptitious glances from time to time. Speaking in a whisper, Beatrice told Ida that she hoped they could go home soon, but that she would probably have to rest here one more day.

"Oh, Sister Beatrice, please do so. I pray you will not try to make the journey home until you are stronger." Ida paused to tear a piece of bread from the small loaf they shared and placed it near Beatrice's right hand. "You know, sister, our rooms are right next to each other." Beatrice nodded and smiled. The young beguine continued. "If there is anything I can do for you, anything at all, please rap on my door, day or night, or else call out." Beatrice nodded again, but Ida feared that the grand mistress would have to be in great pain before she would ask for her help.

After the midday meal, Beatrice and Ida retired to their rooms, each furnished with a cot, a prie-dieu, a table, and a chair. Beatrice's wound made it very painful for her to kneel on the prie-dieu; instead she sat on the cot and focused on the crucifix on the far wall, praying to Jesus for help in responding to the abbot. But her thoughts kept returning to the begijnhof, and soon she was nodding off. Finally, she lay down on the surprisingly comfortable cot and pulled the quilt over her.

Starting up some time later, Beatrice hurriedly smoothed her habit, arranged her cap and wimple as best her one arm would allow, and left the room. She stopped a young brother passing by her in the shadowy hall and asked him to guide her to the stairway that led to Father Paulus' study. The brother helped her up the steps. She knocked on the door and Paulus, trying to look pleased to see her, ushered her into his study and again seated her in the chair by the window.

"Forgive me for ending our discussion this morning so abruptly, Sister Beatrice, but you looked very pale. You look more rested now. So if you wish, please continue. You were speaking about Sister Annalise." Paulus leaned forward encouragingly.

Beatrice tried to sit erect, and immediately felt that sharp pain in her shoulder. She had hoped to answer the abbot's charges persuasively, even forcefully. But this injury made her feel disabled and ineffectual. She took a deep breath, and began again.

"Abbot Paulus, prayer requests for the ill, the dying, and the deceased come to us frequently. We feel it is our duty to respond to such requests, and the alms give us needed income. Sister Annalise would like to spend all her waking hours on her knees in chapel praying for all of us sinners; she could fill many of the requests we receive. I have suggested to my sisters that a life spent in prayer is as valuable a calling as teaching or feeding the poor. If Annalise were to take up that calling, my hope is that any... visions she might have would be confined within the begijnhof walls." Paulus nodded in agreement and waited. Finally, Beatrice continued.

"In the fall of the same year that Sister Annalise had her vision on Corpus Christi, Sister Mergriet accompanied Sister Annalise into Sint Joric. The two crossed the market square after purchasing food and medicine for Sister Annalise's mother, who was very ill. A man who appeared to be drunk recognized Sister Annalise, accosted her, and ridiculed her for professing that she had seen Jesus' face in the monstrance on Corpus Christi. Then he questioned our way of life. At that point, Sister Mergriet stepped forward and vehemently defended not just her sister beguine, but also the life we profess. The man loudly accused Sister Mergriet of preaching.

"Abbot Paulus, we beguines know well that we are forbidden to preach, as are all women. When Sister Mergriet saw that people were gathering around them, the two made their way through the crowd and hurried on their way." Beatrice paused, and to keep her hands from shaking, fingered the prayer beads she had slipped into the pouch sewn into a fold of her habit.

"Sister Mergriet came to me as soon as she returned to the begijn-hof, and told me what had happened. She has a very...forceful manner of speaking at times, but she denied that she was preaching. I believed her. However, I cautioned her to control her emotions and be more careful in the future, and she promised to restrain—that is, to submit to our rules. And to abstain—"

"I agree with you, Mistress Beatrice. I do not think that the church would consider her action 'preaching.' But others who were there might disagree." Paulus interrupted her, then continued calmly. "Tell me, do groups of beguines often go into the town together?"

"Oh no, we seldom go into Sint Joric, but when we do, we usually go in pairs, and never alone. When we leave our walls it is for good reason; a family emergency such as Sister Annalise's or to purchase needed supplies. And the sisters must first come to me for permission to leave." Beatrice stopped speaking; suddenly her throat felt thick. Why had the abbot so rudely interrupted her? Did she sound defensive, trying to explain begijn-hof rules to a person already familiar with the community?

"Please, go on, Mistress Beatrice." Beatrice bent her head, coughing, trying to clear her throat. Now she must speak of Sister Clare.

"Father Paulus, one of our sisters is enamored of a gentleman whom she met at the begijnhof gate one morning when our day pupils were arriving. The gentleman's son is a student at our school." Beatrice spoke hesitantly, as if she were attempting a confession. "The two met again at the Corpus Christi celebration I spoke of earlier. You have probably heard about this already, since Father Johan saw them talking there."

"Nevertheless, Mistress Beatrice, I would like to hear about it from you." Paulus fixed her with a steady gaze. Beatrice described what she had seen of the meeting between Sister Clare and Mijnheer von Lede at the celebration. Then she continued, recounting their meeting at Sint Agustin.

"Much later, I sent Sister Clare and Sister Celie into town to be fitted for new shoes. I know now that choice was a grave mistake. Sister Clare was to watch over Sister Celie, whose vision is very poor. But it turned out that it was Sister Clare who needed watching. In any case, Sister Clare's behavior was unseemly, and she knew it. Finally, she came to me for coun-sel. I warned her that her reputation, her family's, and that of our commu-nity would be maligned if she continued to meet the gentleman." Beatrice began speaking more rapidly, praying that this inquisition would soon end.

"Sister Clare asked me to arrange for her father and the gentleman to meet, and I agreed to try to help her. That was just before my journey here." Now Beatrice's hands were clasped tightly in her lap, and the ache in her shoulder was increasing. "Abbot Paulus, Sister Clare has no vocation as a beguine, and as I am sure you are aware, she can leave us whenever she wishes. Her situation is one reason I wish to leave for the begijnhof as soon as possible." Beatrice looked down, unable to meet the abbot's eyes. Sister Clare's leaving the community would in no sense be a punishment, since that was her desire. But it would solve a problem for the grand mistress.

"I understand your desire to return home, Mistress Beatrice, and I appreciate your...frankness in describing your difficulties. We will arrange for the safest and most comfortable transport possible when you are ready to leave." The abbot felt somewhat weighed down by the torrent of words. Surely he had heard enough about the beguines.

The two had one more brief meeting the following morning. Beatrice had awakened from a sound sleep and felt stronger and more alert. She resolved to depart the following day if arrangements could be made.

"Abbot Paulus, I will think and pray about the responsibility you have given me. I will take whatever steps I deem necessary to address the actions of the sisters who have brought disfavor on our community." Paulus smiled and nodded his agreement. Then he looked directly into Beatrice's eyes, his voice grave.

"Mistress Beatrice, I profoundly regret the pain, both physical and mental, that this journey has caused you. I will, in future, visit you at the beginhof, and I will come with a new understanding of your community and its relationship to the people of Sint Joric." Paulus rose, signaling the meeting's end. As Beatrice turned to leave, Paulus spoke once more. "I will write to Bishop Christophe and tell him that he need not be concerned about the beguines of Sint Joric, and that you and your sisters will continue to serve the town by praying for the community and providing for those in need." He bent his head as Beatrice left the room; her face flushed at his expression of regard.

It was only later that she would bend under the burden he had placed upon her.

CHAPTER FIFTEEN

Late Fall 1334

Celie lay down on her cot piled high with castoff quilts worn to downy softness by long use, and sank into a cloud of constantly shifting memories. Her tiny, windowless room at the top of the stairs was across the hall from the girls' dormitory, and she often fell asleep listening to the girls' murmurs as they prepared for bed. The room's only adornments were the three pegs on the wall holding her beguine habits, her shifts, and her prayer beads. But this night sleep would not come, even after she had murmured the paternoster and all the psalms she knew by heart. She sat up, plumped up her quilts, and pushed a favorite one under her head.

The grand mistress had returned from the abbey a different person, of that Celie was sure. She stepped more carefully now, there were new lines in her face, and her voice sounded hesitant at times. Celie thought Sister Beatrice's injuries were not just on the outside, but hidden inside too. She had always been so strong, and now she seemed vulnerable. But distressing as those changes were, they were not what kept Celie awake.

Sister Clare's trouble was her fault. She would never forget that day not long after the sisters ended their isolation, when the two of them had set out for town to be measured for new shoes. The sky was a milky blue, and the day warm, but Celie began to tire almost as soon as they passed through the begijnhof gate. She walked slowly, her skeletal frame bent over even more than usual. Clare, patient as always, slowed her pace, and when the tower of Sint Agustin came into view, she suggested they stop and rest on the bench near the church. Celie, grateful, carefully sat down on the stone bench closest to the steps leading to the sanctuary doors.

A short time later Mijnheer von Lede appeared, and suggested a walk through the churchyard. Celie did not even try to get up. She had simply waved to them as they walked away; the tall gentleman in a dark, fashionably short tunic, and the slender, plainly dressed beguine, whose beauty was apparent no matter what she wore. Why had she not gotten up to accompany them, as was her duty? Instead she had rested on the bench, and after a while her head drooped and she nodded off.

When she awoke Sister Clare was bending over her, saying that it was time to go to the shoemaker's. Then Celie saw Father Johan striding up the path to the church, and by the look on his face it seemed as if he had eaten something that disagreed with him. But she knew why his mouth was twisted into its most disagreeable look; he had seen Mijnheer von Lede and Sister Clare walking together.

Celie's face flushed, as it did every time she remembered that day. And now she had heard that Sister Clare was thinking of returning to her father's house. She carefully turned on her side and tugged a quilt over her thin shift, whispering the paternoster. As usual, familiar prayer words comforted her, and soon she was asleep.

Sunrise came late on cold fall mornings. The children snuggled under their covers as the dawn light began to outline their cots, and waited for Sister Celie to shuffle across the hall with her candle to rouse them for morning prayers. Celie's room had its door propped open so she could hear a child crying out in the night, or so she said. But the children knew that she could hear very little now. She used to be first at the bedside of a child who awoke with a nightmare, or one crying with the pain of illness. Now, the sisters hoped that the open door would ensure that someone would come to Celie's aid, should she call out in the night.

At last Hilde, the eldest at thirteen, got out of bed and walked quietly across the hall to Celie's room. A close look at the still form, and she knew. Death was a familiar visitor; even children were well acquainted with him.

Hilde ran downstairs and knocked on the door of the sister whose room was closest to the stairs. Swiftly a sister carried the news to the beguine mistress's little house. The sky was streaked with rose-colored clouds, and a breeze blew a few lingering leaves from the chestnut trees across Beatrice's window. She was upstairs dressing when the words reached her: "Sister Celie has gone to God." She felt a stab of pain and for a moment could scarcely breathe.

156

"I will be right there," she finally whispered, but sat down on her bed as the sister left. Celie had always been her champion, had seen her strengths as a leader even before she herself recognized them. Celie, whose own mother had failed her so miserably, had become the chief comforter of the children in their care. Could she really be gone?

Thanks be to God, Father Matthias was coming tomorrow to say mass, Beatrice thought. Her tears fell, but she brushed them away impatiently. There was too much to be done: the body to be prepared for burial; the children calmed and kept busy, as usual; and a soup made, strong enough to carry the sisters through the daylight hours. When night came the sisters would gather around Celie's body and read psalms and prayers to begin their vigil. Then, in pairs, they would keep watch over her through the night.

When the funeral mass ended the next afternoon, the sisters and the children gathered at the small graveyard behind the begijnhof chapel. A weak sun cast shadows that looked like long, gray fingers pointing from the graves of those who had gone before. Soon a new, small headstone would be added, but now there was only the open grave. As Celie's body was lowered into it, the sisters sang the Song of Simeon, their voices quavering.

"Master, now you are dismissing
Your servant in peace,
according to your word;
for my eyes have seen your
salvation,
which you have prepared in the
presence of all peoples,
a light for revelation to the
Gentiles
And for the glory of your people
Israel."

As always, they ended with the "Gloria".

Sister Beatrice was the last to leave. She knelt there in the dirt, fingering her prayer beads, memories of Sister Celie interrupting her attempts to pray. Celie telling her at her investiture as grand mistress that she might be "the best grand mistress ever." Celie throwing her head back, laughing at one of Mergriet's stories, and forgetting for the moment to hide with one hand her few remaining teeth. Celie taking the hand of a child who had fallen, raising her up, then holding her close and telling her one of the

157

children's stories she had memorized, not having any happy stories from her own childhood to draw upon. Celie smiling, looking at her with such love and trust.

Feeling Marie's hand on her shoulder, Beatrice finally got to her feet and followed her out of the graveyard, one hand reaching forward and constantly moving, as though searching for that comforting presence.

Sister Celie's death had shocked the beguine community in spite of her advanced age and rapid decline. It was one more thing to add to their distress and uncertainty. They waited and waited for Sister Beatrice to tell them what punishment Father Paulus and Bishop Christophe had laid upon them, but she had said nothing of consequence since her return from the abbey. Would the bishop try to dismantle their community? Not knowing what was to become of them seemed the worst punishment of all.

No one, not even Elisabetta, wanted to go into town, where they might be greeted with questions about Father Johan's tirades against the beguines. Or with eyes that slid away from them, perhaps doubting they were what they claimed to be: chaste women who fed the poor, and prayed for those who sought their intercessions for themselves or others.

And the children were bewildered. Why was no one smiling? Where was Sister Mergriet, who was always ready to enter into their games? Why was there almost total silence at meals? Was it because Sister Celie had died? Sister Celie had been like a guardian angel watching over them as they slept, and now she was gone. But, they told each other, she was very old. They had never known anyone that old. And now she truly was an angel. So why was everyone so sad?

For days Beatrice did not leave her house, and ate very little, in spite of Ingrid's urging. "No, thank you, Ingrid, perhaps just a mint infusion, nice and hot." Ingrid would leave, shaking her head, and return with a piece of day-old bread glistening with drops of honey, or dipped in sugar; always the bread carefully laid on a scrap of linen and placed close by the mug, to share its warmth. She allowed herself a thin smile when she came back later and only crumbs remained by her mistress' mug.

Sister Celie's death, following not much more than a week after the disastrous journey to the abbey, had shaken Beatrice in body and spirit. It was an effort just to get out of bed in the morning. She was haunted by the burden Abbot Paulus laid upon her, and now she feared him. At night she dreamt she was back in the abbey, his eyes burning into her as he ordered her to "discipline your sisters!" Once she had viewed the abbot as a benign, protective ally; now she knew him to be a cleric with the power to over-rule the actions of the grand mistress, and thus threaten the independence of the entire community.

Beatrice slept little. But she continued to lead morning prayers in the little chapel. Then she spent hours on the prie dieu in her bedroom, praying for Celie's soul and for forgiveness for her own sins.

Marie appeared at her door unannounced late one morning. She spoke in her "schoolmistress" voice: soft, but firm and authoritative, looking directly into Beatrice's face.

"Your sisters are worried about you, Grand Mistress. All of us are in mourning for Sister Celie, but we must continue our work. Work is the best way to ease pain. And we have all known pain and loss." Beatrice held the door open and stepped back.

"Please, come in." The two walked slowly to the window and sat down in the old chairs, the seats formed to fit their bodies by frequent use and faded by the morning sun that slowly warmed them.

"I am glad you are here, Sister. I knew Sister Celie was dying, we all knew that; but I could not bear for her to go to the 'waiting room,' no matter how gentle the sisters there may be with those in their care. Perhaps they could have eased her path, but I knew that she wanted to be in her own tiny room with the door open, listening for any child in distress. That duty seemed to keep her with us, and she could not bear to let it go. Nor could I take that charge away from her." Now Beatrice was weeping openly, wrenching sobs that shook her whole body, her face red and her shift dampening with tears. "Should I have denied her that comfort?"

"Of course not, Sister. Sister Celie died in peace; we could see that in her face." Finally Beatrice's features began to smooth, and her body relaxed into the chair. As always, Marie knew how to soothe her. The two sat quietly for a time, and then Marie got up and went to the door.

"Shall I look for you when we make our usual visit to the infirmary this afternoon?" Beatrice nodded in response. She went back upstairs to her prie-dieu, back to constantly berating herself. How could she not have known what was happening with Sister Clare? Why in God's name had she sent poor, half-blind Sister Celie with Sister Clare that day, her only concern that Celie get the most comfortable design for her new shoes? Above all, why could she not see that frail Celie made an inappropriate companion for a lovesick girl? At last, Beatrice began her prayers for Annalise, Mergriet, and Clare.

Annalise spent her days sweeping the chapel's stone floor, polishing the marble altar, dusting the crucifix and the wooden triptych behind it, and kneeling in prayer for hours. No one asked more of her, nor complained aloud that she was not doing her share. But Beatrice had come upon several sisters muttering their disapproval of Annalise, spending so much time isolated from her beguine sisters.

159

And Mergriet seemed unable to calm her fiery temperament. She kneaded the bread dough on the big worktable with far more force than necessary, her face red with the effort. The end product was coarser in texture than it had been, but her sisters chewed their bread without complaint, dipping it into the broth from their midday pottage to soften it. Mergriet, always attuned to events in the town, now declined the opportunity to go there. She slept little, tormented by nightmares about seductive women in beautiful, translucent gowns.

As for Clare, her father had agreed to meet with Mijnheer Von Lede, and the meeting would take place in a few days. Beatrice had given Clare permission to be there also.

At last, as she lay in bed one night, Beatrice's tears fell in spite of her effort to contain them. "Lord, I am unworthy to remain beguine mistress. It is my pride that keeps me here, my unwillingness to admit to my sisters that I have failed them. Please Lord Jesus, be my strength. I am weak and full of pain." Beatrice gradually sank into a dream-like state between waking and sleeping, her lips moving as she repeated the paternoster over and over.

After a time she felt warmth flow over her, covering her gently, almost weightlessly. Then she felt the crown of her head cupped in two large hands, hands that held her firmly. Could they be Jesus' hands? The Jesus who said "I am with you always?" The Lord God himself? Was this, at last, the kind of divine presence Sister Annalise had experienced?

At dawn, Beatrice woke to find herself lying on the floor beside her bed. Slowly she got to her feet, her body moving as if to untangle itself from the burdens that had pressed it down. She felt renewed, her strength regained. She dressed herself and wiped her face and hands with the water Ingrid had left her, wound her long hair, and pinned it under her wimple. Slipping on her soft shoes, she smoothed her habit and went to the door, her back straight and her head high.

High clouds scudded across the sky, and the bare chestnut branches swayed in the breeze the next morning as the sisters and the children walked to chapel. Beatrice led morning prayers with unusual fervor and after the beguines sang their final hymn, she asked one of the sisters to take the children to gather the fallen chestnuts, now smooth and glossy, freed from their prickly burrs. Beatrice could hear their laughter as she stepped in front of the assembled beguines. Her voice was clear and confident, and gained strength as she spoke.

"Dear sisters, please forgive me for waiting so long to give you the news of my visit with Abbot Paulus." The sisters sighed, a palpable sound as if they were exhaling in one breath the pain that wait had caused them. They shuffled their feet, looking at each other with sidelong glances, trying to read each other's faces before turning their attention back to Beatrice.

"Abbot Paulus informed me that both he and Bishop Christophe believe it is my duty to discipline any beguine who fails to keep the vows she made when she came into this community. And they are right: I took on that burden when I became grand mistress. Perhaps I have not been observant enough, nor strict enough. But I have thought and prayed for many days about my responsibility as grand mistress. And I say to you now that I do not believe I have need to punish any of you." The sisters sagged with relief and then smiled, tentatively. There were murmurs of satisfaction, but also some grumbling that those whose behavior had caused the abbot to censure their grand mistress would be freed from punishment. Beatrice lifted her head and raised her eyebrows, and the chapel was silent again.

"However, I believe that we must make some changes in the way we live our lives. I have been advised by Abbot Paulus that beguines in other places are sometimes criticized, or even defamed, when they appear in public. And so we must... adjust." Beatrice chose her words with great care, speaking slowly and distinctly so that all, even those hard of hearing, could understand her.

"I believe we must change the face we present to the world outside our begijnhof walls. At first some of us, when we have need to go into town, should give up wearing our beguine habits and wear simple wool dresses, rather than the coarse, gray-and-brown wool that we are known by." Beatrice listened for murmurs of dissent; all eyes were fixed on her, but there were none.

"Eventually, we will all dress like townswomen when we leave these walls. We will wear soft woolens in muted colors—like the dresses we wore when we first came to visit here." The sisters looked at each other, astonished. Not wear their habits when visiting the town proper? Would it not seem as if they were disguising themselves? Then again, how pleasant it would be to feel the softness of fine wool and wear colors like mauve, pale gray, even lavender. A visit to the cloth merchants, in small groups of course, would surely be in order. The sisters relaxed, their expressions reflecting approval of Beatrice's decision.

"Above all, we should make these changes in a way that will draw as little attention to ourselves as possible. In the same way that leavening, flour, and water are blended into the smooth dough we bake into loaves to feed both ourselves and the poor, so will we blend into the community, and continue to feed and strengthen it with the bread we make and with our prayers."

"However, within these walls, we will dress as before and continue as before." Beatrice raised her voice as she continued, but her features softened as she tried to reassure her sisters that they would not have to forsake the life they had chosen, that gave them the strength to live as devout Christian women apart from men. "We will continue to live under our own rule, supporting ourselves with the work of our minds and hands, with Jesus' teachings as our guide. Thus will we prevail against those who oppose us." The beguines had leaned forward, listening intently. "In the years to come, God willing, other women will continue to seek us out, and finally take our places. Little will be spoken or written of us, but we shall not be forgotten." Beatrice was close to tears, and her voice was almost a whisper. "Once more, sisters, let us pray." The beguines knelt again on the stone floor, their skirts making only a slight shushing sound.

The changes in dress the beguines made did in fact cause some of the townspeople to view them differently. A shopkeeper recognized one of the sisters and wondered out loud, "Why is that beguine not wearing her habit?" In their new anonymity, the sisters sometimes overheard people criticizing them. "Those beguines give bread to the poor when I can hardly afford to pay for bread to feed my family!"

Occasionally they heard exaggerated accounts of Annalise's "vision," or Mergriet's "preaching," the story followed by a side glance toward them. Or did they just imagine that they were recognized? The "blending in" the grand mistress spoke of would indeed take time.

The sisters knew their reputation had been damaged but they would not admit, even to themselves, that Sister Beatrice might be at fault. Rather, they were grateful to her. She had saved them from rebuke by the bishop, or worse. Any blame they felt was directed at Clare, the one who had never fit in, never truly become a beguine, and she would soon be gone. Sister Mergriet and Sister Annalise were innocent victims. So they told each other, and so they believed. But Beatrice knew better.

~~~

Holding their coats tightly around them, Clare and Ida made their way to Clare's home in the afternoon of a day that was cloudy and chilly. The large house and its beautiful grounds awed Ida. She had come straight to

162

the begijnhof from a small village, and all she really knew of Sint Joric was its center streets on market day or the town square on a special feast day. Her family owned a prosperous farm; at least, it had been until lately, but this place was very different. She suddenly felt awkward and ill at ease, and spoke tentatively. "Sister Clare, ah…perhaps I should wait for you in the garden."

"No, no, Sister." Clare smiled. "You are welcome in my father's house." Clare knocked at the door, and was greeted by a servant, who bowed and led them to the large parlor. Henri rose and embraced his daughter and greeted Ida warmly. She took a deep breath and tried to calm herself. Then Marta appeared with a wriggling baby in her arms, and greeted both women with a regal air. She soon handed the child to a servant girl.

"It is a pleasure to meet you, Sister Ida," she said, and Ida bent her head and curtsied. "Welcome, Sister Clare" she smiled, greeting her step-daughter.

"Mijnheer von Lede has not yet arrived." Henri cleared his throat. "Please, let us wait for him in the library. Come, come." He led the way into the room Clare had so often pictured in her mind, the room that had once meant home to her. It remained unchanged, to her surprise and pleasure. Comments about the weather and other inconsequential matters were exchanged, but the conversation was awkward. Henri was very much aware of the tension between his wife and his daughter, and time and distance had not eased it.

At last Michiel arrived, apologizing for his lateness, explaining that he had been waylaid by a colleague with a legal question. Introductions were made; then Marta rose and suggested that she and Ida stroll in the garden. The two took their leave, Ida quaking at the prospect of making conversation with this formidable woman.

Henri, Clare, and Michiel settled in their chairs as a servant brought wine and small cakes. Clare and Michiel exchanged glances and Clare blushed. Henri could feel the attraction between them and stirred uncomfortably. Michiel spoke fondly of his son Jan's affection for Clare. He described his work as a lawyer, and Henri, speaking stiffly, made clear that he was aware of Michiel's reputation in the town.

Finally Clare spoke, explaining the reason for wearing a simple gown that was clearly not the beguine habit. She described the atmosphere at the begijnhof as somewhat tense, everyone wondering how they could regain their status in the community.

"Much of what has happened is my fault, father. The others were completely blameless." Henri shook his head and frowned.

"Ah, no, Mistress Van Aelst, the fault is mine. I was indiscreet. I knew better than to walk with you unchaperoned. I was caught up—that is, I took your hand..." now Michiel's face reddened and he held her glance for a moment, aware that he sounded like a love-struck youth of twenty.

Henri remembered his feelings when he first met Marta, how over-whelmed he had been by her loveliness and charm. No wonder Mijnheer von Lede was so taken by his daughter; her beauty and intelligence were apparent to all who met her.

"Mijnheer Van Aelst, I know that it is customary in families such as ours for marriages to be arranged by the parents or guardians of both parties, with mutual benefit in mind. But I would like to dispense with those discussions and simply declare in all humility, that I wish to marry your daughter. I can provide for Mistress Van Aelst in the manner to which she...ah, was accustomed when she lived under your roof, and thus no dowry is necessary. I am a widower with a young son whom I believe would be delighted at the prospect of my marriage to her. I would be honored if you would consider me as a suitor for Mistress Van Aelst—"

"And I would consider it an honor to be your wife." Clare could scarcely believe those words had slipped from her mouth. How rude of her! She had not even given her father time to respond. But she had wished for this moment ever since she and Michiel touched hands in the graveyard of Sint Agustin's. Her mind was in turmoil, her hands pressing the folds of her pale gray linen dress. What would her beguine sisters think if they could hear her?

Clare acknowledged to herself to herself for the first time that she did not care; that she wanted to leave the begijnhof and beguine life. Sister Celie, the one sister she truly would miss, was gone. She wanted to spend her life with this man whom she barely knew. But then, how many women were given the opportunity to know the husbands chosen for them? In her naïveté she felt she knew all she needed to know.

Henri was shocked at their frankness. But Clare's happiness was of paramount concern and she would be living nearby, where he could see her often without disturbing Marta's dominion over his home. Her eager reply to Mijnheer von Lede's declaration and her shining face should be all the affirmation he needed. "I will consider your proposal of marriage, Mijnheer von Lede. I know your family's reputation and I recognize that you are quite capable of providing for my daughter. I will send you word of my decision." Henri rose, and the meeting was over.

Clare and Ida walked back to the begijnhof in silence. Ida was commit-ting to memory the details of the grand house and the attire of its queenly mistress. Clare was thinking about the dress she would have made for her wedding. It would be silk of course, in a rich plum color rather than the more popular blue. Long ago, her father had given her a large amethyst brooch which had belonged to her mother; she would wear it on a long chain around her neck. Or perhaps fastened to the bodice of her dress. The dress's design would be simple; close-fitting to below the waist, then a gored skirt flowing to the floor. Her hair would be loose, flowing over her shoulders. Perhaps a crown of flowers on her head. The two sisters, lost in their thoughts, stopped; they had reached the begijnhof gate.

One month later, in the largest and most important church in Sint Joric, the banns were read for the marriage of Clare Van Aelst and Michiel von Lede. Henri hosted a small reception for both families in his garden to celebrate the occasion. Clare was already arranging for her furnishings at the begijnhof to be moved to Michiel's house.

~~~

Beatrice paced the floor of her tiny bedroom, a fruitless exercise since she could take only two steps before she had to turn back. It was time to talk to Sister Marie; she could not put off the conversation any longer.

Marie shook off her cape at the doorway and Ingrid carried it to the kitchen to dry. Then the two sisters warmed themselves in front of the small fireplace in Beatrice's parlor, each wrapped in a thick wool shawl. A cold rain beat against the nearby window, as if it were seeking to gain entry. But the silence between them was not the usual comfortable silence of two good friends. At last Beatrice took a deep breath and began.

"My dear sister and friend, it is time for me to step down as leader of this community."

Marie was appalled. She knew that after refusing to punish any of her sister beguines, Beatrice would likely undertake some form of self-punishment. But give up her position as Grand Mistress?

"I have thought and prayed about the abbot's accusation, albeit unspoken, that I failed to ensure that the beguines of Sint Joric were keeping our vows. The vows of frugality and service have never been in question: I think we all, even Abbot Paulus, can agree on that. But as to our vow of chastity I—I failed to achieve the trust and confidence of my sisters, so that all would feel they could come to me should they need...have need to speak of...I kept my receiving room door open, but perhaps they saw me busy with accounts and so on, and... thus did not feel they would be welcomed. I assumed that all would remain chaste whether inside or outside these walls. Beatrice clenched her fists and the outrage she felt spilled out.

165

"Why did I not see what others saw at Corpus Christi? I did not see Sister Clare and Mijnheer Van Aelst standing too close to each other: I simply saw them amongst the crowd watching the procession. And the idea that Sister Clare would take advantage of Celie's near blindness to do—heaven knows what!" She took a deep breath and tried to calm herself. "I—I still believe that it is the responsibility of each sister to honor her vows, and to report to the Grand Mistress when she has failed to do so." Ashamed of her outbreak, Beatrice sat back in her chair and took a sip of the chamomile infusion Ingrid had left them. Again there was silence. Then Marie spoke.

"Sister Beatrice, did not Abbot Paulus expect that you would continue to lead the community? Did he imply, or order you to step down?" Marie's voice sounded almost plaintive.

"Abbot Paulus expects me to take action to restore the reputation of the beguines of Sint Joric and that is how it should be. He left it to me to decide how it should be done." Beatrice's hand shook; she lifted her mug and then set it down again. "He said it was my responsibility to guarantee that we not draw attention to ourselves when we venture into town. He made clear that I had failed in that responsibility." Beatrice hurried on. "And so I will take steps to make that happen in as discreet a manner as possible.

"As to the individuals whose behavior was questioned, it is true that Sister Annalise and Sister Mergriet attracted unwanted attention to themselves. But I believe they were helpless to prevent what followed, and thus should not be punished. I truly believe that." Beatrice straightened. "And I think Abbot Paulus acquiesced in that regard."

"Sister Clare is another matter. I think she knew the risk her behavior might do to her reputation, and simply yielded to her…feelings. In any case, she is leaving us, which some might consider a punishment." Beatrice kept her eyes down and her lips pressed together, holding back the words that might reveal her true belief: that Clare was completely unable to imagine the effect of her actions on others. Or worse, that she did not even consider the reputation of the beguine community when she walked through Sint Agustin's graveyard hand in hand with Mijnheer von Lede. After a long pause, Beatrice continued.

"As for my role as Grand Mistress, I think I can best help in restoring the reputation of our community by fading from public view for a time. I think people remember faces, and then the stories those faces bring to mind. My face is, unfortunately, well known in Sint Joric. Perhaps it would help our beguine community if my story as grand mistress were gradually to wither away. And so for now I shall not leave these walls except in

166

a family emergency. When I need an herbal remedy I shall ask Brother Pieter or Father Matthias to bring it when they come to say mass. When I need new shoes I shall ask the shoemaker to come here, if that is possible.

"And please, Sister Marie, do not see this as a punishment for me. Truly, it is not. Being the Grand Mistress of the beguines of Sint Joric is a great honor, and I hope in these past months I have learned how I can become a better one. Now my door will always be open to my sisters--and my heart as well.

"As you know, I came here with the hope of teaching children, and I wish to continue using that gift God gave me. It gives me such joy. And please, Sister Marie, think and pray about some day about becoming the Grand Mistress.

That same day, Father Johan was busy in his dusty study, packing his belongings: a few books, his Bible, his clothes, including his new cassock. The pile was pitifully small, he thought. He could carry it all in a pack behind the saddle of the sturdy, if slightly aging horse he had bought for the journey. Bishop Christophe had named him priest of a slightly smaller church, in a slightly smaller town. The bishop had promised to reimburse him for his travel expenses, which he hoped would include the horse.

It was time to go.

CHAPTER SIXTEEN

Winter, 1334

Beatrice, frowning, sat at her desk in the receiving room. The heat from the little fireplace did not begin to reach her desk by the window, and Beatrice had pulled her warm, purple shawl so closely around her body that she felt constrained by it. The kitchen was running short of flour. She had sent one of her sisters to look for Sister Mergriet; perhaps she would have an explanation.

"Thank you for coming so quickly, Sister." Mergriet entered at her usual lively pace. "Here, sit next to me. Can you tell me why our supply of flour is so low? I understand that we may not have enough to last us until the next delivery, a week from now.

"Well, as you know, we have been feeding more poor souls than ever. This past week alone, there were three new families in the queue, all with young children or babes in arms, and they came every morning." Mergriet shook her head her head slowly, and exhaled audibly, expecting so see her breath in the cold room. She too wrapped her shawl more closely around herself. "I think we should ask Cousin Willem to send us an additional sack of flour, to tide us over. Perhaps, by the grace of God, we will have fewer souls to feed next month." Looking doubtful, she pursed her lips and paused.

"Meanwhile, I can make the loaves slightly smaller and add a little oat flour, as it is more sustaining—though as you know, oat flour is also very dear." Again, Mergriet waited, but the grand mistress did not speak. "I could go to the warehouse for you, and speak with Cousin Willem."

"Oh yes, that would help, Sister. Please, go as soon as you can. And why not take our newest beguine sister with you. It will be a chance for her to go into town; she has been too long within these walls for one so new to us." Mergriet could not remember the last time the grand mistress herself had left the begijnhof. It was obvious that even when the opportunity presented itself, she had no desire to leave.

The two beguines set out for the warehouse the next day after the midday meal, the sky dark and the wind rising. They held their coats tight against the breeze as the few leaves left on the chestnut trees rained down on them. Willem's warehouse was some distance away in a part of town near the wharf, and the women arrived there accompanied by a cold drizzle. As they approached the heavy door, which was slightly ajar, Mergriet called out. No one answered, so the two pushed back their hoods in order to see better, and then shoved the door open. The drizzle had turned to rain and seeing no one, they stepped inside and shook out their coats. All was quiet; there was no sign of Willem.

Suddenly a man appeared, tall and thin, dressed in a ragged shirt and pants too big for him, held on with a threadbare rope tied at his waist. Mergriet gasped and stumbled backward. And seeing who it was, the man jammed his cap down over his eyes, gesturing deferentially, aware that the woman had seen his face and remembered him.

"What is your business here? Have you come to steal from my father's warehouse?" Mergriet had seen the scar, how it pulled the corner of his eye down, and even in the dim light she recognized the intruder from that night years ago. Her heart was pounding, but her voice was strident.

"I—I mean no harm, mevrouw. My name is Geejs. I am here to keep things safe and clean the stalls, fork down hay for the horses, give them drink. I come in the afternoon, when Mijnheer Van Belle leaves. And I sleep here at night, in the loft. The mijnheer is kind; he gives me a few coins for food. But—he left early today, told me he had to meet someone at an alehouse down on the wharf." The man's voice was unsteady, his hands hung loose at his sides, and there was no sign of a knife or cudgel about his person. Mergriet was not appeased; his abject manner emboldened her. In that moment she decided to let him know that she had recognized him.

"You should not be here!" she hissed. "Not in my father's warehouse, nor on the streets. Why did you not leave town after you attacked my sister beguine that night?"

The intruder stepped back, his jaw slack, shocked that she had spoken of that night he had tried so hard to forget. His shoulders slumped, and for a moment he was struck dumb. Then he stammered a reply. "I—I had had much to drink, but nought to eat. I lost my head lookin' at—"

"Why did you not go back where you belong?" Mergriet was at once furious and fearful. He had begun describing behavior that was unspeakable. She clenched her jaw and stood her ground. "Answer me!"

"There is none there for me now. It was just me and my ma, livin' together since my pa died o' the fever." His voice sounded as if all the strength had been beaten out of it. "When the troop grabbed me she cried out, begged them to leave me be, and one of them swung round and s-struck her real hard on the side of 'er head with his cudgel. She—she went down. She dint move. They wouldna' even let me see to her, but it mattered nought. I could see she was dead."

He bowed his head, fearful that this woman might have the power to take away the first secure place he had found since he escaped from the troop. Mijnheer Van Belle had hired him, but the master was too young to be the father she spoke of. Perhaps her father would sack him, and he would be out on the streets again.

The young beguine tugged at Mergriet's coat. "Please, Sister, let us go. We can come back another time, when your brother is here." Mergriet did not move, yet she felt her anger subside. He was a young man, and hardly appeared the tool of the devil she had imagined. But one never knew. Now his fists were raised, he was frowning, and looked threatening. She took a step backward, and tried to think what to do. She must get away and go to Willem, and tell him about this man, what he had done.

"I will speak to Mijnheer Van Belle another time." Mergriet spoke loudly, and tried to adopt a withering tone, her whole body a rejection of the man's plea. She turned her back and walked away, and her sister beguine hurried to catch up to her, lifting her skirts to avoid the mud. Then Mergriet, hearing heavy footfalls behind her, whirled around, her eyes widening as she faced a pair of dark eyes glaring back at her, the one scarred.

"You are a religious, is it not so? Do you not believe in forgiveness, in givin' a sinner a second chance?" He was almost shouting. "If I be banished from this town, flung out into the countryside, I mought be impressed again. At the least I will have nowhere to go an' no food. In these hard times few folk have food enough to share, even if they would. You will have me on your conscience." With that, the intruder turned and stomped off into the gloom of the warehouse.

171

Mergriet's mind was in turmoil, her body stiff. She started down the street, her arm about her sister beguine, who was shivering and saying not a word. The rain had subsided to a drizzle again as they headed toward the center of town.

Forgiveness? But think what the man had done. Think what he had intended! What if she had not been in the room that night? Yet she was there, in the corner. Mergriet pushed those thoughts away, but more questions pressed on her.

What if Sister Beatrice had not given <u>her</u> a second chance? What if she had not made the pilgrimage to Chartres, the journey that changed her life forever? She had been forgiven, had received Christ's blessing as she gazed at his image over the portal of the cathedral on that unforgettable day. Had she, thus, the right to deny forgiveness to another sinner when it was asked of her? How could she condemn him, when she herself...

Mergriet yanked her thoughts back to what she should do next. She could not face looking for Willem now. What should she say to him about that man? She needed time to think.

"I will return to town tomorrow, after the bread making is finished." The young beguine sighed with relief. All she wanted was to get back to the safety of the begijnhof. It was a long walk and the light was beginning to fade, but by the time they reached the begijnhof it had stopped raining. The porter greeted them and they passed through the gate.

After evening prayers, Mergriet went straight to her small room under the eaves of Sister Beatrice's house. She had only the faint light of the tallow candle she clutched to help her find her way through a night without moon or stars. For once she looked forward to being alone. Willem knew nothing about that man Geejs' misdeeds. So how to get him to dismiss him? To get him out of Sint Joric?

Mergriet said her prayers and got into bed, but she lay sleepless. Finally she got up, pushed open the dormer window, and leaned out. The night was quiet except for the occasional drops of water from the eave above her, splashing on the stones below. The usual noises of the town seemed far away, though the begijnhof wall was not far from their townhouse. She knew that night belonged to the spirit world and she should not be at the open window, but the air was crisp and clean after the rain. Then something flitted close by her, a dark furry ball with pointed ears, making a small chirping sound. Was it a messenger of Satan? A warning that she herself was laden with sin, and one day would face judgment?

Quickly she closed the window and went back to bed. Comforted by the distant call of the night watchman and warmed by her quilts, she finally fell into a restless sleep, and dreamed of a huge black ball

172

pursuing her down a dark street, rolling faster and faster, getting closer and closer.

Mergriet woke with a jerk to a gray dawn, thankful to be safe in her bed. After morning prayers she again left for the town, this time with Sister Lisbette, who wanted to visit her ailing cousin. Mergriet could hardly sit still as they prayed for the slight figure, motionless on a cot in a small house near the center of town.

Finally it was time to leave, and they set off for Willem's shop. How well Mergriet remembered the heavy door with the needle carved of wood and painted gold. She pulled open the door and the two women stepped inside. Willem sat on the stool behind the counter of the elegant shop studying his ledger; Klaus, the young man who now ran the shop, chatted with a customer. Lisbette leaned toward the skeins of yarn that hung behind the counter, fascinated by their deep purples and blues. Mergriet spoke softly to Willem about her need to speak with him in private. He motioned her to the small storeroom behind the main room. It was stacked with large bags containing spools of thread, and hung with more skeins of yarn in colors that glowed even in the dim light from the small window. She remembered as a child hiding behind those skeins, hoping to escape the lessons she found so boring.

"Cousin, I apologize for disturbing you. But I went to your warehouse yesterday, hoping to ask if you could increase our delivery of flour by one sack next week, and perhaps the week following. There are new families at our door almost every day, and we need to bake more loaves in order to feed them."

"Of course, of course we can help; I know that Uncle Hans would agree." Willem scratched his head. "You say one bag more? Fine, I will see to it when I go back to the warehouse this afternoon. I am only here to check on things; Klaus does a fine job managing the shop. But cousin, you look troubled. Is my mother unwell?"

"No, she is well, though her injury and the difficulty with Abbot Paulus still burden her." Mergriet paused, and tried to choose her words carefully. "She has decided to confine herself to the begijnhof, unless there is a family emergency. She is more open to the sisters, however, and loves spending more time teaching...and she smiles more now." Willem's face reflected his surprise, but he said nothing.

"Cousin Willem, I spoke with your—your watchman at the warehouse yesterday. He has a strong country accent, and was a bit hard to understand. And he seemed a bit...truculent. How is he with your customers?"

"Ah, yes, Geejs is a man of few words. Perhaps that is why he seemed unfriendly. But you are right; he is not much help with the odd customer who comes in when I am not there. He has no learning at all, and even simple sums frustrate him. But he is steady, a hard worker, always waiting when I get there and grateful for the little I pay him. And he is a good hand with the horses, old faithful nags that they are." Willem paused and mopped his forehead with a cloth pulled from his sleeve. The room was small and crowded with just the two of them there.

"I'm thinking he might be better suited as a drover. We need someone to bring the crops from Uncle Hans' farm to the warehouse. And there is need of someone to help with the animals at the farm during the winter months. Our cousin and his wife have lived there a long time; they are getting old and need help. Thank you for bringing the matter to my attention, Cousin Mergriet. I have been meaning to speak with Geejs, and you've given me the nudge I needed to get it done."

As the two women took their leave, Mergriet thought how much Willem had changed; he was no longer the shy, quiet youth she remembered. Walking back to the begijnhof, she felt a measure of relief about the man Geejs. Willem would surely send him back to the countryside, where he belonged.

On an unusually warm late winter afternoon a tall, slightly bent figure sat on the schoolhouse porch, sheltered from the cool breeze and feeling the sunshine seep into her bones. Beatrice was dressed in her beguine habit, with a warm shawl over her shoulders. She did not miss wearing "town clothes," though some of the sisters wore them all of the time now.

Beatrice was comfortable with her decision to stay inside the begijnhof walls. She smiled to herself. Now she felt blessed, and at ease. On days like this she welcomed visitors to the long porch, rather than inviting them into the receiving room or her little parlor.

Only yesterday Willem had come to the porch, sat down next to her, and told her that her grandson wanted to go to school 'where grandma lives.'

"I told him he was not quite old enough," Willem had said and they both laughed. Now she watched the younger children playing tag; soon they would go inside to rest, and it would be quiet again. Her beguine sisters often came to sit with her in the late afternoon, seeking her advice, most often about a problem with another sister. Beatrice would listen and reply, always asking the sister to pray with her before leaving.

Now Sister Marie was walking toward her under the trees. Sister Marie, too, seemed to feel most comfortable seeking her out here on the porch. They nodded to the sisters passing by on the path and watched the children play at running games under the trees.

"Ah, Sister Beatrice, how well you look; at peace, too."

"I am so much more comfortable as grand mistress now, Sister. And I find I have more time to do the work that God truly called me here to do: teaching children. When one of the older girls seeks me out with a question, or the youngest gather around for a story, then I am most content."

"Well, as usual, I have something I would like to discuss with you, Sister. Long ago, you assured me that you would listen if I had a knotty problem to resolve. You see...."

The sun was sending slivers of light across the pathway when the two sisters left the bench and made their way back to the main building. The friendship that had begun so long ago in this place was as strong as ever.

~~~

A figure dressed in shabby clothes sat hunched over on the seat of the battered wagon, his cap tilted down over his eye. He held the reins in one hand; the old dray horses had an easy task, as the wagon was almost empty. They had begun to pick up their pace, sensing that the farm was not far away, when a band of horsemen appeared out of a copse nearby.

"Hey there, what's in that wagon, man?" one of them called out. Geejs stiffened and drew a sharp knife from his belt.

"I'll not be taken agin," he muttered to himself. A man in a faded uniform rode his horse alongside the wagon and tried to grab the near horse's bridle. Geejs whipped the horses up, but they were slow to respond. He aimed a blow at the rider with his crop, but he knew he had no chance. They were too many. The horsemen surrounded him, stopped the horses, and dragged him from the cart's seat, leaving the horses to lumber away down the dirt track. The riders had their hands full with Geejs, who slashed at them with his knife and took one down before they overpowered him.

"Ah, he's no use to us now, you've cut him too deep," the leader growled. "Drag him off the track and let's be gone. Those old nags ain't worth chasin' after." Then he saw that the injured trooper was bleeding profusely. Those wounds had to be fatal. "Oh God, poor Kendric. We'll have to do a proper job burying him." The boss sighed and got down from his horse.

"What about the drover, boss? Shouldn't we bury him, too?"

"Aw, find someplace in the underbrush a good distance awa', scrape out some soil, lay him out, and cover him over. Then pile some branches over him, and help us dig the grave for Kendric. Get going!" Thus Geejs, bleeding and unconscious from the wound in his shoulder, was left half buried under some shrubs well away from the path, dirt and brush tossed over him. The first flakes of the last snowfall of the season sifted down through the darkening sky, until the brush and the body beneath it were as one.

The horses and the battered cart finally arrived at the farmhouse with the goods sent from town, but there was no sign of the drover. Willem's cousin asked a friend in the hamlet nearby to help him search along the track, but they found nothing.

The following day a traveler with a dog trotting beside him came down the track. Suddenly, the dog left his side and began madly scrabbling in the field by the track. Thus a body was found, and it was assumed to be that of the missing drover. He was buried in a small graveyard outside the hamlet, the plot marked by a crude wooden cross.

Willem's cousin sent word of what had happened to the drover and Willem mentioned the loss to his mother when he made the extra delivery of flour to the begijnhof. When Mergriet woke from her nap the following afternoon, Beatrice was in the parlor downstairs with two mugs of mint infusion.

"Sit down, please, Sister. I have news of the intruder whom you met at the warehouse not long ago." Mergriet, unaware that Beatrice knew about her encounter with Geejs, felt as though she had received a sudden blow to her stomach. "Willem told me he sent the man Geejs to your father's farm, but he never made it there," Beatrice continued. "Evidently he was dragged from the cart he was driving and killed, his body hidden nearby. But a traveler found the body, and it has been buried in a graveyard in the hamlet near the farm." Much to Beatrice's surprise, tears were rolling down Mergriet's cheeks.

"I—I never meant for that to happen. I had wished him dead many times, and for certain I wished him out of Sint Joric, but when I talked to him that day at the warehouse, he challenged me. He asked me if I believed in forgiveness, in second chances. And I do, of course, so how could I judge him so harshly?"

Beatrice rose, went to Mergriet, and put her arms around her, holding her close. "You have come so far," was all she said.

Some days later, a sturdy cart carrying a gentleman and a plainly dressed woman appeared in the hamlet by Hans' farm. Several men stopped their work to stare at them.

"I say, I don't mean to interrupt you, but we are seeking the grave where a stranger has been buried recently." A man doffed his cap, and agreed to take them to the spot. He heaved himself into the back of the cart, splattering mud generously around himself and the cart's bed. The graveyard was but a few leagues away.

"Here's the grave, but mind ye, we've no idea who he is." The gentleman helped the lady down and the two stood at the foot of the grave. The peasant shrugged, puzzled that such well-dressed townsfolk would come asking for a man whom all assumed to be the ragged drover headed to the nearby farm. At last the gentleman spoke.

"My name is Willem de Belle. The farm nearby belongs to my cousin. The man Geejs was working for me in a warehouse in Sint Joric. I sent him out here to help the old couple."

"Oh, aye." The peasant lingered, hoping the gentleman would say more, but the only sounds were the ones he heard every day: dogs barking, children shouting, mothers calling them. The man gave him a coin, and the peasant thanked him and turned away.

At last Willem helped Mergriet climb back into the cart and turned the horse down the track toward the farmhouse, where they would have a meal and perhaps stay the night before heading back to town. Not a word was spoken, each deep in their own thoughts. Again, Mergriet had tears in her eyes, but she would not let them fall.

~~~

Far away a man in rags, boots with no socks and a cap pulled down over one side of his face, left the road and stopped to rest. He had heard the sound of water trickling over stones, and made his way to the stream just off the path. Carefully he got down on one knee, and cupped his hands to drink. "I've come this far," he muttered to himself, looking up at the abbey walls not far away. "I'll clean m'self up an' go pull the rope. The monks jest might take pity on a starvin' man with a hole in his shoulder." Taking his time, he got to his feet, and using the staff he had made from a sturdy branch, climbed back on to the path. With luck, he might get to the abbey before dark.

18408324R00105

Made in the USA
Middletown, DE
08 March 2015